Pictures of the Past

by

Deby Eisenberg

Studio House Literary

For Michael, my husband

From the beginning, his truly energizing passion and support for the story never wavered. He provided me with the opportunities to visit so many fascinating venues in America and abroad, which eventually found a home in the novel.

Provenance

n. the place of origin or
earliest known history of
something; a record of
ownership of a work of
art or an antique

Oxford Dictionary of English,
Second Edition, Revised.
Oxford University Press.

Gerta Rosen

Chicago

September 2004

Slamming her hands on the rotating tires of her wheelchair, she abruptly stopped its slow progression. "It can't be." Her words were soft and almost unintelligible at first. "Oh, my God." She spoke louder now and the small group with her, previously drawn in many directions, began to form a circle around her. "It just can't be." Louder still and more disturbed, her accent became thicker with each repetition, as she searched out her eldest daughter. "Darlene, now... please . . . I need you. Come. I need you to read me the plaque."

Darlene left the small Degas she was studying and came to her mother. "What a beautiful painting—I can see it's by Henri Lebasque. I believe he is French." She reached for reading glasses. "Yes, 'Henri Lebasque, French 1865–1937'; it is '*Jeune Fille à la Plage*, Girl at the Beach.'"

"No, not that. I know that." Her delivery was uncharacteristically irritated. "Now you tell me this—how did it get here?" Leaning forward in her seat, she was perceptibly impatient for the answer. "Tell me now who donated it. Read me that."

Darlene focused on a second small sign accompanying the work of art. "It reads, 'Donated by Taylor Woodmere, Woodmere Family Foundation, Kenilworth, Illinois.'"

The elderly woman resettled in her chair, straightening her posture to elevate her small stature. Her normally sweet, complacent countenance took on a stone-faced frown. "Who is this Taylor Woodmere? What kind of a name?" The questions, though directed toward her daughter, now successfully sliced the hushed cadence of the entire gallery; the other visitors stopped and stared at their group.

"Now you must listen to me," she continued in the crackling higher pitch that years add to voice modulations. "This one thing I know. This painting hung in the Berlin house of my dear neighbor, Sarah Berger." The agitation in her voice was escalating as she continued. The adults moved closer to her side as if afraid she might slide from her chair in a faint, or worse yet, attempt to bound from it.

"Mother, please. What is it?" Darlene asked anxiously.

And then her mother, in a rare, accusatory tone and with a fervor she had not exhibited in years, cried out, "Liar, liar—this is enough, enough. They cannot take my family, my friends, and now my memories!"

Gerta Rosen had asked for one special treat for her eighty-second birthday. She wanted, yet again, to visit the Art Institute of Chicago and her beloved Impressionist rooms. With her elderly and brittle body so evident, few would guess what this strong woman had endured. But her family knew. And they believed that what small pleasure they could give her would never compare to the gift of life she had given their generations by tenaciously surviving the Holocaust. Although there had been years, maybe even decades, of silence after Gerta began her life in America, eventually she recognized the need to share her past with her family. And in due course, she participated in the video biography projects crucial to Holocaust documentation.

Her love for the Art Institute itself, the powerfully positive feelings that each visit to the site evoked in her, was a result of the aesthetic roots of her childhood. When she was a young girl in pre-World War II Berlin, Gerta's parents were major supporters of the arts. Her neighborhood had been home to some of the most educated, wealthiest families in the city. In her earliest memories, she is kneeling on the vanity chair in her parents' bedroom, watching them dress for a night at the opera or the Berlin Philharmonic. Sorting through items in a beautifully carved jewelry box, she would try on earrings and bracelets, and then she was proud to help choose which intricately designed piece her mother would wear. As her mother raised her hair from the nape of her neck, Gerta loved the way her father would secure the necklace clasp and then place a tender kiss on her shoulder, and she longed for the day when she would be old enough to join them for a concert in the evenings. But often on afternoons when the weather was most inviting, they would all stroll the boulevards of the bustling city of Berlin and would visit the art museums and private salons together. At all of the galleries she would run past the large, somber Renaissance works, and she would coax her parents toward the multihued, vibrant paintings from the turn of the century, the French Impressionist works, and she had memorized the names of her favorites artists. When she would point to the canvases by Max Lieberman, who had led the movement of German Impressionism and had been president of the Prussian Academy of Arts, her father would laugh and remind her that Max, himself, had been a family friend, had often sat in the same dining room chair next to him that she would now occupy.

The Rosens and their friends were assimilated Jews, a vital part of the German cultural nation—or so they thought as they were lulled into their false sense of security.

And so on this day, as Gerta had requested, the women of the family planned a beautiful afternoon for their beloved matriarch, including the granddaughters and the five great-grandchildren. First, Gerta enjoyed her favorite light lunch of salad and soup in the courtyard restaurant. Then, while the young mothers followed their children as they ran up the Grand Staircase to the Impressionist rooms, her three daughters, accompanied by some baby strollers, escorted her on the elevator.

Naturally, her family immediately went to the main Pritzker Gallery, where Gerta loved viewing the masterwork, Georges Seurat's *A Sunday on La Grande Jatte*, surrounded by van Goghs and Renoirs and Monets. Only at the Musee D'Orsay in Paris, did she feel there was a collection that rivaled that of Chicago's Art Institute.

But today she asked to be wheeled to a side room, which she now realized she had neglected all these years. And then she spotted *Jeune Fille à la Plage.*

"Mother, please calm down. Please tell us what's upsetting you so. We want to understand." Darlene's words were calming, were accompanied by an interested, rather than patronizing tone. She knew from attending seminars and group sessions for children of Holocaust survivors, that when victims wanted to talk, they must not be silenced.

Gerta fought to regain her composure. Even the youngest ones settled down, as if they sensed the importance of the moment. The two babies continued quietly sucking bottles.

"My children, this beautiful work of art hung in the Berger home during my last year in Berlin." Then she turned to her oldest again. "Darlene, you know from my telling you, maybe 1937 to 1938. Until shortly after Kristallnacht. The Nazis were taking everything precious, objects and souls." She was speaking slowly now and her eyes were no longer focusing on those present. "I was often at the Berger house. The daughter, Sarah, was maybe three years older than me. She was my . . . how do you say . . . idol, role model. Her father was an important businessman and she was a beautiful, intelligent girl." Now her eyes seemed to return to the present. Her softer tones had invited the group to circle closer to her chair and she reached out to one of the teenage girls, who bent to the level of her grandmother's chair as an adult would to a small child, and Gerta continued as if she were speaking only to her. "Eventually, I found that Sarah had left from Hamburg on the ship, the famous ship, the *St. Louis*, which was turned back when it reached the Americas."

Now she raised her gaze and the young girl stood and Gerta focused on her own three daughters. "You know my story—I have told you many times. Our family went into hiding and then we were 'relocated.' Only my protective older brother and I made it through the camps." There was a longer pause now, as the loss of her parents became fresh again. "Yes, so many gone. It never leaves me. And I never did know what happened to Sarah. Sarah could easily have been slaughtered by the Nazi filth."

Once again she made a gesture that signaled the group to re-shift and allowed more of the children to be at her side, each wanting to comfort her in some way, touching her hand or her arm or stroking her hair, as they imitated their mothers.

"But they did not destroy great works of art—these they valued above life, especially Jewish life." She stopped to catch her breath.

Understanding where her mother was leading, Darlene took her cue. "We know how many masterpieces were stolen by the Nazis, hidden, and then sold."

Gerta nodded and regained her forceful voice. "This painting is a theft from my Jewish heritage. If I could not help my friends then, I will seek justice now."

"Mother, I understand. We'll continue our plans for today, but I will return tomorrow and relate your story to the museum director, and I promise you—this I will do for you—I will make sure they find the provenance of this painting."

Within the next four months, this accusation of impropriety would set into motion a series of events that would bring controversy and scandal to the revered Woodmere name.

Jason Stone

Chicago

September 2004

"I know you're tired. I know you're hungry. But don't even think of settling at the table yet. I have a strange story to tell you." As Jason Stone entered his lakefront condominium after a stressful day at his law office, his wife, Lara, greeted him, anxiously, with these words. His young son, his little clone, came running into his arms, a "My Name is Marcus" sticker clinging to his shirt.

"Am I allowed to first hug Marcus, my new kindergartener?" he teasingly asked, as he grabbed and tickled his son. Then he reached to raise Lara's face to his. She smiled at him. She would never deny him his welcome home kiss, but she was intent on telling her story.

"OK, now listen to this," she said, grasping each of his hands with hers as they rested at the small of her back, and she looked into his eyes. "The craziest thing happened today at Marcus' first day of school." She was conscious that her husband was anticipating a light-hearted story. He began walking toward the stack of mail on the hall table as she spoke. She backed up slightly and placed herself in front of the pile so that he would have to focus only on her words. "Jason, just listen. It was really strange." Finally, she had his attention. "There was this lady, another mom—never saw her before. But when she saw Marcus, this woman literally left her own daughter with one jacket sleeve on and one off, and turned to Marcus with what seemed to be tears in her eyes. She bent down and then grabbed his arms and began to either embrace or examine him—I swear I was a moment away from calling security." Lara could tell that her husband wanted to interject a comment, but she raised her hand in a halting motion and continued.

"And then, as if in a trance, this woman said, 'Rusty—my God, Rusty, I have been looking for you for so long.' I thought she was insane—I thought—oh, my God, maybe her child was kidnapped and I'm going to have to prove that Marcus wasn't adopted and that I gave birth to him. Then the mom backed off and seemed to be in deep thought for a moment and then she simply introduced herself. But I swear it was more so that she would hear our name. When I said I was Lara, she quickly asked . . . 'and his dad is?'—But then she just retreated when I said your name was Jason. I guess she finally remembered she had her own child to tend to."

As Lara finished telling her story she didn't see the peculiar narrowing of Jason's eyes as the name "Rusty" registered on her husband's face. If it weren't for his trained self-control practiced in the courtroom, he would have shown that he was shaken. He spoke so softly when he composed himself that she could barely hear him ask his question and so he cleared his throat and repeated a second time, "And what was her name?"

"I only remember her first name, Sylvie."

Then it began, once again—the memory that had followed him most of his life. It would waft from soothing daydreams to tormenting nightmares. It was always the same—the image of a mansion and a winding staircase with a thick black and beige carpet runner. And a picture on the curve of the wall, an oil painting he realized later. And the girl, younger than he was, saying, "Hi, I'm Sylvie"—then following her up the stairs to a playroom. And then, a short time later, him responding to the words, adult words, "Rusty—we're leaving—now."

The next memories were vivid ones, déjà vu moments at the Art Institute of Chicago. The painting again—knowing he has seen it or it is part of his history, but always dismissing it. It began first on a class field trip when he was twelve years old. He simply had a double take when he passed it, and returned quickly to clowning around in the gallery with his friends, not paying attention to the teacher and docent—almost embarrassed within his clique that art had drawn him in.

He saw the same painting again, this time at the age of sixteen, actually proud to be with his beautiful, intelligent mother, Rachel, who was whisper-narrating the history of paintings. She too stopped at the same painting, first pointing out its beauty, with no recognition like he had, but then halting when she read aloud the adjacent plaque and then the donor nameplate, finishing in midsentence—moving on quickly, pulling him as if he were five again.

Sylvie Woodmere Hunt

Chicago

September 2004

Loosely curling masses of hair cascading over her eyes, Sylvie had no free hand to hook them back behind her ears, as was her habit. Although at the moment she was walking with a slightly bent posture and with a less than graceful step, it was still obvious that she had the tall, slim, long-legged physique, and certainly the face, of a fashion model, the radiant hues of her hair apparent even in the dim light of the office corridor. But she was not reaching for the door to one of the many advertising agencies that populated the building; rather, she was turning the knob beneath the elegantly etched glass panel that read, Dr. Sylvie Woodmere Hunt, Clinical Psychologist.

Sylvie had left her daughter's new classroom dazed. Even she didn't understand the tears in her own eyes, but she knew that they were not for her daughter's first day of school. She was unsettled and disturbed on the one hand, yet some sense of happiness also enveloped her. Something about her young life, one that was privileged, but tormented, was resurfacing, some isolated happy memory that she stored among the frequent recurring sad ones of a dysfunctional father and absent mother.

And now, she could barely remember boarding, riding, and disembarking from the city bus, when suddenly she was opening the door to her Michigan Avenue office.

"Lisa, is my first patient here yet?" she asked her receptionist.

The young woman, who worked part-time while completing her own degree work in the field, was taken aback at her boss' appearance. Immediately, she moved from behind her desk, seeing that Dr. Hunt needed assistance at the door, her jacket, briefcase, purse, and some pink object all almost falling to the floor.

"Well, I thought you might be irritated to hear that Mrs. Aronson just cancelled, but now I am thinking this news may be welcome." She was helping her with the door now, catching what appeared to be the fleece jacket of a young girl. "Don't they have hooks in the classrooms these days?" Lisa teased, knowing that somehow Dr. Hunt was still inadvertently holding onto her daughter's coat.

"Oh, no. One more problem. I can't run back now—but she'll be cold at recess."

"Don't worry. It's early September," Lisa reminded her. "An hour from now, it will be warmer."

Instead of proceeding to her inner office as was her custom, Sylvie sank into the single waiting room chair, one that she remembered carefully selecting for color, size, and texture when she had decorated her new office three years ago, yet she had never actually sat in once since it was delivered. Now she found, as she had anticipated, that it did, in fact, present the perfect balance of comfort and firmness to ease her anxiety-ridden patients as they waited.

"Can I get you something?" Lisa offered, confused at Sylvie's uncharacteristic actions.

"No—no. You stay where you are—we're role-playing now. I am the patient."

With barely a hesitation, Lisa played along. "But you don't even know my fees."

"Fair enough," Sylvie responded. "I treat you for lunch today."

"But you always do," Lisa said, slightly laughing.

"But not at the 95th." Sylvie was referring to the pricey panoramic venue down the street at the top of the John Hancock Building.

"That sounds good. I am Dr. Lisa at your service."

They each settled into their positions—Sylvie leaning back in the comfortable chair, and Lisa, seated at the receptionist's desk, but leaning forward, posing with pencil and pad in hand, like a television psychologist.

"Lisa, do you see me as organized and controlled?"

"Anal—oh, sorry—I'm just supposed to be listening and nodding, not judging."

"I lost control today."

"Welcome to the real world."

"Lisa, I did something crazy today. Out of character. Out of control."

"Go on."

"At the school today . . . I saw this little boy, and I had the strongest sense of recognition in my life. I felt that I knew him. I felt that I knew him from the past, from when I was his age." She was honest in describing her actions now. She couldn't let go of the episode, her almost accosting the child. She didn't even know what had overcome her that she would act out like that. She knew she must have seemed like "stranger danger," if not to him, then certainly to his mother.

She had been staring blankly, slowly shaking her head, but now she focused on her listener. "You know that right after my mother died, we moved in with my grandparents and they really raised me."

"Yes, I know, 'poor little rich girl,'" Lisa blurted out and then had a sickened look on her face, fearing she had antagonized her mentor.

Sylvie, realizing her distress, lightened the moment. "I know, don't worry. It seems ridiculous to complain, but I was an extremely lonely child." Sylvie had shared pieces of her history with Lisa, as she probably spent more waking time with her than anyone else, even her husband. In fact, Lisa knew to address her simply as Sylvie when there were no patients around.

There was no need at this point for Sylvie to elaborate. Her story was known not only to Lisa, but was well documented for all those familiar with Chicago's society circles. Sylvie's grandfather, Taylor Woodmere, the wealthy industrialist from exclusive suburban

Kenilworth, had been her one savior; even now she worked with him at the charitable Woodmere Foundation. Her grandmother's depression, though she was aware that she only knew pieces of the story, was intensified by a remote husband, and a son, her father, who had spent much of his life in one rehabilitation facility or another. So Sylvie tried so hard as a child to be sunshine in a grand mansion of gloom.

She had worked her whole life to be dependable, responsible, and controlled—all those things her father was not . . . all of those things that would bind her to her grandparents so at least they would not reject her as her parents had.

"Reject" was a strong word and truly the wrong word—years of her own therapy had clarified that. As is often the case, Sylvie had become a psychologist to understand the complexities of those closest to her and of her own life. And she did understand them better now. She understood that after her mother died in the car accident, her father was incapable of handling the responsibility of a child.

"So at the school today," Sylvie continued explaining, "when I saw that little boy, I became around four years old again, reliving a wonderful childhood memory in my solitary upbringing. I remember a special afternoon with my grandfather, spinning the globe in his study, when the doorbell rang and then a woman entered with a child about my age." At this point she glanced up to see that Lisa was intrigued and was nodding for her to continue. "I remember an instant connection to an auburn-haired little boy. I think I grabbed his hand and I pulled him up the stairs to the playroom. But he stopped me on the steps—pointing to a painting on our stairwell, a picture that I had never noticed before. He said he could see a little girl in the picture—wanted to know if it was me." She stopped her narrative without looking up and almost closed her eyes, as if she were intently concentrating to relive the specific moment. "I remember Grandfather's houseman, Reed, saying, in his very British accent, something like, 'My goodness, young man, that is not Sylvie.' Whatever else he said, I couldn't understand." She raised her head to Lisa once more. "It's crazy, I know, such a vivid memory," but then she continued without allowing her to respond. "And although he may have said the name of the artist at the time, it was only through the following years when I actually focused on it, that I knew it as *Jeune Fille à la Plage*, by Henri Lebasque."

She finished the story slowly, not for dramatic impact, but wanting to hold on to the memory even for a brief time. "Before long, the mom was calling out 'Rusty' and the two of them were down the stairs and out of the house."

Once again she settled back in the chair giving Lisa more time to digest the scenario. "You know I've discovered, Lisa, that those children who spend their lives surrounded by many other young family members and friends actually have diminished memories of specific childhood encounters. But to me, they were isolated and therefore paramount." At this point, Sylvie slowly left the chair and walked over to Lisa's desk. "Let me ask you something," she said, establishing this more intimate distance. "What is your earliest real memory?"

"OK . . . Let me think . . . Yes, that's easy," Lisa responded after only ten seconds of contemplation. "I'm five and in kindergarten and dancing with a cute little boy, Barry, at the graduation party."

Sylvie prodded her further. "OK, now I ask you to really think. Is that a true memory—or a recollection when looking at a photograph of the event?"

"Well—no—I remember it—I think—or maybe I only do remember the photo." Now Lisa took the time to transport herself back in years, leaning slightly on her elbow, her eyes in the upward, distant glare of contemplation, her closed fist, still encircling the pencil, momentarily covering her mouth. "Sylvie, you are so perceptive. You know—I think my real memory is of sitting on the living room couch with my mom. I am about ten years old and we are looking at albums and pointing to that picture. You may be right." And she focused once more on Sylvie, allowing her to continue.

"Well, this morning I had such a strong feeling of familiarity with the little boy at my daughter's school. When I came to my senses—barely—I thought that maybe the little boy I remembered, named Rusty, could have been his father—this little boy's father. I guess it's laughable now—how ridiculous that reach was. But the father's name was Jason, not Rusty." She started to turn away from her listener and now spoke only to the air. "Perhaps I should apologize and try to explain . . .if only I could explain it to myself."

As Lisa moved in her seat, she seemed to gesture with her pencil that she was ready to interject a comment, but Sylvie, facing the opposite direction, did not take her cue, and continued with her own thoughts.

"I've played this memory game with others before—friends I made at camp or my first year at college out East," Sylvie said. "Those were times that I lived for. I loved that sibling-like camaraderie that you've always had with your sisters." Now she turned back to Lisa as she spoke. "When I asked those friends the same question, it was never day-to-day moments that were the childhood memories. Usually it was vacations, occasions that were out of the ordinary routine—swimming with cousins on the beach in Florida—visiting grandmas and drenching themselves with their perfume bottle collections. But for me—a seasoned world traveler by high school—I was not a stranger to the Hôtel de Crillon in Paris and the Villa d'Este in Lake Como—my most cherished early memory was bonding with a little boy, playing hide-and-seek in my playroom. And there is no photograph of that, only the picture in my mind."

In an almost unconscious move, Sylvie simply left the reception area with her briefcase and entered her private office. She no longer felt the need to verbalize her thoughts; now she just wanted some time alone to collect them. For one more memory of the painting filled her personal history. She was around ten years old and her grandfather was beginning to have problems with his eyesight. Sylvie remembered even the tone of Grandmother's words. "Then, as long as you can't see it well anyway, it is off as a donation to the Art Institute of Chicago. They have been approaching me recently about securing more of our collection and I will be happy, finally, to have this one out."

Sylvie had looked at her grandfather after the exchange and could sense his emotion was resignation. Normally, any charitable donations, she knew, roused only positive reflections of pride in his demeanor. But something was different with this one, she recalled thinking.

And now Sylvie, all grown up and a young mother, understood that this boy might be nothing to her, but his appearance had triggered memories in her that she finally needed to understand. "Closure." As a psychologist, she often used that word with her patients. And now she knew that she needed closure. But how could that come about?

She had no recollection of her father, Court Woodmere, ever interacting with that little boy, and anyway, her father had passed away years ago, his body finally failing from years of drug abuse. Her grandfather, Taylor Woodmere, was present that day in the 1970s, but he was, after all, ninety now. Though he was still an amazing man, she doubted that he would have any memory of this small episode.

Emily and I were just discussing activities for thi

ful day ahead."

She raised her eyes and her index fing

to the uniformed butler who approach

service and refilled her cup before

with his customary coffee. Emily cl

a slight cough so that she might

"A fresh cup for me, if yo

cooled," she said, and th

mother and I have alrea

den, partway down to

At this point, th

a silver domed ca

up behind him

the used sil

assortmen

reveal

garni

me

Then

girlfriend, Emily, who w

behind her, he gave a lighter peck on th

head, adding, "And you . . . you are strawberry jam on scones."

Emily lowered her head and blushed slightly. Louise Woodmere smiled at her only son. "You are an incorrigible flirt," she said, using her fork to direct him to the chair closest to her. "I'm not sure your father will be joining us this morning. He seems quite preoccupied. So that means I can have you both to myself for a while.

s beauti-

er, motioning
ed with the tea
presenting Taylor
ared her throat with
catch the server's eye.
u don't mind—mine has
n turned to Taylor. "Your
dy had a long walk in the gar-
he lake."
e butler returned, briskly wheeling
t in their direction. A maid, keeping
, brought them fresh plates, removing
erware and straightening the remaining
of utensils. Just as the butler raised the lid to
oached and lightly scrambled eggs, beautifully
shed with fresh slices of cantaloupe and honeydew
lon and green grapes dipped in sugar, Taylor's father
ntered the dining room.

Addison Woodmere was an imposing figure by any standards. Even at this early hour, he was elegantly dressed for the day. His three-piece, dark gray, pinstriped suit, the contrasting stark white, crisply starched shirt, and the wide navy cravat were in bold contrast to the muted, casual summer attire of the others. He acknowledged the women first, with a "Good morning, ladies," then stood next to Taylor, his arm resting heavily on the young man's shoulder, making it evident that he had been looking for him and had no intention of seating himself at the table.

"Good morning, Father," Taylor said. "I just sat down myself and I was about to explain to the ladies that I was busy with the material you gave me last night. I was going to be coming to you as soon as I finished breakfast." Taylor felt comfortable with his father, but he also did not want to appear to have neglected any of his directives.

His father's firm grip softened into a sweet paternal pat. "Ladies, enjoy your day. Taylor, I'll see you in my study shortly." He motioned to the maid to pour him some juice, and without further instruction, she took a serving tray from beneath the cart, placed the glass on it along with a pastry on a china dish, and followed him.

Seated behind his oversized, gold-etched, wood grained desk, he cleared a space beyond the rectangle of his black blotter where the maid placed the breakfast tray, then made her exit. Addison Woodmere was a successful businessman. He and his father, the senior Addison, in his eighties in the year 1937, had made prudent investments, came through the crash relatively unscathed, and had actually built their company during the ensuing years with substantial government contracts. Not only an important manufacturer, Addison was also a prominent philanthropist, a well-respected figure both in his affluent suburban community of Kenilworth and in Chicago society.

As promised, Taylor, appeared in the study just a short time later, straightening the stack of papers he carried, and anxious to be the first to speak. "Father," he said, "I can only presume you have given me these documents because you are planning on my accompanying you to Paris. And pleased as I am to be presented with a European trip, I have to say that this is not a time for me to leave. I would prefer to stay at home for the summer."

It had always been understood that Taylor was being groomed to enter the family business. As a very young boy, he would accompany his father on his factory rounds, scribbling in his composition book as if he was taking the most meticulous notes. Later, when he was on school breaks, he was required to put in long hours to be exposed to each facet of Woodmere Industries, experiencing everything from janitorial work, where he devised a time-saving method for garbage removal, to time at the loading docks, heaving containers of corrugated boxes that would serve as packaging for a multitude of industries. Now he was hoping to delay assuming, for just a few months, his post as the heir apparent.

Having recently graduated from Yale University, alma mater of the last two generations of Woodmeres, he was enjoying what he presumed would be his last summer vacation and was focused on entertaining his houseguest, his "almost fiancée," Emily Kendall. Introduced by one of her brothers, a classmate of Taylor's, he and Emily had been keeping company on and off for over two years. They had met at the first Yale football rally of the season, always well attended by the bright and pretty coeds from Vassar. They soon became "an item," hand in hand at many athletic events, and arm in arm for most of their school formals.

"I understand your personal situation and I apologize for that," his father said. He leaned forward, his elbows on the table and his clasped hands, forming a bobbing triangle to emphasize his points. "You have been a leader throughout your school years and I want you to continue to develop into a man of accomplishment, generosity, and open-mindedness." Taylor's anxiety was abating; perhaps he had misinterpreted his father's purpose in giving him the thorough descriptions of each meeting on the European schedule. But Taylor was mistaken. Addison had, as always, skillfully manipulated the interaction to make his case. "I do understand the impact of timing. And that is why I need you to travel overseas now to be introduced to our European associates." He purposely did not look up, not wanting to monitor his son's reaction.

"Herman Lester, our manager of operations, has already left for Paris, and he will have the greater organizational responsibilities." He set before Taylor an array of business papers and personal correspondence with a range of international addresses and postmarks. "There is the possibility that we can align with our European counterparts and create a supply network and shipping chain that could win contracts for us whether nations are at peace or at war. In our uniform supply line, for instance, although we have materials for clothing and boots, we may use their labor or their resources for distribution. This next week I will fill you in completely on my goals, but you know the business, and I have a strong confidence in your abilities."

At this point, Taylor was recognizing the inevitable— that he would do whatever his father asked of him.

"Will Grandfather go with us?" he asked, although he was certain that the senior Addison would never miss the opportunity to spend time abroad.

"You need to realize, Taylor, you will be the on[e] one representing the Woodmere family in Paris." H[is] father's tone turned very serious and now he looked Ta[y]lor directly in his eyes. "Recent developments requir[e] your grandfather and me to deal with labor issues her[e.] You read the papers. You know what has happened [at] U. S. Rubber. We want fair negotiations to forestall an[y] problems at our locations."

Taylor was taking some time now to comprehen[d] what was being asked of him, digesting the weight [of] responsibility, but relishing the tremendous faith i[n] his abilities that his father was implying. For the pa[st] six months, his father had been arranging a multin[a]tional conference that was to be held during the sum[m]er Paris Exposition. Owners of some of the large[st] manufacturing enterprises in England, France, an[d] Germany would be meeting at the World's Fair in hop[e] of planning future joint ventures. His father was prou[d] to be an industry leader and a visionary in the role [of] international cooperation as a means to climb from th[e] Depression.

Addison studied Taylor, who appeared intereste[d] though somewhat overwhelmed, but gave him n[o] opportunity to speak. "Your principal contact will b[e] Emanuel Berger, a Jewish man, who lives with his famil[y] in Berlin."

"Yes, I remember you speaking about him—and wit[h] high praise, always," Taylor said.

Addison nodded. "As you know, there is a great dea[l] of anti-Semitism in the world. But make no mistake; tha[t] is dangerous and misguided. Many of the Jews I've deal[t] with aren't merely bright, but brilliant. They are clever, honest, and resourceful, and as a people posses a rare humanitarianism. You know, of course, of your grandfather's close friend who died some years ago, Julius Rosenwald, who built Sears, Roebuck & Company into a retail giant. He was a German Jewish immigrant—and eventually a great philanthropist—the Museum of Science and Industry is his endowment."

"Yes, of course."

"And I am proud to call Emanuel a good friend. He and I have had many illuminating conversations on a wide range of topics, cultural and historical. I've asked him just how concerned he was with the rise of Adolph Hitler in Germany. He told me the Jews have suffered and overcome great trials throughout their long history; they've looked tyrants in the face before, and this one has the profile of a most virulent beast.

"Once I tried to talk to my group at the club about this, and, God love the 'old boys.' they cracked their stereotypical jokes . . . I will not repeat them for you . . . so I just shut down my inquiry. I'm afraid anti-Semitism isn't limited to Germany."

A post-college European trip was a common "coming of age" gift for his set, but Taylor was not at all excited at the prospect. He had finally captured Emily Kendall's full attention—and won her heart. He would soon give Emily his grandmother's diamond ring that was resting in his bureau drawer.

As they approached engagement, she had granted him (yes, the word "granted" was perfect, as sometimes he felt like a subject in her royal presence) more intimate liberties. How would he live without the taste of her silken lips, without the feel of her soft shoulders and perfect breasts? He had worked so hard to capture her, fighting off the dozens of other suitors and luring her from her home town in Newport for the summer, convincing her that sailing on Lake Michigan was more exciting than ocean sailing, that Chicago society rivaled Newport's. It would be hard to concentrate on business deals abroad when all he wanted was to think about the changing colors of her hazel eyes. He would miss everything about her, even her temperamental, demanding side.

His father saw his reluctance, but he remained firm. "You must go now—Europe is in turmoil—and although it is safe for the time being, I fear it won't be for long. Our business needs to be completed."

Rachel Gold

Chicago

June 1968

It was the magical summer of 1968, the summer of flower children, antiwar protests, of drugs and free love. Rachel Gold had just returned home from her freshman year at the University of Illinois in downstate Champaign. She had always been a quiet and intellectual girl. Her parents were hard-working, sweet people, her dad an accountant at the Lyon and Healy Music Company in Chicago. They were proud that their daughter was at the premier state school and not a city college. Though the dorm costs were a stretch for them, they were able to meet that obligation. And Rachel had earned a full tuition teacher's scholarship. Clothing and extras—this was the summer she was determined to get contact lenses—were paid for by earnings from part-time and summer jobs. Rachel didn't mind; her work ethic was inherited, and like everything else, she approached challenges as opportunities.

For this summer, she'd landed a job at Last Chance Café, one of the new casual eateries that defined the decade, where peanuts covered the floor and local rock bands played (almost for peanuts) in the evenings. It was just off the Chicago area's legendary Sheridan Road, right before it takes the turn from the city into the suburbs.

Sheridan Road was unfamiliar to her now. It traversed an area where village names defined residents, but as a city girl, Rachel, until this summer of discovery, had rarely ventured on it north of Chicago. Later she would be able to recite by heart the suburbs that followed its serpentine route once it exited the city . . . Evanston, Wilmette, Kenilworth, Winnetka, Glencoe, Highland Park, Lake Forest . . .

At Last Chance, she learned to smile and to flirt and teasingly toss her long black hair and wear make-up to distraction. As a late bloomer in many respects except for intellect, she transformed during that summer from an awkward girl into a beautiful young woman. She walked and slimmed down by accident, not by design. It happened that she was just interested in saving some extra money, so she didn't take the bus to work. She missed reading while riding, but the stopping every block and re-shifting of sweaty bodies on the busy route was too distracting anyway. So she began to walk to work. And as she became more intent on applying makeup at home in the morning, not heavily, but perfectly, she found time would get away from her and then she would need to get to work almost in a run. Within the first month, her body, which had not been fat, but somewhat round, soon took on a delicious new form. By July, she was literally turning heads, boys' heads, as she moved from table to table at work. The attention made her feel more powerful than her class rank ever had. This is ridiculous, she thought. I'm not some shallow high school cheerleader. But she didn't let the attention go to her head, and maintained her beautiful, enigmatic quality.

She first noticed Courtland (Court) Woodmere because he seemed so solitary among his group, not as full of himself as the others. They were, obviously, the Northwestern boys. His dark auburn hair was in such contrast to the wheat-colored shags of the others at his table. And there was something about his eyes . . . Finally, the third time he came in with his fraternity brothers, he touched her hand when she brought him his Coke. Then he gently grabbed her arm when she returned with fries. By the time she was serving the pizza, he had his hand around her waist, escorting her to the dance floor.

"Just for a moment," she insisted, whispering. "I'll get in trouble if I'm not working."

"Oh, I don't believe that for a second. You're the reason they're packing them in, not the bands. You should be on display more; it would be better for business," he said, twirling her around and ending in an old-fashioned dip.

After the dance, he suggested they get to know each other somewhere besides Last Chance. He offered to drive her home that night, but she quickly declined. She didn't want to tell him right out that dates with Gentiles were forbidden in her household, but she did say that her dad insisted on picking her up himself each evening. But during the drive that very night, she began thinking of a way to spend time with Court. It's the summer of love and excitement, she thought, and I want something to remember it by. Despite her intelligence and pragmatism at work, she and her friends were mostly naïve and unsophisticated girls, giggling in corners and swooning with crushes.

And as it evolved, three days later, on Saturday afternoon, Court pulled up for her outside the movie theater, as she waved good-bye to her sworn–to-secrecy and frozen-in-astonishment friends, and was off in a red Mustang convertible.

Sitting beside him, she was giddy. My God, he was cute, she thought. Then she corrected herself. Cute did not begin to do him justice. He was magnificent! She tried not to stare at him as they drove, but she needed to reassure herself that he was real, not just another post-adolescent fantasy she had conjured. She kept readjusting her position in the passenger seat, hoping he would not pick up on her self-conscious maneuvers. Luckily, the car had bucket seats and a center console, so she did not have to agonize over how close she should sit to him, as she had on past first dates, trying to calculate the perfect distance between date and door, so as to appear neither too easy, nor too frigid.

Soon she was in a whirlwind of clandestine encounters, and whenever they were together she was magnetized by his charm—his elegant, polished manners. He always escorted her into the car first, closing the door gently, making sure her sweater or purse was neatly arranged on her lap, not dangling where it might be caught. And then he would skip around to the driver's seat and take his place. He would look at her as if she were his precious prize. It was his routine to hold her left hand in his right, and steer with his left hand. He called her princess, and treated her like royalty. And then when they reached their destination—he was equally courtly. She had to remind herself to wait for him to come around and open the door—to conform to what was expected of a well-mannered girl. Hippie dress, music, love, sex, and drugs may be the rule of the day, but good manners never went out of fashion.

For the first time in her life, she felt reckless. And she loved it. She loved the wild feeling of the convertible ride, though she always kept her hair restrained by a peasant scarf so the wind could blow across her face without allowing errant strands to whip in her eyes. From their first afternoon together, she knew that he would want to kiss her, that he was winding his way north on Sheridan Road to Gilson Park in Wilmette, a place she had heard about that was famous for "parking."

First, they watched the players on the tennis courts and the children and families at the playground. Then they sat on the beach and were lulled by the rhythmic swells of the waves. The moon climbed from the east and the sun set behind their backs. They ended up back in the car, top up now in the dark parking lot, and there they kissed. This ritual was repeated three times

that first week they were dating; each time he lured her
to become increasingly intimate. He was gentle, never
forcing himself on her, but he was helping her to discover the needs of her own body as well as his. She
didn't want to appear "easy," but his kisses were better
than chocolate to her. As his hands worked their charms
to tease her with caresses of her body, she felt an intense
physical desire for his touch. After two weeks of being
together, she was no longer a virgin, and she felt glorious and proud of her new womanly being.

She was surprised to discover that he didn't know
she was Jewish. Certainly, she'd known immediately that
he was not. But perhaps in his world, where you are
not a minority, where you are not continually looking
to define yourself among strangers, there was an awareness of only the most elemental stereotypes of Jews. It
was on their second Saturday afternoon outing—lunch
at the Pancake House—when he ordered for both of
them.

"Oh, I don't eat bacon," she said.

"You don't eat bacon?" he asked.

"I don't eat any pork."

He looked at her quizzically. "What are you Jewish
or something?"

Looking back, perhaps she should have followed
her instincts. There was something unattractive about
the way he said it.

"Well, yes, actually, I am—of course—I assumed you
knew that."

"Well, no offense."

"Well, of course, no offense," she responded. Living in Rogers Park with its proud Jewish heritage, she didn't know why anyone would be offended. Even at college her first year, certainly where the greater student populace was not Jewish, she had found her comfortable niche in the world of the "Jewish dorms," and the Jewish fraternity and sorority social scene. She had never personally encountered anti-Semitism.

And then, as the summer drew to a close, only a week before it would be Labor Day and the return to school, she told him she was pregnant. She had not even completely sorted out her own feelings on the predicament. But she felt so close to him, so in love with him, that she knew it was something they would face together—she never thought she would need to handle the problem alone.

He said nothing for the longest time and when he finally spoke, he did not look at her, but surveyed first the cloudy sky and then the small patch of grassless dirt on which he was standing. "I explained to you," he said firmly. "My family—it's different from yours—we have a long history. My God, we've got three generations living in my house. Kenilworth is different from Rogers Park—I never even heard of Rogers Park until I met you." He continued in an almost incoherent rambling pattern. "It's just that I'm really attached to my parents—and my mother—she freaks at anything Jewish—sorry, something about the wartime, something from when my dad went to Europe right before WWII. It just won't work you and me—you being Jewish—you know."

Of course, she hadn't expected him to be thrilled. But she had never dreamt he would be so cold and dismissive.

"I can't believe those words are coming from you," she finally said when she could breathe. "You can't be the same boy I met two months ago, the one who romanced me in the coffeehouse, and made love to me by the beach. I don't even know you."

She struggled to regain her composure, to give him time, as well, to digest what she had said and reconsider his response. She waited for a quick apology, for arms to embrace her, for his hand to brush through her hair and wipe away her tears. But there was no such contrition; he stood very separate from her. Now she wasn't just hurt, she was angry. "Wasn't I Jewish the first night when you came on to me? And how about sitting on the floor of the Folk Lounge on Sheridan Road, and wasn't I Jewish that night at Evanston Beach on the sand and in the car at Gilson Park? Wasn't I your dark-haired beauty then?"

He was smart enough to say nothing.

And then his eyes took on a narrowed look of loathing. And in that instant, her dream became a nightmare. The glorious, passionate heat that had consumed her body day and night froze. And on this dreary evening, her body became one more cloud. She was a rainstorm of tears, a thunderstorm of anger and hurt, a cyclone of torment. She wanted to forget her "summer to always remember." But that was not possible—she had a baby growing inside her.

They met only once after she broke the news to him. Though her college term had started, she came back to Chicago to work for a few more weekends. The money was great enough that it would pay for books and some necessities for the term. But she was still keeping her situation private. Contrary to her usual pattern, she was not attacking the problem head on. She was like any young girl in trouble—confused, in denial, postponing decisions.

It was a week before he contacted her again, appearing at Last Chance at the beginning of her shift, before any of the young crowd gathered. Leaving his car parked in the loading zone at the front of the restaurant, he walked in slowly, without his usual self-assured jaunt, a literal embodiment of the image of "dragging one's feet." He scanned the room with the sparsely filled booths and tables of the early hour, expecting to see her standing and writing an order.

"Rachel," he called, but his voice, too, was without his usual force. And though he was sure that it was her by the kitchen pass-through, donning a black apron with her back toward the tables, sharing a joke with a white-capped cook, she made no move to respond.

"Rachel," he repeated, this time with a volume and urgency in his voice.

Finally, she turned, and he was drawn to the beautiful rose bloom of her cheeks. Excusing herself from the counter area, she began to slowly approach him. As she walked closer, he saw again the innocence of her huge brown eyes, how she unconsciously fluttered her lashes disbelievingly. It almost made him lose his nerve and determination. He stretched his arm in her direction, holding it out as if he could take her hand, although a good thirty feet separated the pair.

Only in the few moments that it took her to walk to him did she believe he had returned regretful and loving. She was too easily recaptured by the familiarity of his thick auburn hair, not close enough yet to see that his smile was partial and insincere. But when her hand was almost touching his, eager to be cradled in his strength, he pulled his hand abruptly away.

"Um, a, Rachel," he stammered. He was turning away from her and so she had to follow him out the door, like an errant child who a parent had just located in a public place and was preparing to reprimand privately outside. "I need you to come with me for a second." It was not a request, but a command.

He turned back to her only briefly, still barely making eye contact, as he motioned her to the passenger side of his parked car. "We need to take a little ride. Just around the block." He was speaking quickly, not wanting her to tell the staff that she was leaving. He wanted her confused and unsettled and vulnerable in his own comfortable element. He didn't want there to be a scene. But if there was one, he wanted it to be on his own turf—in his red Mustang.

Too quickly, he made a sharp turn at the first corner and he drove halfway down the block, taking the vacant space in front of a fire plug. He put the car into park and reached above the flipped-up sun visor to extract something. It was then that she saw an envelope in his hand, and when he finally faced her completely, the sour, curt look on his face.

"Here," he said, handing her the envelope. "There's a doctor's name, someone my mother knew of . . . and money. This should take care of it." And while she tried to digest just what he was saying to her, he was remembering the scene at home the previous day when he had gone to his mother for money for an abortion. He had said only that there had been trouble with a Jewish girl. He was more than familiar with his mother's attitude toward Jews, remembering several occasions when she made snide, anti-Semitic remarks, and he would catch his father glaring at her. And so his instinct was to approach only his mother with his situation. He was relieved to have found her alone in her upstairs sitting room, and although he addressed her quietly, her staccato quick retort, her repetition of his own words "trouble with a Jewish girl," was uncharacteristically loud. And while she was finishing, he thought he heard his father's heavy footsteps approach and then stop just beyond the doorframe. Confirming his suspicions when he furtively looked in that direction, he could see his father's reflection in the hall mirror, but his father's head, like his, was lowered. He seemed to still be processing the words he had heard. Court expected momentarily for him to enter the room with a "What goes on here?" While his mother rattled on and then went to a dresser drawer to retrieve something, he prepared for his father to take yet another opportunity to express disappointment in his only son, initiating yet one more time when Court wished that he had a sibling to help shoulder the tremendous weight of the prestigious Woodmere legacy. But this time Court was spared the lecture. He sensed the quiet retreat of his father back down the hall. Incredulous to have escaped the familiar tirade, his relief was palpable.

Taylor Woodmere never broached the topic with his son, neither then, nor in the future. But it was not because he was indifferent. For Taylor, just hearing the words "Jewish girl," made his own painful memories come rushing back. The years of torment, the years of searching, of fear, disappointment and despair returned in a flood. He wanted to rush toward his son, shake him, slap him, but he didn't. Perhaps he had misunderstood the situation; maybe he was reading his own history into his son's words. But most of all, he did not wish to aggravate his wife. For years now, for what seemed a lifetime, he had worked hard to maintain the peace between them.

For Rachel, Court's final rejection was a sword, a knife—and she emotionally felt its impact. She did not know whether to pray that the baby escaped the pain of it or hope that his words did their trick to expel it before any doctor needed to operate. As Court made an abrupt U-turn to head back to the restaurant, Rachel sat stiff and cold as a marble statue. When she left the car, he turned to her and with a boyish, remorseful face, mouthed, "I am sorry."

What to do? What to do?"Think," she sobbed aloud, walking from his car. He hadn't even opened the door for her as he had since their first date. No. Not today.

Today no doors were opened for her. It was one simple gesture, but it revealed his true manner. After he drove her around the block to talk and they pulled up again at the restaurant, he did not get out. He simply leaned over her and opened the passenger door—almost shooing her out as if she were a hitchhiker, or worse, a whore.

Of course she understood that abortion was the easiest solution—but until now that had only been a word, a concept, a popular cause. Now it was personal. This was a real baby. She had been conditioned to welcome news of a baby—to greet it with joy and expectation. Her own parents had desperately wanted another child. On two occasions her mother had announced that she was pregnant, and each time, just weeks later, Rachel heard her sobbing in her bedroom. Shortly after, a neighbor, the mother of a friend, would come to stay with her, when her parents left overnight for the hospital. The next day, her father would only tell her of a "disappointment," and ask Rachel to be "Mother's best little helper."

What to do? What to do? It took two more days of anguish and then it came to her. And that was the gift that was Rachel—she could turn something potentially bad, a *shanda*, and spin it into a *mitzvah*—a good deed.

The hardest part was telling her parents. She knew it would be a blow, knew they had been complacent in their pride in her. She feared her father—who had put her on a pedestal—might actually need medical attention after she delivered the news. Just telling them she was dating a Gentile boy would be bad enough, but now she was going to tell them that she had been in love with the boy and that she was pregnant with his child. But, perhaps because of their love for her, or because she was so obviously overcome with remorse and fear when she broke the news to them, they responded, after their initial shock, with concern, and tried only to comfort her.

After a few minutes of weeping and hugs, they left her with a box of tissues and spent some time in the kitchen conferring with each other. Ten minutes later they emerged again.

"Will you marry this boy?" her father asked with trepidation.

"You don't understand," Rachel was quick to respond. "He wants nothing to do with me. He said that he loved me, and now he can't wait to be rid of me. What a fool I am—I think he may be anti-Semitic. Here was his solution." She paused and got up from the couch to retrieve her huge macramé purse. Fumbling through it, she pulled out the white envelope and tossed it on the coffee table. "He got his mother to give me $300 for an abortion. Oh, my God," she said, weeping again, "How could I have let this happen?"

"Rachel, good riddance to this fiend. We cannot pretend that we are not shocked or disappointed—but that will pass—our love never will," her father said, as her mother, tears in her eyes, nodded agreement. "We will figure this out together." These two middle-aged people could never forget their own struggle to have another baby, and because of that they could never be complicit in sacrificing a pregnancy.

Rachel straightened herself, smoothing her clothes and hair and rubbing smeared makeup from her eyes. "Actually I have thought this through and I have a plan. I think it is a good idea and would save a great deal of anxiety and embarrassment for you. I hope you will be supportive."

The day before, "Aunt" Ida had come into her mind in an epiphany. Ida was not really her aunt, but a woman for whom they all had great fondness. Rachel's mother and her grandparents had been in an earlier emigration wave from Europe—they did not need a Hitler to drive them out when perennial *pogroms* breached the peace of their village. "Aunt" Ida had been the daughter of her grandparents' neighbors in the old country; she was about five years younger than Rachel's parents. But Ida's family, possibly because her father was of some means in the village and tried longer, too long, to protect his possessions, became victims of the Nazi rampages. Only Ida, less than twenty years old when she finally was liberated from Auschwitz, survived the war. Through agencies abroad and at home, Rachel Gold's family was able to connect with Ida and sponsor her immigration to America.

The plan was that after Ida Lieber arrived in New York, she would then travel on to Chicago. But Ida, still a skeleton from her experiences in the concentration camps, was barely admitted past the gates of Ellis Island. Luckily, a processor misread her information, and thinking she was a little girl accompanied by a guardian, instead of an unhealthy young woman traveling alone, allowed her to enter the United States. But that very day, she fainted on the street and landed in a hospital where she stayed for several weeks. When she recovered, she had neither the will nor the energy to move on, although she was effusively grateful to her sponsors, Rachel Gold's family.

They visited Aunt Ida often. And Aunt Ida, who never married, who said that she had been "violated" by the Nazi beasts, found a contented life in New York. She had made friends with seamstresses during her hospital stay, had quickly picked up English from them, and secured a job in the fabric industry. She had lost her family, but she had made a family of friends in New York.

Rachel remembered conversations with her when she was so small that she didn't even understand their meaning—"Rachel, my sweet one, you are the future. You are the hope. I will look to you—pray that you help to replace those we have lost. Please may I be 'Aunt Ida' to your children one day—and please –may your parents still be living—that you would one day bring alive again the name Jacob, honoring my young brother—through your children."

Rachel

New York

October 1968

So Rachel let go of her carefree college days of sororities and late night parties, said to herself— "Here is Rachel, Part II," and she embraced the new situation. As it turned out, New York was a gift to her. She had visited several times when she was younger, after long car trips with her parents, but she didn't remember the city outside the Greenwich Village apartment of her aunt. Now she loved exploring everywhere, the cacophony of the streets—the vendors' cries, and construction work whistles, the taxi cab horns, and police sirens—was a symphony of enchantment.

True, Chicago was a beautiful city with a world-famous skyline—but nothing compared to New York. She loved Chicago and knew she would return there one day—but now she was a person who was ready to be lost in the anonymity of New York City.

Aunt Ida herself turned out to be a wonderful surprise. When the taxi arrived at her apartment building just blocks from the Village's iconic Washington Park, Rachel chose the first load of luggage to carry up to the second-floor landing, one suitcase full of clothes and her first of three small cartons of books. She spotted Ida waving to her from the window, and wondered for how many hours she had been pacing the apartment awaiting her safe arrival. When Rachel climbed the stairs and was at the front door, Ida was there too, with an offering of flowers in one hand and a plate of double fudge brownies in the other. She lifted both arms high so she could accept Rachel's enthusiastic embrace, but she could return only kisses on the cheek at the moment.

"Aunt Ida," Rachel said with a laugh, "I'm the guest. I'm supposed to come bringing gifts for you. And I have many things, but I don't know which suitcase they are in." As she spoke, drawing in not only the warmth of Ida's greeting, but the familiar scent of chicken soup and old rugs that pervaded the apartment, she felt at home already.

"No, darling," Ida insisted. "Your coming here . . . this to me is an honor . . . you are to me from a royal family . . . you are a princess and you will be treated as such . . . end of discussion." And so Rachel accepted the flowers graciously and nibbled some brownies, savoring each bite of the deep chocolate flavor. In the moments she stood facing Ida with smiles and nods as she chewed, she took a really good look at her. Rachel saw immediately that Ida was not the old-world guarded individual she remembered from her youth, but a sweet, perky, middle-aged woman, younger looking than she had anticipated, with a petite frame and a possibly good figure hidden beneath an outdated wardrobe.

Rachel knew a little of Ida's history in Europe and had previously witnessed her quiet, yet contented life in New York. But now as she walked through the same apartment that she had visited two or three times as a child, her focus was different. She wasn't looking out the windows; this time she was also looking at the apartment—at Ida's memorabilia—plates and linens and crackled pictures. She wanted to know more about Ida's story and the wisdom in her years. "Aunt Ida," she coaxed, "please tell me about all of these pictures."

"No, my dear," she answered almost abruptly. "You think they are mine, my real memories. But they are gifts from other people, thinking they can replace what I have lost." Her back was to Rachel now, as she scanned her own apartment. "Over the years, when I was reunited with neighbors from our village or relatives from neighboring communities, people who had made their way to America before the war would share with me pictures they would insist included my mother or father or even me. I would thank them graciously, for I knew they had only the best of intentions, but my father would never have had a beard of that fashion, my mother would never have worn that dress, and I certainly was not a towering, husky child."

"Aunt Ida," she said again. "Won't you please tell me your story?"

Ida looked at her chosen niece with sweet adoration and tried to be soft in her response. "Rachel, my Rachel—you have always been a unique child—and now a woman. It is so easy for me to see how you would love and be loved." (This would be one of the only references Ida would make to Rachel's predicament.) "One day, my darling," she continued. "Perhaps, one day I will tell you my story, though it is a sad one." But to herself, Aunt Ida hoped that Rachel could help her create new good memories of birth and push further back the memories of death.

Taylor

Paris

July 1937

Although this was not Taylor's first European trip—twice before he had accompanied his parents on summer holidays in the south of France—this would be his first exposure to the metropolitan life of a European city, and his first independent passage. The itinerary was well planned and seamlessly executed. He boarded a train in Chicago and his first-class Pullman accommodations afforded him ample comfort and privacy to review his father's instructions and all that had transpired in the last week.

Surprisingly, he was not consumed with thoughts of Emily. Initially, he had been worried that she might return to Newport immediately upon his departure, and he pictured her recaptured by the patterns of her youth, dancing in the arms of any number of young men who had pursued her through the years. And so, he was extremely relieved when she assured him she would remain in the Chicago area while he was abroad. She would still use her guest room at the Woodmere Estate in Kenilworth as her home base, but she would spend time with a rotation of girlfriends from school, as well as a cousin's family, all in adjacent North Shore communities. He chose not to interpret her sullen mood and tearfulness as emanating from a lack of understanding and support, but just the disappointment of separation that tugged also at his heart.

"When I come back, I will have something for you . . . something very special," he told her the last morning. He had dressed at 5:00 a.m. for the long car ride to Chicago's Union Station, and while the chauffeur placed the suitcases in the black Packard, Taylor had quietly opened the door to Emily's room and gently rubbed her back to wake her.

She heard the words as she emerged from sleep and with her eyes still closed there was a slight smile on her face. "You will have something for me?"

"Ah, ha. I knew that would improve your mood and chase away your frowns."

She maneuvered herself to a more upright position against her considerable collection of pillows and made no attempt to adjust the bodice of her nightgown, which revealed a generous glimpse of her right breast. Taylor kissed her there, then drew her to him in a tight embrace. He planted more kisses in the rich thickness of her glorious hair before his lips finally settled on hers, and then he pulled back for a lingering look into her eyes.

"I love you, Taylor," she said. "I will miss you so much."

"Wait for me . . . I will come back to you soon," he promised.

A representative from the *SS Normandie* was waiting at Grand Central Station in New York when he arrived to take him to the harbor and assist with his luggage. The *Normandie* was twice the size of the *Titanic*, and was built to be the most powerful and fastest ship ever constructed, boasting modern turbo engines and a new hull design.

Taylor was not one of those who let out an audible gasp when he ascended the boarding plank and entered the foyer of the grand ship, nevertheless he was truly awed. There was a museum quality to the structure, with sculptures and paintings that were rarely seen in public spaces. And this was a deliberate new direction for the models of such luxury liners. While refugees to the United States had previously filled ships with lower-class passengers and even steerage, the declining immigration quotas had now influenced the steamship line to design a ship geared mainly toward amenities for first-class passengers.

Carrying just his briefcase, he approached the purser's desk where there was only a short wait until it was his turn and he presented his boarding papers.

"Mr. Woodmere," a young, uniformed officer of the ship addressed him after glancing at them for his name, "Welcome to the *Normandie* and please tell me any way I might be of assistance to you during the cruise." The purser did not speak with the French accent that Taylor had anticipated and so he surmised that among the special considerations that would make American first-class passengers feel most at home was the hiring of employees who spoke their language and understood their needs. The European traveler might require a fuller bulk to his pillows and duvets, might expect a larger meal at lunch and lighter fare in the evening, and might want to begin that repast at an hour when the Americans would be folding their napkins and pushing their chairs from the table. The French would want their morning café, the English their afternoon tea, and the Americans an enormous dessert display.

"And I'm glad to know that you will personally be available to me," Taylor said in the friendly, joking style that sometimes only Americans can understand. "I am traveling on business to Paris and I may need to communicate with Chicago during our crossing. Is that possible or do I sound impossibly naïve to even ask?"

"Sir, that is a reasonable question. Every ship will have its own capabilities, but not every ship has the efficacy of communications as does the *Normandie*." He went on to explain that the ship was fitted with the most advanced technology that would well service his needs. Thanking the purser for his help, Taylor left the desk while reviewing a simplified blueprint that he had been handed. He was anxious to explore the vessel, but lingered to overhear the conversations of the other passengers now waiting in the growing line.

"How y'all doing? Told my friends I was booked on the largest ship afloat," one man said with a thick, colorful Texas accent. "And in my first hour I have not been disappointed." He continued speaking to no one in particular, perhaps waiting to catch a response from a fellow passenger. "Did you see the dining room? I mean they say it is more beautiful than the Palace of Versailles." His mispronunciation of that venue was so egregious an assault on their language, that the group of returning Frenchmen passing by exchanged incredulous glances and grimaces with each other.

Behind the man, an elegantly dressed middle-aged woman in a sleek royal blue skirt suit, unaware of the unattractive run snaking up one leg of her textured nylon hose, bent down to the child behind her. "Oh, just wait, young man, until you see the pool. There is even a shallow beach end for you, honey." Rising back up while cautiously trying to maintain her balance on her thick high heels, she addressed his mother next. "And I know that I am ready to use that hydrotherapeutic steam bath for myself."

"Tell her about the animals," the little boy said, looking up at his mother and pulling on her sleeve. "Tell her not to be scared—they are not real." The young mother then explained how they had seen only a small portion of the ship and that her son had been mesmerized in the children's café, where enormous images seemed to have leapt from the pages of a *Babar the Elephant* book onto the walls.

Taylor had studied his ship documents on the train from Chicago and had seen the reviews of the *Normandie*, promoting it as the pride of France, a floating wonder featuring the best in French design and craftsmanship, and offering the finest French cuisine. Now, with the ship's schematic in hand, Taylor stopped first for a peek at the dining room. Twelve soaring columns of Lalique's signature frosted crystal were the focal masterpieces along the ornate glass sculptured walls. A waiter who was putting finishing touches on a table setting told him that each evening the room would accommodate over seven hundred passengers. As if he captained the ship himself, he proudly explained that despite the summer temperatures, the guests would be content in their formal attire, enjoying the presentation of courses in the comfort of air-conditioning.

Passing next through the grand salon, Taylor found red, black, and white floral upholstered chairs, settees, and chaises, and a brilliantly polished ebony piano. He was once again impressed by the ship's interiors, and understood why its moniker was "Ship of Light." Following this theme in the salon, four oversized torchieres illuminated the room where rich wood pillars alternated with the art deco murals.

He spent another hour just walking the outer perimeter—around the impeccably maintained decks of the ship. He began on the lower levels and worked his way to the top, where against the backdrop of the city skyline, the men below, busily hauling passengers' suitcases and trunks, looked like worker ants. As an experienced sailor himself, he was intrigued with any seagoing vessel, but the boats that had crossed the Atlantic from Europe and had navigated the channels of the Great Lakes to reach Chicago were more often old, rusted cargo carriers. Standing now in the bustling harbor of New York, he was instinctively turning to his father to share this experience. It was the first time on his trip that he absorbed the impact of being alone, that he understood just how much he needed to be an adult now.

Inside once again and in search of his cabin, he tipped his hat as he passed clusters of lovely young ladies and their mothers. After he passed, he could hear one group stop and discuss him, making no effort to keep their voices discreet. "He's soooo cute," he heard them say before he was out of range, and when he turned slightly back toward them with a smile, they quickly spun around, covering their giggles with gloved hands. Once, a pair of sisters, probably no older than fourteen and fifteen, followed him down a long corridor until they finally had the nerve to address him. "My sister says that you are an American, but I think you are French," the braver one said. And when he answered them smartly with "*Je ne comprehends pas*," the one phrase he used most often on his past trips to the *Cote d'Azur*, they stood dumbfounded and then, laughing, mimicked the swoons of actresses.

It was no wonder that Taylor Woodmere inspired such reactions from impressionable young ladies, for at twenty-two years of age he was a perfect specimen of a young man of good breeding. He was six feet tall and his physique was athletic, but not overly so. His full, medium brown hair was highlighted by blond strands left over from his summer sailing on Lake Michigan. Sometimes he slicked it down with tonic and combed it to the side to present himself formally, but just as often he left it natural and casual. He had the habit of running his fingers through his hair when in conversation and more than one young woman wished her hands could follow that path.

He was unusually handsome, his eyes the startling sapphire blue of his mother's side, the pupils edged by a light brown. Back in Chicago, he had frequently been sketched or photographed for the society pages, his likeness often featured in reports on theater or charity events. Since his college years, he had become a favorite of the Chicago gossip columnists. But Taylor Woodmere's true gifts were less superficial and these he assiduously cultivated—his intellect, his strong sense of responsibility, his sincerity. He had the gift of truly listening to others, not with that appeasing quality that many have when they are waiting for their turn to interject a thought, but with a truly interested and empathetic ear.

Few people would have believed that as an adolescent Taylor was prey to all of the emotional insecurities typical of that age. By the time he was a junior at University Preparatory, his boarding school in New Haven, Connecticut, the students and faculty alike had identified him as a leader—bright, confident, ambitious, and popular. They had no idea, however, that the young man behind that façade, the young man who saw in the mirror the same exterior that others perceived, when lying alone in his bed at night, conjured fantasies of mediocrity. He longed to be able to blend rather than excel, to receive less than perfect grades and be praised for "good tries," not only for successes. He longed to escape from the demands for perfection and the burden of being an only child.

Only his mother could read the fear behind his eyes. "Taylor, you do not have to be perfect to be fine—even to be great," she would assure him. She would sit on the edge of his bed when he returned home during school vacations, and affectionately stroke the side of his face even though the softness of his childhood cheeks now was roughened by the bristles of puberty. She would push the thick strands of hair from his forehead and massage his temples as he pretended not to be listening, as he stared out the window. But they both knew that he drank in her words—"Don't judge yourself so harshly, so strictly," she would say. Eventually he would turn his head back toward her and she would love capturing the smile that would emerge. "Don't be afraid to make a mistake—it's not the end of the world—just smile when you do and the world will smile back at you. My darling—people will be more attracted to you if you are more approachable and more like them—human—with all that it means."

Her words meant a great deal to him and would reassure him for weeks—at least until he received the next letter from his father.

I understand your team took seconds in crew—and I am thinking now that they should choose a more assertive coxswain. But that would be a waste of your talent and could be filled by a smaller boy; truly, your place is at stroke position. You do have the most fluid, strongest motion, and there you can best help the team increase their strokes per minute. I will drop a note to your coach on that. I assume you will be captain next year.

And then the anxiety would resurface and the pressure would mount and the distance between the Taylor in the mirror and the Taylor in his soul would return.

Taylor did not lack for company during his days and nights aboard the luxury ocean liner. During the days, he would try to relax on a deck chair away from the bustle of the pool and attempt to study his materials. But after a short time, an energetic crowd of college students would seek him out and lure him to participate in a game of water polo or shuffleboard. With the distractions of endless meals, professional concerts, cinema and live stage, a vibrant nightclub and stimulating conversations with the impressive list of passengers, the time moved as swiftly as the Blue Riband pennant-winning ship. In four days they had reached Southampton and by early the next morning they arrived at Le Havre, the gateway to Paris.

Monsieur Francois Benet was holding the "Woodmere" sign when Taylor arrived.

"Bonjour, *Je suis Francois Benet*," the man said, extending his hand as Taylor approached. "I hope your trip was easy and I would like to be the first to welcome you to France."

"*Bonjour, Je suis Taylor Woodmere*, and that may be just about the extent of our conversations in French," he replied.

"I am delighted to be your translator and your tour guide during your stay, as I have done often for your very gracious father and your grandfather, as well. May I please inquire first as to their health?"

"Oh—*très bien, très bien*—I'm surprising myself—maybe a few courses in French were not wasted, Monsieur Benet."

"Francois, please. And I shall help you to expand that vocabulary as we travel—but not so much that you would no longer require my services."

"Your job is safe, of course."

"Of course—*bien sur*," Francois replied almost automatically.

And Taylor repeated, "*Bien sur.*"

Monsieur Benet was a slightly built man, his finely chiseled face and wiry hands protruding from a loosely fitting three-piece suit. With a flamboyant ascot and matching pocket handkerchief, he presented a spirit that seemed much stronger than his physique. Taylor was reluctant to hand him his small bag and briefcase and was relieved when he directed another man, the driver and valet, to take them and then to lead the porter with the rest of his luggage to the waiting automobile.

After a three-hour car ride, they arrived at the Hôtel de Crillon, perfectly located at the cultural heart of the city on the Place de la Concorde. The former palace of the Comte de Crillon and his descendants, it had been converted to a luxury hotel in 1909. Not surprisingly, it was even more opulent than the ship, with an expansive inlaid marble floor, glistening chandeliers, and Louis XV style décor. After Taylor was settled into his suite, however, he had no interest in exploring the hotel; he was eager to finally visit the city of Paris and the World's Fair.

Having accompanied Taylor to his room and sitting momentarily at an elegant writing table, Francois pulled from his own briefcase the most updated conference schedule and saw that they would have enough time for a first look at the Exposition if they went at least partway to the entrance by automobile. The driver brought them to a location on the Champs de Mars, and after quickly exiting the backseat, Taylor immediately began perusing the paintings and wares of the street displays of the artists and merchants. Even when Francois encouraged him on toward the fair, he was reluctant. He kept lagging farther and farther behind as they walked, and Francois had to retrace his steps and try to hurry Taylor along.

"But look at all of these," Taylor said, pointing to the inventory where he stood. "I do know a little about art—they are intriguing and accomplished, not really amateurish. Francois, just wait a moment. Indulge me." He would not be coaxed from the stall of one young artist, with dozens of oils on display and with splashes of paint adorning every section of his clothing, including his shoes, as if he were a mobile canvas. Taylor studied a number of pictures and finally settled on one. In it, a woman was walking along the bluff overlooking a lake, and the beauty of the landscape, the trees swaying in the heavy wind with the woman tightening her shawl, reminded him of a fall day in his own back yard. "Look at the colors. Emily would love this. That's my girlfriend, back home, in Chicago." Francois let only a small smile show, but inside he was extremely amused by the suddenly adolescent enthusiasm of this very mature looking young adult.

"Could you please ask him how much it is? I would love to bring this home for her. Do you accept a price? Do you negotiate? I'm sure you do. We could settle on a price and I could return with the French francs."

Instead of answering him immediately, Francois took Taylor aside. The French artist would unlikely have a command of English, but he had such a burgeoning optimism in the anticipation of a sale that Francois felt sorry to have to be the spoiler. "I am guiding you in many ways on your stay—and now I am just asking you—to take time in making a selection. Do not buy the first thing you see. Become more familiar with the offerings."

"But everything is so beautiful. How could there not be a thousand great paintings, when there are a thousand beautiful scenes here, everywhere I look? The Seine, the bridges, the parks, the buildings, there is such character here . . ." And he would have continued if Francois had not interrupted.

"Mr. Taylor. I do not mean this disrespectfully to you, as I am honored by your praise of my city, of everything Parisian. But I assure you, you will find many more wonderful objects for your discriminating tastes." Within hours, he would be proven right on two counts.

When they entered the fairgrounds, they immediately procured a map of the area, and stepped aside from the moving throng to review their choices.

"Ah, exactly what we want. We will have time now for one stop only and so I see where we should head." Francois continued speaking as they walked in the direction his finger was following on the map. "In a short time already I feel your tastes. Today, we will enter only the Exhibition des Maitres d'Art Independants at the Petit-Palais, where it is said the Impressionists have an inviting showing."

It seemed to Taylor as if Francois had read his mind. He understood that this initial visit to the exposition would have to be brief, as he felt that in the days to come he would have many opportunities to visit the international pavilions with the rest of the group and to study the technological advances at the exhibits. But first the art galleries were a magnet to him. He had loved studying the many works of art that hung at his parents' home in Kenilworth, impressive works that his grandfather, the senior Addison, both loved and shrewdly invested in. Paintings by many famous artists were on view in the gallery on their upper reception level at home. Among Taylor's favorites were two oils by the American expatriate Mary Cassatt, each featuring a pair of women relaxing on couches at tea time. He knew that Cassatt herself had spent most of her productive years with the other Impressionists in France. Another treasured painting was by Alfred Sisley, a landscape at Argenteuil. But Taylor loved most Claude Monet's rendering of a French boulevard leading to the Seine and he wondered if he could find that very location during his stay. Taylor's grandfather, who never boasted about the financial success of his corporation, was validly proud of his acumen in art speculation. His crowd had challenged one another to build their own collections and to become benefactors for museums, especially the

Art Institute of Chicago. They had followed the lead of Bertha Honore Palmer, a charismatic socialite and philanthropist and the widow of real estate developer and hotelier Potter Palmer. She had been instrumental in bringing art to the Columbian Exposition in Chicago in 1893, and is said to have returned from her European tour with eleven Renoirs and twenty-nine Monets, one of which was eventually purchased by her friend Addison Woodmere.

The Paris Exposition was housed along the shores of the Seine, and unlike many previous world fairs in outlying areas of a city, this one molded itself into the existing urban landscape. New buildings mixed with existing edifices to house the attractions. On the site of the old Trocadero, the new Palais de Chaillot was constructed, with a portico of over one hundred and fifty columns. People would enter the grounds through the space between its two massive wings, which curved as if they were holding the entire fair in a maternal embrace. The fair extended from the Place du Trocadero along a wide-open esplanade to the Eiffel Tower, which, itself, had premiered at the Paris World's Fair of 1889.

But underneath the serene beauty of the fair were undercurrents of a world on edge. In this tumultuous year of 1937, the pavilions themselves seemed to symbolize the rising tensions among European nations. The towering buildings for the Soviet Union and for Nazi Germany, both huge and grandstanding, faced one another across the walkway pond, posed as if not only ideological, but also military battles were already

underway. They each looked like colossal trophies. At
the summit of the Soviet building, two enormous sculptured figures, a worker and peasant by Vera Mukhina,
held the hammer and sickle in a triumphant stance;
atop the Nazi German roof, perched a huge, arrogant
metal eagle.

As he followed Francois through the fairgrounds to
the major art exhibit, Taylor was struck by the diversity
of the crowd. Nationalities were easily identifiable by
their attire. Here was a stereotypical Parisian, bereted
and goateed, dressed as if he had just walked out of his
studio on the Left Bank. And there was a frumpy, cheery,
rosy-cheeked mother of three, chasing after her *enfants*,
as if they were still at their farm in the Loire Valley. The
businessmen were easy to spot. Walking in groups, holding briefcases or notepads, they pointed and nodded in
waves of agreement and switched directions like schools
of fish.

When they finally entered the Petit-Palais, Taylor
could not decide which way to look. He was drawn first
to one artist, and then he would turn and the vibrancy
of another display would call to him. Continually, he
exchanged glances with Francois, who was finally allowing him to enjoy the art at his own pace, and he could
sense that his fervor was entertainment for the man.

The hall was large and well stocked and people were
in lines of two and three deep, barely moving along as
they rocked slightly in place with the rhythm of small
boats tied at the shore, captured by the ebb and flow of
the waves. First, they would walk close to see the artistry
of the work, and then pull back, because an Impres-

sionist painting was best viewed from a distance, when the vibrant individual brush strokes would suddenly become cohesive and the scene would be revealed. He was reluctant to become part of the main lines and so he stood almost in the middle of the room surveying the entirety, perhaps finally following Francois' advice, slowing down, getting an overview of the presentation.

And that was when he came upon it, when he first saw the painting, *Jeune Fille à la Plage* by Henri Lebasque. It called to him with an extraordinary voice. It was not, however, identified as one of the artist's major works hanging on the gallery walls. It had been leaning in front of the director's desk in the middle of the room, among a secondary group of paintings available for sale. Taylor had, literally, stumbled upon it as he backed up to view an enormous landscape on an adjacent wall.

"*Excusez-moi. Soyez prudent,*" the man at the desk had admonished him when he heard the slight knock of Taylor's heel against the frame.

"Oh, sorry, sorry," he was quick to say. "It didn't fall. It was leaning precariously. No harm done. I'll set it right again." But as he bent to just readjust its position, he was immediately captured by it. "Sir, may I put it here?"

There was an open easel, likely there for this very purpose, and so without waiting for an answer, Taylor placed the painting gently on display at eye level, as Francois, having witnessed this last part of the exchange, came toward him.

Taylor had been drawn to the painting immediately, as if it were a play for which he arrived late and he was anxious to take his seat. The painter had not only illustrated a poignant moment in time, but had touched his audience with an unmistakable impression that they had come in at the middle of the story, that they needed to know the beginning and to follow it through to the end. Francois translated the title for him, as "Girl at the Beach," and Taylor understood that the artist meant for the central point of view to be that of the little red-headed girl sitting to the far left of the canvas at a beach café table, with possibly her young mother, or more likely an older sibling. Sitting close together in their turn-of-the-century attire, the pair reminded Taylor of those in Auguste Renoir's *Two Sisters*, the colors equally as vibrant as that master's. They are watching a group of young couples dancing. Perhaps the little girl's fascination with the scene is because she is envious of their age and wishes she could be part of the fun, but more likely she is trying to understand the exchanged looks she is witnessing. A handsome young man, his arm around the waist of his partner, is not focusing on her eyes, but is staring instead beyond her shoulder directly at the older sister, the longing in his eyes unmistakable, as is the desire in hers.

Taylor was so moved by the painting that he turned to Francois and insisted that this was the one—and Francois could only concur with his choice. Taylor knew that this painting would be the beginning of his collection—that he would present it as a gift to Emily upon his return.

Speaking to the artist's representative, Francois explained that his young American tourist was interested in the painting, but would need a good price in exchange for extending the artist's reputation to Chicago in the United States. Of course, the dealer was anxious to reduce his inventory and even Francois was surprised at the modest price he named.

Although Taylor would have liked to have had the painting in his possession immediately, would happily have carried it carefully through the crowded walkways of the fair, instead, they arranged for the painting to be delivered to the Hôtel de Crillon the following morning, at which time a remittance would be left with the hotel cashier.

Taylor's guide, well aware that they were running late, rushed him along. Even without the purchase, they had to delicately maneuver the crowded promenade of the exposition area, as many people were heading in the opposite direction to enjoy the evening at the fair.

When they finally reached the restaurant where the conference would have its opening dinner, Taylor found it to be a dark and weathered-looking place, not at all worthy of the accolades that Francois had advanced. But once they were led past the maître d's stand in a dimly lit alcove, it opened into the most elegantly appointed space, with an adjacent sunroom of glass panes and wrought iron moldings.

He was greeted with a strong hand patting the top of his shoulder in a friendly gesture. "Hello, young Mr. Woodmere." He recognized immediately his father's friend and colleague, Emanuel Berger. With his thick German accent, he was exactly as his father had described, not tall, perhaps five feet eight, and with a full build that might have seemed plump, if not contained by the perfect fit of a finely tailored suit, which gave him a distinguished appearance. He had a broad moustache and thick hair, both black, with graying strands. His face had a friendly character, handsome, but with the lines of the trials of life.

Taylor had taken time to prepare himself to address each man at the conference with an individual comment. But just as he was beginning to inquire about the business climate in Berlin, Emanuel's attention shifted away from Taylor. Now Emanuel held out his hand to a young lady who had just entered the room. Perhaps because of his own movements or perhaps alerted by the sweet floral hints of her perfume, Emanuel could see immediately that Taylor's attention was diverted, as well. Beneath the shade of his moustache, Emanuel's broad smile was evident. He was used to this reaction. "And may I introduce to you my daughter, Sarah."

Taylor felt as if someone had pulled on his heart, as if he were frozen, mesmerized by her beautiful face, paralyzed by the brilliance of her blond hair, which was embellished by a topaz rhinestone comb, lifting one side of her coiffure in a stylish curl to reveal a small, perfect ear.

"Sarah, I would like you to meet Mr. Taylor Woodmere, from Chicago."

She held out her hand to him, but he did not see it. He could only focus on the shimmering blue pools of her eyes. "Pleased to meet you, Mr. Woodmere. I am

Sarah Berger." When he did not respond, she said, "I apologize. Is my English perhaps unintelligible?"

He was shaken from his trance by the soft, pleasing touch of her hand. "Oh no, my God, you . . . I mean your English . . . is perfect." Taking her hand without moving his gaze from her eyes, he repeated, "Yes, perfect."

Emanuel, sensing he had become invisible, laughed, and seamlessly moved to another circle of colleagues.

"I am glad you think it is perfect," Sarah said. "At home we have an English tutor . . . for Papa and Mama and me. Father has insisted on that since I was twelve years old. He wants us to be able to travel to England and feel as at home as we do in France, because we know French. Here my family has not just business associates, but friends and relatives, and so we come often."

He was compelled to extend this brief introduction into a lengthy conversation and so a barrage of topics sped through his brain, but in an unbelievably incoherent pattern, leaving him embarrassed and speechless for perhaps the first time in his life. He, who had been garrulous even as a toddler and had developed into a master conversationalist, a decorated debater in college, was momentarily incapable of formulating a single sentence that might initiate even the most mundane response about the fair weather.

It was Emanuel Berger, returning to them, who finally broke through Taylor's dreamlike fugue to introduce him to other colleagues, and Sarah excused herself to allow her father to be the focus once more.

"Mr. Woodmere," he said, approaching with two other distinguished gentlemen.

But Taylor, after a brief frown, an involuntary reaction to Sarah's quick departure, responded respectfully, "Please, Herr Berger, I would be most comfortable as Taylor."

"Oh, yes—that casual, American style surfaces already."

"Perhaps that—but I will need everyone to see me as an individual and judge, themselves, if I am a worthy substitute for my father and grandfather."

Emanuel Berger nodded his head, already warming to his friend's son. "Then, Taylor, I would like you to meet Mr. Richard Hammersmith. He is one of our British colleagues. Richard, please. This is Addison Woodmere's son, Taylor."

Now Emanuel motioned toward the second man and continued. "And this is Monsieur Pierre Bouchet, our host for this evening."

After shaking each of their hands, Taylor stepped back, bent his head pensively, and then addressed the British gentleman. "Yes, Crown Industries with—metal cookware and leather goods, two factories, one under construction."

"Taylor, you have done your homework," the man answered, putting his arm around the shoulder of Emanuel Berger. "As we discuss our international business relations, we are not naïve to problems that may lie ahead for our dear friend in Germany. We proceed with discussions as if all is normal—'business as usual,' but we assure Emanuel that whatever happens in his homeland, he will have a home with us."

"I do understand this. Again, as my father prepared me for the meetings, he did not skirt that issue." And then Taylor addressed Monsieur Bouchet, but with a lighter note, further showing his easy eloquence. "My father spoke mainly about your food processing factories and the refitting of your packaging equipment to meet the needs of the military. But I was drawn to the success of your many vineyards and wonder how you can even work at all in a country with cafes beckoning you to sit and relax wherever you turn."

"You are right about that," he acknowledged, and then his voice rose as he addressed the entire group. "*Bonsoir, mes amis.* Let us fill the wine glasses for our first toast for our conference." He motioned for the waiter to begin pouring from his private stock, already displayed on a nearby table. Lifting his own glass high, he rotated his body in a semicircle. "To us—let us drink to our joint ventures promoting international commerce," he began with a strong tone, but then added with his head lowered, "and let us pray for peace." A brief silence followed and then more of the guests approached the small group, anxious to be introduced to the handsome young American representative.

Knowing the importance of first impressions, Taylor tried to be as cordial as possible—but he was more than distracted; he was desperate. Where had she gone? His guide, Francois, sensed his impatience. Francois, already, had become attuned to the rhythms of Taylor's speech, and however impressed by his maturity, he sensed that Taylor had suddenly lost his focus and he thought he knew the reason. He could see Taylor scanning the room, just as he watched Taylor's eyes when he first met Sarah. In support of his young charge, he became generous in his translations with the group, adding depth and sincerity to cover for him.

Soon Herman Lester, the Woodmere Industries manager from Chicago, came up to Taylor and greeted him enthusiastically, and then Francois excused himself. But Taylor was unable to process the words Herman was speaking, even though they were in his own language. Through the windows of the glass porch, Taylor had spotted Sarah just outside of the restaurant. He saw that she and some of the wives were eating hors d'oeuvres in the beautiful garden area, enjoying the coolness of the last hour before sunset.

He tried to concentrate on what Herman was saying, but it was almost impossible. "There have been some changes to meeting locations, due to the late opening of exhibits and so I have had these memorandums delivered to your room . . ."

"Herman, would you excuse me a moment?" Taylor was following Sarah's movements over and in between the crowd of men in their suits. Herman, who had tried to ignore his odd actions, now turned to follow what Taylor was watching, and when he saw Sarah, he gave a sympathetic nod. Undoubtedly, he had been happy to meet Herr Berger's daughter earlier in the evening; even a married man with three small children would have found that introduction pleasing.

"Yes, Taylor. Please, do what you need to do. We will have plenty of time to talk." Taylor patted his shoulder, moving past him with the jaunty initial step and stride that football players take when called from the bench by the coach.

Taylor stopped first at the table where there were still unused wine glasses and open bottles from the toast. The waiters having moved on, he poured two fresh glasses himself. He needed a reason to approach her.

"Miss Berger," he called, catching her attention, as she came back inside.

"Please call me Sarah," she answered, accepting the wine he offered and then clinking glasses with him in a mock toast.

"I was thinking you were avoiding me," he said.

She gave him a doubtful look. "Well, no, just being friendly. I am substituting for my mother, you must understand. She was too busy at home with a charity event to accompany Papa—and she knows how I love Paris." She paused before continuing. "Nevertheless, I am sure you are teasing me. You have been quite occupied, yourself, Mr. Woodmere." She smirked when she said it, knowing what he would want her to call him, and so she added, "Taylor," without his needing to ask.

"Well, perhaps, but . . ."

"And anyway didn't I just meet you? . . . And didn't I just meet, for instance, Monsieur Lester, your manager? And yet he is not chasing me to ask if I am ignoring him."

She had the most intoxicating, naturally flirtatious manner, he thought. "You're funny."

"You think so?"

"Yes—and that is a gift. Funny in a foreign language, even. And, by the way, Monsieur Lester seemed very sympathetic to my cause."

"And what cause is that, Mr. Taylor Woodmere?"

He had been standing at least two feet from her as they conversed, but now he moved closer, establishing a greater intimacy. "What cause? At the very least to capture your interest," he said, taking her wine glass and placing it with his on a nearby table, so that he might be able to hold both of her hands as he continued to repeat his words. "At the very least, to capture your interest . . . at the very most, to win your affection." He continued bringing her hands to his lips for a cursory kiss.

"Well, you are quite forward."

"But it's the French custom, isn't it? I have seen it in the movies. I am just being polite." Reluctantly, he let go of her hands.

She was trying to remain cool and composed, but the feel of his kiss on her hand had sent a warm shiver through her body. She tried to play with him to cover her reaction, cautious not to read too much into it. "So I am still wondering was there something specific that you wanted to discuss with me?"

"Well, I just wanted to tell you that . . . I love . . ." He had been drinking in the deep water-blue of her eyes and wasn't even cognizant that he had begun saying those words, "I love," aloud. He didn't know where the sentence would go when the words were released. He understood it was premature to say "I love you," but it was the only way to express what he felt. And now those two words, "I love," were hanging there with no immediate object. It was too late to sweep them back out of the air and into his private consciousness and so he let them land on her attire. "I just wanted to tell you that I love your dress."

"Why thank you. It is by Chanel. Do you know her in America? Coco Chanel. Very expensive, *tres cher*. Papa has allowed me this special treat because he knows that once we are back in Berlin, it will be a part of my mother's wardrobe. I am lucky; we wear the same size."

He said nothing and just looked at the way the black and cream gown followed the contours of her body, unaware that the colors and textures of the dress were the signature of the Chanel line. She held her dress out to the sides, grasping the fabric with her fingers as if she was about to curtsy, but instead she twirled around like a ballerina.

"It is beautiful," he said. He suddenly remembered the comment he had advanced that led now to this action that was further intoxicating him, when he had started to say "I love you," but had settled for "I love your dress." And now, almost involuntarily, he began a sentence with "I was just wondering . . ." And again he did not know the appropriate words to follow. He wanted to say, "I was just wondering if you are tired of hearing that you have the sweetest smile?" or "I was wondering, do you know your hair smells like a fresh garden?" But everything he wanted to say was too forward, too personal, and so he just searched for anything to say, until he finally came up with what he thought might be an acceptable compliment. "I was wondering . . . if the designer were here now if she would ask you to be her professional model."

Taylor had two goals in mind at this point—to remain by her side until they were called for dinner and to secure the seat next to her. When the announcement was made and the group moved toward the elegantly set table, he followed her in the direction of her father, who was standing behind a central chair and motioning for her to come to the one to his right. Taylor assisted in pulling out her chair and then moved to occupy the next seat, but he was frustrated by a calligraphed place card that said instead, "Monsieur Roger Lamont." Discreetly, he backed away and he proceeded to check each card until he located his. And to his delight, he found he was seated directly across from the irresistible Sarah Berger.

The following day, when the conference ended in the early afternoon, there was time for Taylor, with Francois, to accompany Sarah and her father to the Eiffel Tower and to ascend the structure with them for a spectacular view of the fair and the city beyond. This outing that was heaven for him, simply because he could be by her side, had actually been her idea.

"Have you seen the fair yet?" Sarah had asked at dinner the night before. He could barely concentrate on what she was saying, so absorbed he was in memorizing the details of her face, the contours of her neck and shoulders. When he responded that he had indeed been down the promenade, visiting just one building, she persisted. "No, have you really *seen* the fair—seen it from the Eiffel Tower? That is the only way."

She was right. The view was breathtaking, but not the sites she was pointing out—the highlights of the fair, and then the famous landmarks of Paris—the Louvre, the Arc de Triomphe, the Seine snaking through the city. The view of her perfect face and figure framed by the strong rays of the afternoon sun was all he cared to see.

When they returned to the street level, Sarah pulled her father close to her and whispered something in his ear. And then she repeated it aloud to Taylor. "I am telling Papa that I think this tour has taken a toll on him and he looks tired and a bit out of breath." She patted her father lovingly on his chest and kissed him on each cheek. "Papa, I would understand if you had enough for the day. Would you allow me please to have dinner with just Taylor this evening? We will be fine."

He looked at her as the most loving parent, proud, yet cautious of his precious princess, as he considered his answer. "Well, of course, darling. I promised your mother not to overdo," he said.

The services of Taylor's guide, Francois, had been excellent, not just in the translations necessary when conversing with the conference participants who did not feel comfortable speaking in English, but also for helping to navigate from one location to another. He also helped Taylor acclimate to the French culture, from ordering breakfast to converting the U.S. dollar into French francs. But at this point, Francois, also, was gracious enough to take his leave from the young pair.

"Mr. Taylor," he had said quietly to his ear. "Perhaps you would not mind if I attend to some pressing business."

Taylor was delighted when they entered the café. The decor was exactly as he would have imagined from what he had seen in magazines and movies. The windows were etched with an arch of thick gold letters reading *Café du Couer*. Inside, there was the requisite blackboard easel, wood framed with soft wisps of canary yellow, listing the menu choices. The painted ceiling had a marbleized quality that imitated the clouds of a spring day and was bordered with robin's-egg blue arches that gave it a gift-wrapped feel. Linens of blue and yellow adorned the small round café tables. Against the wall, surrounding a protruding window affording a view to the kitchen, were shelves eight rows high, filled with jars of marmalade and other preserves, bottles of wine, and cans of olive oil. The wood-paneled walls appeared a bit chipped and battered, either aged purposefully to give it a timeworn look, or the natural result of generations of diners. The floor had sections of the same old wood planks, alternating with black and white tiles.

A pleasingly plump matron, presumably the owner's wife, stood at the cash register, greeting the guests and managing the business. The proprietor's corpulent stature was obvious even though he was half hidden behind the kitchen opening, his chins so numerous and full that he appeared to have ingested the yeast of his own recipes, and had become as fully risen as his newly baked loaves.

The waiter, returning with the soup they had ordered, exited the swinging doors of the kitchen with too broad of a sweep, and splashes of their vegetable bisque joined the dots of red wine already visible on the folds of his white shirt. They watched him by the server's stand perfecting the presentation of the dishes by wiping them carefully with a napkin, and then he self-consciously and apologetically served their first course.

"Please enjoy," he offered and turned abruptly, undoubtedly anxious to soap down his shirt or exchange it for a spare.

There was a certainty that he would not be returning momentarily to refill their wine glasses or offer a second croissant and so Taylor reached for Sarah's hands across the small table.

"I was just wondering what you are doing after this," he said.

"After this? You mean later this evening? I think by the time we finish this dinner . . ."

"No, not later tonight. Just later."

"Later?"

"Yes, *fraulein*, later—after this—and for the rest of your life . . ."

She tried to think of some funny retort, but nothing came. "Well, that is a hard question."

"Not for me. Ask me."

"But I know what your answer will be."

"Then just say you feel the same way."

"Can we take one day and then think about the next?"

"No—because I feel . . . I know it seems crazy, Sarah . . . but I felt from the moment I saw you, when I first looked at your beautiful face, when I heard the melody of your beautiful voice, that I have known you my whole life."

She knew what he meant; last night, sleep had eluded her. She too had felt a certain anticipation, an excitement, accompanied by an unfamiliar anxiety.

"But we only met yesterday," she said. "You have known me for one day—less than one day—not even twenty-four hours. So you meet a German girl—in France, with a face you have never seen before and an accent you have maybe never heard before and you say that you have known her your whole life."

"I know it's implausible. But I need you to understand—I have known you my whole life . . . because yesterday was the day I was born." He had been holding her hands and gently caressing them as he spoke, but now he released them. "Everything before that was prelude, preparation, all to be in that place at that time . . . to meet you."

She couldn't look directly at him. She didn't know how to answer. But she knew what he meant, though she was too shy or cautious or confused to say it. It was impossible not to be seduced by this handsome man, by the masculine elegance of his demeanor, by the quiet tones of his voice, by the hypnotic gaze of his dreamy eyes, by the sincerity of his smile. When she finally looked at him again, there was no need for her to answer. He answered for her. He leaned farther across, knocking a small bud vase to drip into the bread basket, and he kissed her gently on the lips. When he could see the delight in her eyes, he moved his chair closer to hers and they kissed once again.

Taylor believed one thing now—that the only true love was "love at first sight." With Emily, he had been proud that she finally accepted him as her intended—he felt triumphant parading with her on his arm. His parents were pleased, his friends impressed, and he felt happy and satisfied.

But since he'd met Sarah, since last night, everything had changed. She was the girl he wanted, he desired, the girl with whom he was meant to spend his life. He now knew that "happy" and "satisfied" were not the true emotions of love. Suddenly, with Sarah, he felt things he'd never felt before; he was "elated," "exhilarated," and "impassioned." He wanted her more than he had ever wanted anything before.

He had always considered himself to be a cautious, rational person. How could such a transformation occur within him in such a short time? This sudden, but profound love, these overwhelming new feelings, were a shock to him. But he was certain that she was his destiny, that just as allegiances were shifting on the larger world arena, so in his own heart and mind, the wheels of fortune and of fate were realigning. First, it was his father needing him to travel abroad, introducing him to the world of international commerce, and then making a point of praising a Jewish businessman from Germany, Emanuel Berger, who would just happen to have his thoroughly enchanting and beautiful daughter accompany him to the conference.

By the third day, Taylor couldn't name one thing about Sarah that he did not love. "You are perfect," he would say to her. And she would wave off the words with a flick of her fingers, which he found adorable. He loved that she asked permission from her papa each time they were left alone. He too had always wanted to please his father. He briefly wondered if his new intentions might tarnish the sterling reputation of the Woodmere family. Would there be society talk of him "jilting" poor Emily Kendall? Though he had been enamored—besotted, actually, with Emily—now he admitted to himself that he had hesitations about her before he'd left. Why else would he still be hiding her ring in his bureau drawer instead of displaying it on her finger?

He was often irritated by her spoiled manner and insensitivity. She was steering him always to friends she thought more acceptable than ones to whom he was drawn. She had admonished him for the almost brotherly way he treated the younger staff. "*My family has always believed in setting boundaries,*" she would say.

She was constantly shopping. He was forever apologizing to the maid or the cook for her endless demands and harsh criticism. And this, while she was just a guest! What would it be like when she was managing a household?

"*At Newport we can't go ten feet without another tray of fresh lemonade brimming with ice . . . at Newport we never carry our own bags to the beach . . . at Newport, Daddy wouldn't consider joining this new club or that (not our type of people).*"

He knew what he wanted from life now, but he was apprehensive about displeasing his parents. And so he began to formulate strategies that might lead Emily to leave him and therefore spare her any indignities.

However flattered by his loving attentions, Sarah often tried to divert Taylor's fascination with her to a more worthy subject. She loved Paris and she wanted him to know and love the city also. Although Taylor's father had arranged for his French translator to accompany his son, Monsieur Francois Benet was often left in the late afternoons and evenings to his own devices, while Taylor explored the city with Sarah. Over the course of the conference, as he spent an increasing amount of time with her, meeting her for walks and meals whenever he had free time, he came to appreciate that her mind was not, like Emily's, an inventory of possessions, but filled with ideas.

In the Louvre, she took his hand and led him to her beloved masterpieces. But he said that Mona Lisa's smile did not approach Sarah's own and that he felt no passion for the Venus de Milo, who could not fully embrace him with her arms. "I expected more from you," Sarah said as they left the museum. "You sound like a silly schoolboy," she chided him.

"Well that is your fault. Show me no more women; they will only pale in comparison to you."

With that she remembered how she had been told not to miss the Spanish exhibit at the fair, which was rumored to be a controversial showcase of the most influential artists of that country.

Sarah and Taylor approached the pavilion with the eagerness of children in line for an amusement ride. But even at the entrance, they understood that this exhibit would be different. People were emerging with disgusted looks, shaking their heads. Sarah interpreted for Taylor as one pair passed by. "We did not come to a world's fair to see such misery. People should be warned."

A group of Spanish intellectuals and artists were brought together by the architect Jose Luis Sert to create this first ever Spanish exhibit at a world's fair. These artists, however, did not wish to show the world the beauty of their country. They were united by a need to show the world the gruesome reality of the Spanish Civil War. Joan Miro and Alexander Calder were among the most celebrated artists of their country who had contributed work in support of the Republican cause. Protesting Fascism, they had all created statement pieces, graphically or symbolically depicting the horrors of war. Photographs, films, and paintings exposed the brutality of Franco's army. But it was Pablo Picasso's enormous *Guernica*, a black, gray, and white abstract interpretation of the devastation of the German and Italian bombing of Guernica in the Basque region and the suffering of the innocent townspeople that drew the most attention.

Over the weekend, when the conference was not in session, Sarah took Taylor to her favorite places. After the grand concourses, the Champs Elysees, the Boulevard Saint-Germain, the Place Saint-Michel in the Latin Quarter, she led him to the narrow passageways off the Rue de Rosiers in le Marais, the Jewish quarter. There, poor Jewish immigrants had settled—rabbis, tailors, butchers, and shopkeepers. She wanted to introduce Taylor to the smells and fabrics of her heritage.

"You know how much I care for you, Sarah, more than care," he said to her, as they shared a traditional *latke*, a delicious potato pancake. "I know how close you are to your father. I feel he likes me, but I know that sometimes there are boundaries that are hard to cross. Would he ever accept your being with someone who is not Jewish?"

"Taylor, you are so funny and sweet," she said, tilting her head in the most coquettish manner. "We are not *shtetl* Jews from some small villages in Russia. We are part of the German cultural nation—only now, that madman Hitler is singling us out. He began by organizing boycotts of our businesses, and then placing more restrictions on our lives. We cannot own land, we cannot work in many of our professions, we are restricted from many schools . . . But, still we are different. Of course, my father accepts you—You are not aware, but my mother is Christian. In Jewish law—I am not even considered Jewish, as I do not have a mother who is Jewish either by birth or conversion. Although you must understand already, I feel Jewish and I have been raised Jewish and we do identify with the Jewish community in Berlin."

"Sarah," he said, as tenderness and relief washed through him, "if something could possibly build between us, I would never ask you to give up your legacy. And my father—before I came—told me how he respects Jewish people, and especially, your father. I am confident there would be no objections from my family either. My parents will be as drawn to you as I am. Of that I am sure."

Sarah bent her head, then looked up. Their eyes met and locked and there was no mistaking the electricity that passed between them.

Though Sarah was powerfully attracted to Taylor, unlike him, she lacked the experience necessary to identify her feelings as love and she was often confused by her new fierce emotions. This was not the first time that a boy had fallen for her. She knew she was considered pretty. People were always remarking on how she looked like her mother, with her dramatic eyes and blond hair and curvy figure. As a schoolgirl of seventeen, fumbling schoolboys were often stuttering in her presence. But now, for the first time, she too felt the fluttering butterflies in her stomach and her heart that she had read about. She found this handsome, smart, and personable young man irresistible.

On Saturday, Taylor accompanied Sara and Emanuel for a special exposition presentation by the symphony and the ballet. Taylor waited in the lobby for them to come down from their suite at the Hôtel de Crillon. When Sarah emerged from the elevator, she took his breath away. On this night she had chosen to wear her hair pulled back in an intricately twisted knot. He missed the dazzle of the shock of blond curls that previously framed her face, but he found this new look surprisingly appealing. The depth of her eyes and her high, radiant cheekbones were accentuated.

During the concert, Emanuel sat between Sarah and Taylor and the young couple exchanged only occasional glances. At intermission, they were both careful to engage Emanuel in their conversations about the powerful music and the beautifully choreographed dances. But after the concert, as they stood in a line awaiting their car and driver, without even consulting Taylor, Sarah addressed her father. "Papa, it is such a beautiful evening and the hotel is not so far. Wouldn't it be lovely to walk back instead?"

Her father, already showing a slight limp from negotiating the grand staircases of the Concert Hall, momentarily played with her. "What a wonderful idea, my *liebling*. I would just love a long walk." But when he saw her eyes widen incredulously, he could not extend the joke. "No, no. I have a better idea. I am ready to retire. Why don't the two of you go on ahead?"

Once more she kissed his cheek, and saw him give Taylor a slight wink as she did so.

Paris on that July night in 1937 was a contradiction of terms, alive with *joie de vivre*, but also shrouded by a smog of dread. The rumors, whispers, cries, and shouts of European neighbors did not go unnoticed on Parisian streets. Walking with the many attendees, tuxedo-clad gentlemen with beautifully coiffed and coutured women on their arms, enjoying a stroll on the boulevard, they were shaken by posters and graffiti that they passed.

Taylor could not read their words, but that was not even necessary. You could understand what they alluded to—an undercurrent of unrest on the continent. "The time I am spending in Europe is opening my eyes to more than just the business at hand. There is a terror here—not yet as palpable as what we have seen the Spanish are enduring, but present nonetheless. And if you can feel it here, I can only imagine that it is worse in Germany."

"But there is so much beauty in my country—so much culture in Berlin. If only I could take you there. You would see beyond the ugliness that Hitler has been spreading. Papa says that we will still be all right." Sarah insisted. "But I will tell you that I sometimes think my father has more in mind than just social and business objectives in providing us with our English tutor. I am thinking now that he has a master plan. There is a saying that I know in English—my tutor has told me—'one foot out the door'—when you are planning to leave something." She looked up to see Taylor nodding.

"My tutor told me about him and his wife—'I tell you if she does that one more time, I will leave her. I already have one foot out the door.' I laughed when I heard it, and I love using the expression. Well, my father and his pursuit of English, I think reflect not yet, 'one foot out the door,' but opening the door and peeking out."

Taylor had been holding Sarah's hand as they walked, but now he placed his arm around her waist and pulled her close, initially, in a protective reflex. But then after they walked a few blocks farther away from the graffitied walls, their closeness took on a romantic quality and they let the cares of the world escape them once more as they stopped for a long kiss.

Approaching the hotel, Taylor became anxious again. More than once in the past few days, he tried to broach the subject of Emily with Sarah, but she would be distracted by an intriguing exhibit or a store window and she would pull him in one direction or another.

"Sarah," he finally said, "I am going to have to tell you something that you may not want to hear. Something about me."

At this, she stopped and turned to him. "If I would not want to hear it, then maybe you should not tell me."

"I wish it were that easy." For once, he had no desire to look in her eyes, focusing instead on the pavement, his head down like a freshly disciplined schoolboy.

"What? You are a thief, a murderer—an escaped convict?"

"No, not likely," he said, finally looking up at her with a slight grin.

"Then how bad could it be? You have a wife and three children? Should I be sitting down when I hear this?"

"No—walking is better—purposefully walking so you will listen and digest my story."

"OK. Continue," she said, resuming her stride. "I am walking now."

"Before I came here, I had a girlfriend."

She didn't miss a beat in the pace of her step.

And so he reiterated, "A serious girlfriend."

She stopped now and turned toward him.

"You were to marry?"

"We weren't engaged, but it was understood we were heading in that direction."

She considered this for a few moments, and then said, "I am not surprised."

He didn't know how to interpret that and so he said nothing, and just looked at her quizzically.

"Why would this surprise me? Do you think I would fall for a man with no appeal?"

But then she continued. "Would it surprise you to know that I had a boyfriend?"

He had not prepared himself for this revelation and it blindsided him. What had he been thinking, he asked himself—that she been sitting at home waiting for her prince to ride in? Finally he said, sheepishly, "If I am to be honest . . . that upsets me."

"Well then, I appreciate your honesty, and I will return your trust." She paused now and offered him the most little girlish swaying of her head from side to side. "There is no boyfriend. I was just postulating. Truly, I only know boys my age, and they are cute, but too immature. When I am older like you . . ."

"Twenty-two," he interjected.

"Twenty-two, then. I will have a boyfriend for you to be jealous of."

"Not likely," he returned.

"You think I will be old, withered, and unappealing already."

"No, I think you will be married and with children—ours."

"Oh, you are quick to change your direction. And so this girlfriend . . ."

"She is no longer a girlfriend."

"All right then. This girlfriend, who is no longer . . . her name . . ."

"Emily . . . Emily Kendall."

They had reached the Crillon and they entered the hotel lobby. Taylor led her immediately to a secluded corner with a small couch. He took her purse and diaphanous cream shawl and placed them on the coffee table and they sat down together. He had no intention of letting the evening end too soon. Taylor loved every word of this conversation, the fact that she could tease—this young girl could turn the tables on him.

She said nothing for a while and just whispered the name "Emily" two or three times, as if that act would conjure a specific image. Finally, she said to Taylor, "Blond hair also, I am wondering?"

"No, not blond, darker, reddish actually, but very dark—auburn, we say."

"You know, I just don't feel that you make a good boyfriend. If I were to take someone's boyfriend, I'd want assurance that he was worthy."

"I was loyal and true for a long time."

"But you come abroad and forget her immediately."

He knew she was being dramatic and sarcastic with him, but certainly there was truth in what she said. He tried to think of a way to escape from this tangle of words, and then it came to him. "You are wrong. I did not forget her, well at least not immediately. The first day, when I arrived, I could think only of buying the perfect gift for her."

"Now, finally you are talking like a good boyfriend," Sarah said enthusiastically, her eyes angling up to meet his.

"As a matter of fact, I bought her a painting, the most beautiful painting I had ever seen. And I was so excited. For an hour, I was so thrilled just thinking of watching her when I gave it to her."

"An hour only?"

"An hour only."

"And why that short a time?"

"Because at the end of that hour . . . I met you . . . I saw your face." He let the words float toward her and said nothing more for a moment, just held her gaze. And then, as if reacting to the sting of a bee, he jumped up and pulled her with him off the sofa. "I must show it to you. I know you will love it. It's crazy. It's like I was meant to give this painting to you. Now I see it perfectly."

"You are crazy."

"Say nothing. When you see it, you will understand. You must come with me to my room."

"Taylor, wait. You are getting too excited. I hardly think I can go up to your room with you. I'm sure you understand that. Papa is giving me a great deal of latitude as it is. I cannot betray his trust."

"Of course," Taylor said. He was trying to slow down and be rational. "Of course you are right. But I am going to bring the painting down to you and you must promise to stay here."

When he left abruptly, she retired to the ladies lounge, where she powdered her face and reapplied her lipstick, and had a brief conversation with two of the other occupants about highlights of the exposition. By the time she returned to the couch, he was back and had almost finished unwrapping the painting.

As if their moves had been synchronized, they looked at it first from two feet away and then moved back another five feet. He was silent, waiting for her response.

"It is magnificent," she finally said. "It is everything anyone would want in a work of art."

He knew what her reaction would be, and yet, he was ecstatic to hear it from her lips. "Go on . . . tell me what you are thinking."

"It has all the beauty of the Impressionist style. All of the brush strokes, the colors, and the romantic theme as well. But there is also a story here."

"Exactly," he interjected. "I knew you were smart—and sensitive. Help me to understand what is going on here. There are so many ways to read this. Is this the beginning of a story? Have they just seen each other for the first time? Is this the middle of the story? He has not yet told his partner that he is in love with someone else. Or is it the end of the story? He has had to say good-bye to his true love; he had no courage to leave his girlfriend or fiancé or wife. I even asked the collection curator if there was a series of these paintings and perhaps that might clarify the story."

"There are no others?" She was as curious as Taylor.

"Not that he was aware of. He explained that it seemed to be a solitary effort, so different from Lebasque's other works, which were much less detailed, where rarely did faces emerge from the canvas. So we have only this painting and its little mystery, seen through the eyes of the little girl." Taylor sucked in his lips and shook his head. He looked back at Sarah and saw her smile. The painting had been clear to her immediately. Maybe he did not understand it when he first purchased it—when he thought of it hanging in the home he would share with Emily. But now just these few days later, he could see what she saw. She studied the painting one more time and then turned to Taylor.

"I think it tells the story of the day they were born," she said softly and slowly, but confidently.

Taylor considered her words and drew her to him. It was impossible to believe that the dim light of the hotel lobby was responsible for casting her entire face in a brilliant glow. He brazenly removed the one large clip holding her hair back in its tight chignon and he ran his fingers through the loosely falling blond locks. "I have wanted to do that all evening."

She looked around quickly at the spirited hotel lobby, but saw that none of their group was present. With the soft pressure of his fingers along the nape of her neck, their tender touch brushing her ear so that a tingling sensation disarmed her from any ability to resist, he brought her head to his and she closed her eyes and accepted his kiss. But after only ten seconds, she pulled away and straightened her dress. She retrieved the hair clasp from the coffee table where Taylor had dropped it, nervously fumbling to reattach it so that it could once more hold her hair away from her face.

He stepped back and allowed her to compose herself.

"I spoke to your father and asked him a great favor."

"Really?"

"Yes. Not when we were all together, but at a break this morning, during the conference. We had just signed off on the papers creating International Goods and Services. We had acknowledged the success of our conference, and so I took him aside," Taylor said, trying to be businesslike. "I asked him if I might accompany you both back to Berlin for a stay . . . a brief stay, I assured him . . . an opportunity to see his operations firsthand."

"Oh really . . . and what did he say to this proposal?"

"He was open to it . . ."

"But I think you insult my father with these words."

Taylor was puzzled; he bent his arms at the elbows with his palms open and angling outward. His head went side to side in the recognized pose of confusion. "Insult him. I think you misunderstand. He seemed pleased . . . maybe flattered that I was so intrigued by his factories."

"Insult his intelligence." She was smiling and laughing slightly. "You think that you are not transparent to him, that he is unaware of your true motivation."

"Oh, and now I ask you what you think that motivation is."

"I think that you are not yet ready to put an ocean between us."

Rachel

New York

January 1972

This time love came to her in quite a different manner. There was no immediacy of love at first sight. She would never allow herself to fall into that trap again. Well, that was not totally true—she had fallen for love at first sight just once more—about two and a half years before—the moment that Jason was born.

Following the Jewish tradition, she was thrilled to honor Ida's wish and she chose a name for her son with the same first initial of the brother that Ida had lost. After Jason Gold's birth, Rachel—just like Ida so many years ago—was not eager to leave New York. She had become comfortable sharing a household with her aunt, had made many wonderful friends, and was extremely vested in her educational path at New York University.

And that was where the love, that wasn't at first sight, was slowly and carefully nurtured.

It was her last semester of college. It was his last class to teach as a graduate student, prior to receiving his MBA. Sometimes he found it exasperating. "Accounting for Non-Business Majors." Yes, he was teaching bright students, but they were generally in the literary and fine arts sectors. This class was for the layperson—regarding how to really exist financially. In other words, if you finally landed a role in a Broadway play, wrote a screenplay, or sold a painting, how should you successfully handle that first windfall, in case there were bleak times ahead? He always thought he should walk in the classroom the first day and simply say, "I have three words for you—hire an accountant," and then not show until the final exam where he would hand out papers that ask—"what are the three words that sum up the class?" You would get an A if you wrote "hire an accountant." But, of course, he couldn't do that. That would be condescending, and even a little mean, two qualities that did not define Richard Stone.

And since he was teaching this course almost by rote after having taught two classes for each of the previous three semesters, Richard was quite caught off guard by this young woman in the front seat, right aisle. Oh, he was familiar with beauties. NYU was, after all, a premier school for the budding actors and actresses of the time. But most of the girls, especially, were thin little waifs who acted like they wanted to be anywhere else but in his class. And he was used to rejection by beauties. In fact, he was recovering from a major setback in the romance department. A girl, Sharon Lee Stein, who he had dated for two years, who seemed to like his quirky humor, his just-above-nerdy looks, his Wall Street potential, left him (with a ring in his pocket) for another man.

So now he was completely surprised by this enchanting young woman in the front row, staring at him with eager eyes (for his knowledge). For Richard Stone, the feeling was as if he had been hit by a car. It was that rush of anxiety that overpowers you when you see it coming, the deep thud inside upon impact, and then the relief that you have survived, and that you will be OK. But in cases of love, there is the potential that you might even be better than ever.

Later, as his mesmerized state abated, he began to analyze her powerful attraction. She was beautiful, young, and radiant looking, yet it was evident she had a certain maturity to her. And he kept feeling he might have recognized a slight vulnerability behind that self-assured façade. Whatever her story was, he knew he wanted to be part of it. He set his goal to attain Rachel and he knew he would structure a plan as he would any project for his graduate degree. Soon Richard would have his MBA from the university and he had already accepted an offer from the financial analysis department of the Goldman Brown Trust.

In class, he tried to be professional, tried not to look at her too much. But it was almost impossible. The thick waves of her hair, her large, inquisitive brown eyes, the way her sweaters clung to the beautiful curve of her breasts, made it a challenge to concentrate. Eventually, he tried to think of teaching just for her (without looking at her), as the eccentric student mix went in many distracted directions and only Rachel seemed to be responsive and to soak in his lesson. In a sense, the class reminded him of the years he spent teaching junior high math, while awaiting his draft status. They were not the preteen gum chewers and letter passers, but the actors were "acting out," whispering about tryouts and rehearsals, the dancers were stretching legs and pointing toes, and the artists were doodling or sketching instead of taking notes.

Finally after the first month, Rachel, to his amazement, actually stopped Richard on the street to talk to him. "I don't know how you do it—I mean teach seriously while everything is going on."

"Oh, you noticed that too. Well here's my trick, Rachel." He was caught off guard hearing her voice, feeling the touch of her hand on his shoulder to gain his attention. He only willed his mind to function to prepare logical words for a response. "I realized from the first time I taught this type of class for non-finance majors that most of the class were taking the course Pass/Fail. This is not the student population that I am used to. In my sections for finance majors, the kids are quiet, unless they are obsessively asking questions, and they're serious about learning the material and getting a good grade.

"So when I get a class like yours, I just block out the shenanigans of the 'artistically gifted' of NYU and try to teach to whoever is listening—which, in this case, happens to be you—and maybe only you."

"Oh," she returned softly, obviously taken aback. She was surprised that he had even noticed her, since he barely looked her way even when she asked questions.

He tried to keep his cool; he was so practiced in looking away from her in class that he didn't know how to handle himself now. "So I guess I need to know if you've learned anything, to assess if my system is working," he finally said.

Rachel's relationship with Richard stayed at a controlled distance until the end of the term. Their feelings were never verbalized those first months, and they interacted in an acceptable student-teacher manner, although he did invite her to his office two or three times for tutorial sessions and another two or three times she sought his help before a test. But both of them were aware that there was no need for tutoring, no test anxiety; Rachel could have excelled even in the class for finance majors.

By their first real date after the course ended, they knew only the most elemental things about each other— that they were both Jewish, both bright and directed, both valued a sense of humor. And they knew the most important part of each other's history.

From the beginning she didn't want to mislead him or take him by surprise. So very soon after their initial connection, the week after they spoke on the street, she knocked on his office door.

"I won't be in class on Thursday; I just wanted you to know."

At first he didn't understand; he thought she meant not ever after Thursday. She could tell that from the reaction on his face. "Just that day—you see—it is Parents' Day at Rusty's school. I have a son Rusty, Jason really. He's two and a half, and he is the light of my life. I have no husband."

There, it was out. In the past two years she had not been truly interested enough in anyone to even reveal this much. Solitary dates had occasionally been entertaining—that was all. But she wanted Richard to know who she was from the start. As she spoke, she pulled out a preschool picture of an adorable rusty-haired boy and placed it in front of Richard.

"Well," Richard said almost choked up that this catharsis on her part indicated that she too thought they might have a future. "You're ahead of me—I've been rejected by love and I have no wonderful picture to show for it."

It was then that he told her about Sharon Lee Stein. "Since you have been so honest with me—I will tell you about my experiences with Sharon Lee Stein." He sat back in his chair, twirling his pencil in his hand and focusing intently on the act without looking up at her. "Obviously, you see me as a handsome, charismatic lady's man, but it was not always so."

She smiled broadly; did he truly not know how attractive he was? His allure was not because of his face or body, but his general bearing, his wit, and the charm of his personality.

Lifting only his eyes to assess her expression, he felt assured enough to continue. "Now, as I was saying . . . in high school I was a big team player, but we're talking the Debate Team and, oh yes, the local Math Olympics team. The ladies were not truly falling all over me.

"So when Sharon Lee started paying attention to me at the beginning of my junior year of college, I was an easy mark. It started slowly—peaked grandly—and ended badly. When I was little, they called me four eyes. Truth be told, I **was** blind—blinded by her."

This time he was not afraid to look at Rachel's eyes, and he was pleased to see her sympathetic expression. "Have you ever been with a date in a room, sitting on a couch at a party, sitting at an intimate dining table, and the person you are with isn't looking at you when you talk? He is looking past you—seeing who is better behind you—over your shoulder.

"Actually she wasn't even that great looking—nothing like you. But I was a late bloomer, over-ready for love, and an easy target." She nodded with understanding and pondered silently her own past.

"My parents who are kind of 'old country' saw it easily," he continued. "'She's too made up . . . too much bust showing . . . her language is not refined,' they said. And this from two people who, although successful in business with a good place in Jewish society, still spoke with the accents of immigrants.

"But they only voiced their feelings once—my parents are good, supportive people—they've always let me find my own way," he said.

She was struck, again, by similarities in their lives.

By the last weeks of class, all Richard could think about was kissing her. He longed to envelop her sweet full lips with his own, to touch the cashmere of her sweater, to outline the curve of her breasts with his hands. He was counting down the days until school was over like a fifth grader awaiting the vacation bell.

Finally, on the last day of the term, after grades were distributed so that there would be no hint of impropriety, Richard asked her out. Just a few months later, they were an established "item." By that time, Ida insisted that he call her "aunt," and he was gaining weight from her noodle kugels, and bonding with Rusty while playing with presents of trucks and coloring books.

Soon Rachel began spending evenings with Richard's parents and small extended family. His parents recognized a new positive energy in him as he emerged from his depression following his last romantic relationship. And Rachel knew to be grateful to his "rejection by Sharon" for helping her, an unwed mother, young son in tow, to be easily embraced by them. Rachel was especially drawn to Richard's uncle Charles, who they called Chal, a sweet, charming man who had lost a young wife and child in the Holocaust. A diamond cutter in the New York industry that was becoming dominated by Jews, he lived alone and had never remarried and frequently was a dinner guest at the Stones' home. There was something tender about this thin man, whose sadness was reflected only remotely behind his bespectacled eyes, but not worn outwardly as a heavy coat. He had a broad knowledge of European history, although he skirted any references to his own plight. He loved following the newspapers with a diligence that titillated and educated everyone around him, and he extended their exposure to the fascinating culture of New York City, often inviting them to join him in prime seats for the symphony or ballet.

Her acquaintance with Chal soon led her to devise a plan. She had long been trying to think of something special she could do for Aunt Ida to make her understand not just how much she appreciated her, but how much she and Rusty really loved her. Rachel still felt extremely close to her parents, and they had continued to contribute to her living and tuition expenses through college, just as they would have if she had remained at the University of Illinois, but Aunt Ida had certainly become her closest source of emotional support and help with her son. After so many years working in the garment industry, Ida had moved from seamstress to supervisor to part-time bookkeeper for a midsized operation, and was so invaluable an employee that her boss accepted her request for an even more flexible work week once Rusty was born. Through his early years, she was always available when needed. After a long day away at class, and then at the library studying, Rachel would come home to see Ida sitting on the sofa listening to a very soft television with the toddler asleep on her lap. Rachel would come up behind her and envelop her shoulders and neck in an embrace. And Ida would apologize to her—"Oh, I am sorry. He fell asleep while I read him a story—in the middle of a sentence—he was listening and even asking questions and then he just closed his eyes. My fault—I wore him out at the park after dinner."

"You wore him out? I would think he would wear you out."

"Just the opposite, darling. He energizes me. Please don't be upset. He was too precious to put back to bed," she would say. "I just couldn't part with the feel of his soft cheeks on my arm."

"Aunt Ida, what would I do without you? You are an angel. I have imposed on you constantly, and yet you never complain."

"Complain? I should complain to the person who has saved me by bringing the joy of life back to me? I should complain because now I have people to cook for? Was I happy with wonderful recipes in my memory and no one to join me at the table?"

Rachel wished she had the means to send Ida on a wonderful vacation, but she doubted that she would even accept such a gift; when she treated her to dinners out, Ida would try to fight her for the check. Gifts of sweaters and dresses remained in their boxes or were returned with the money back on Rachel's dresser.

And then she thought of the gift of Uncle Chal! Richard approved of her scheme—it wouldn't be a planned double date—just an evening out with the pretext of going to an art exhibit. The men would simply stop for a moment to pick up Rachel in the Village on their way to the gallery, and Ida and Chal could meet each other.

As the evening played out, only minutes after Uncle Chal was introduced to Ida, they were babbling in Yiddish, with Chal showing coin tricks to Rusty (quarters behind ears, disappearing nickels) that sent him into giggling convulsions. When Rachel and Richard told him they would miss the opening if they didn't leave soon—he just waved them on.

"You two go ahead. I like the show right here," Chal said. As it turned out, he and Ida had lived mere miles apart in their youths, and shared a wealth of collective memories. And soon Richard and Rachel would stay home with Rusty, and the older couple would catch a symphony or Broadway show. And eventually, Ida did not resist the touch of Chal's hand to hers.

The Woodmere Estate

Kenilworth

July 1937

The cable from Taylor arrived by messenger around lunchtime and Addison Woodmere walked to the foyer from the sitting room to read it. His houseman, as was his custom, stood with him in case it elicited the need for an immediate response.

FATHER I MUST STAY IN EUROPE LONGER STOP I AM GOING TO BERLIN TO TOUR FACTORIES AND CONFIRM JOINT INTERESTS WITH EMANUEL BERGER STOP

"What?" Addison Woodmere, Jr., exclaimed rather loudly, as he read the latest cable from his son. "What—on to Berlin—I never condoned that—I apprised him of the European situation. Damn me. I had second thoughts the moment he left about sending him into precarious territories."

YOU SPOKE HIGHLY OF THE GERMAN INDUS-TRIALIST STOP I AM GOING TO SEE HIS OPERA-TION STOP PLEASE TELL EMILY STOP

And as he read the last words aloud, Emily who had been visiting for the meal approached him. "Tell Emily what?" she inquired as he started toward his study to sink back into the leather of his chair. He was rubbing his forehead in his familiar pose of frustration.

"Please say he is on his way home," Emily said softly.

He sat down and read the telegram to her, trying for her sake to hide his own disappointment and apprehension at the words. Bravely, she heard the message and then sat blank faced at the conclusion, as if waiting for more words. First, there was a quizzical look and then a stone set glare in her eyes. Her thoughts and those of her prospective father-in-law's echoed similarly.

Just "Please tell Emily," not "Please tell Emily I miss her or love her." And as their minds had merged, their thoughts were tandem now. For Addison Woodmere remembered himself at twenty-two and in love, and Emily Kendall, had the fresh images of her almost fiancé seemingly tormented to leave her just three weeks ago. But now he was extending his absence with no words of regret. What kind of business was this?

Taylor

Berlin

July 1937

Relieved and elated that his suggestion to accompany the Bergers back to Germany was so genuinely welcomed, Taylor felt he was the luckiest man in the world to be seated beside Sarah on a train admiring the European landscape. Their ride to Germany was an illuminating experience, spanning a beautiful portion of the continent, beginning in France, passing through Belgium and on to Germany, traversing fields, mountains, rivers and lakes, villages and cities. Not only did Taylor feel it was a geography lesson come to life, but Emanuel narrated histories of kings and queens and unions and divisions as they proceeded.

"I still can't believe how you travel such a short time and you are in another country. It's not like that in

America at all, especially where I live," Taylor said, as they crossed their first international border.

"In Europe, we are all family," Emanuel answered. "You did not know this, I am sure. From King George in the 1700s through George V in this century—every monarch in Great Britain chose a German royal for a spouse."

"I've learned just a little European history—marriages are often political matches—not love matches—is that it?"

"Often. But like any family, what do you think happens? Still conflicts, still wars. In this century, so much tension and hatred between Germany and England—that after the war, the English royal family changed their German resonating surnames to Windsor, more British."

"Can you tell already? Papa knows everything," Sarah said, adding anecdotes of family travels as they continued, smiling and laughing with her father at certain memories, and often comfortably taking Taylor's hand in hers. In Brussels, she insisted on leaving the train to run into the station house for boxes of her favorite chocolates from Bruges.

When they retired to their private sleeping compartments after a late dinner, Taylor could not bear the hours of separation from Sarah and tried unsuccessfully to lure her images—her voice, her smell—into his dreams. He lay awake much of the night, his hand pressed against the wall of his bed, as if hers was present just on the other side. In the morning, when they emerged simultaneously from their cabins to meet at the dining car, they exchanged a curiously provocative look that validated Taylor's impression that she was there, beside him.

The chauffeur met their train in Berlin at the Lehrter Bahnhof, a station built like a palace in the French Neo-Renaissance style. He supervised the transfer of their suitcases and a few boxes of presents. Taylor himself carried the painting he had purchased in a most protective manner, making sure that it was situated upright next to the luggage and wouldn't be crushed or compromised in any way. The three travelers settled in the backseat with Sarah in the middle, and she pointed out certain sites along the route from the train station, but having to do more with parks and favorite restaurants than the imposing buildings and monuments of history and government they were surely passing. Taylor twice saw groups of brown-shirted military men marching stiffly in long columns, eight abreast, as if they were in a parade. And along the widest boulevards, elongated red banners, with the Nazi swastika imprinted in bold black, were stretched several stories tall. On this ride, Taylor was surprised that Emanuel barely spoke. He faced away from Taylor, staring out his own window and continually shaking his head. More than once he emitted an "aach" of disgust, and eventually he yelled to the window, "What was I thinking? In a few weeks away do I forget? It makes me sick to see Berlin defiled with his people and his signs."

Taylor wondered if Paris had not been a brief respite for Emanuel, away from the political climate of Germany, and this was a reawakening, with any loose ends of the banners that were flapping in the wind acting as a renewed slap in the face of normalcy for Emanuel. Taylor was hesitant to broach the topic, presuming there would be time ahead for that, and then, surprisingly, Emanuel began talking with his recognizable lightness of tone, as if he snapped out of his depression.

"Here we come upon Oranienburger Strasse. See there, to your right, we pass now the Neue Synagogue. It means new synagogue, which it was in the 1860s. You see, we were not always out of favor in Germany; the Bismark was even there for the inauguration," he said, putting a boastful emphasis on the leader's name. There, just at Krausnickstrasse, where we will turn for our home. It is a palace, is it not?"

"Very beautiful—very ornate—it looks Moorish."

"Taylor, you are a student of architecture also?"

"Not really. It's just that the dome reminds me of the Baha'i House of Worship near my home, actually farther down our main street, Sheridan Road. It's been under construction for years, but you can tell it will be beautiful when it is completed."

"Oh, I see . . . and now we come to our street. Did I tell you? Already you are a favorite of my wife, Inga." The automobile left the main thoroughfare and approached the residential neighborhood. "When she can prepare a room for a guest, or so direct the staff, she feels the house comes alive. She was from such a big family, and yet we were blessed only with Sarah. So a guest gives her more purpose and fills the hollow halls of the upper floors with welcome footsteps."

"And I was going to ask if I was imposing," Taylor responded. "Funny. What you describe is surprisingly familiar to me—so like our own situation at home. Only my mother centers on the emptiness of the long dinner table. I guess this is the universal sadness of a family with an only child."

"But then we work harder than most children to fill that emptiness, don't we Taylor?" Sarah interjected.

"And you succeed; you both succeed," her father assured them. "But now, in minutes only, you will meet my lovely wife." Emanuel was looking past Taylor, pointing out the window to indicate to him which residence on the street was theirs. "Perhaps your father has told you as my own did. Always look at the mother before you choose the daughter."

"Oh, Papa, you are too presumptuous. You are embarrassing me," Sarah immediately groaned, her hand covering her eyes.

But Emanuel answered with, "Shu, Shu. Never mind. Taylor knows what I am saying. This is man talk."

When the car stopped, it was in front of a three-story building with a high front stoop, and Taylor was thinking it was not at all like their residence in Kenilworth, but resembling more the large townhouses that lined the streets of New York's Upper East Side. It was nestled in a neighborhood that seemed to alternate similar homes with apartments and duplexes. The two men gathered their briefcases while Sarah raced immediately to greet her mother who was waiting at the top of the stairs, and Taylor understood what her father was talking about. Inga Berger was the obvious star that had spawned the ray of sunshine that was Sarah. Emerging from the front door, she stood briefly in an unconsciously elegant pose, one hand still on the door handle. Her blond hair, so like Sarah's in color, was shorter, but had a similar bounce and bob. She wore a casual black and white print dress with an oversized red silk flower near one shoulder that perfectly matched her dramatic lipstick.

Inga did not greet Taylor stiffly or formally, but with a warm hug, indicating either that her daughter had held her in close confidence by phone during her time in Paris, or that she felt a maternal connection with Taylor through her closeness to his father.

"Taylor, welcome to our home. It is as if Addison, himself, has come to our doorstep; the resemblance is so strong."

"It is my pleasure, Mrs. Berger. Thank you so much for allowing me to come."

At this point, Emanuel climbed the last step, put down his briefcase, and took Inga's face in his hands. He planted a quick kiss on her lips and then turned her chin toward Taylor. "I have told you the truth, have I not?" he said, winking at the young man.

After Taylor was shown to his room and they all freshened up from the long trip, they were called to the dining room for a full meal of chicken schnitzel and cabbage with noodles. They described details of the fair and the conference to Inga, and then Sarah left the room briefly, returning with the exquisite Chanel dress that she had already worn that would be now be a gift for her mother.

"Oh, that is just beautiful," Inga said, rising and taking the hanger from Sarah and then moving to the mirror over the dining buffet, where she held it in front of her and swayed with it in a dance move. "Sarah, I have taught you well," she continued, speaking into the mirror, "and thank you, Emanuel, darling." She then motioned for the maid to take it from her.

After the dishes were cleared, Sarah addressed her father. "Papa, I know that Taylor has come here to spend time at your factories, but can I please show him the city as well? You know he has never been to Berlin or even to Germany. We don't want him returning with memories only of dark, massive machinery and their thunderous roar."

"That sound, my dear, is the symphony of my work and the substantive support of the food that just graced our very table."

"Oh, Papa. You know I understand that very well and appreciate it," Sarah began, and then looked pleadingly at Inga, who followed her cue and continued.

"Emanuel. Our guest will be just that . . . a guest, introduced to all aspects of our lives in Berlin. And he will receive the royal treatment. I will work with Sarah on an itinerary. Of course, you know that, dear, and you choose to be obstinate," she said with an exasperated look and then turned to Taylor. "Taylor, let us start first with your choices—what would you like to see?"

It was momentarily an uncomfortable question for Taylor, though posed with the best of intentions. He was a very educated young man who always needed to feel prepared when he entered a new situation.

Before Paris, for example, he had familiarized himself not only with conference materials, but with a general idea of what locations he would explore. But his impulsive decision to go to Berlin was a decision of the heart and not the mind, and the only research that had accompanied it included analyzing the texture of Sarah's hair and examining the features of her angelic face.

He struggled to even think of a famous site of Berlin that was familiar to him. You didn't need to be a student of France, and yet mention Paris and you immediately conjure images of the Eiffel Tower and Notre Dame; in Rome, there is the Coliseum; in London, the Tower and Buckingham Palace.

And then he remembered the Olympics that had taken place the previous year, and he felt proud to appear worldly. "Oh, yes. One thing for sure. I would love to see that enormous stadium—where they held the Olympics last year—our Jesse Owens was a star—what did he have—four gold medals? I remember seeing pictures in our newspapers—and some newsreel coverage too."

When he said this, he looked up from his previously shy pose, expecting to see three smiling faces nodding to his great idea. But he was met only with blank looks and an uncomfortable silence. Inga and Sarah exchanged glances, knowing that Emanuel would soon begin his tirade. His voice, however, was quiet when he finally spoke.

"The Olympiastadion in Charlottenburg? Never. No, Taylor. This you do not understand from such a far distance as you lived. Never will I be escorting visitors there."

"I apologize. I had no idea . . . I think I still don't understand."

"No. And it is not your fault. You see . . . or we see now, just as we thought, how Hitler's tricks of propaganda are working—how your typical person in America and other countries would think how wonderful Germany must be from watching these Olympic Games, attracting an audience through newsreels to glorify our country—to show the guests, the participants, the people from around the world that Berlin is a sophisticated showplace—that Hitler has done so much for the country—that he is revered. But we will not be a party to propagating that illusion."

Emanuel paused to take a drink of wine, and then continued. "Always, when an Olympics is held, there is a cleanup of a city—a whitewashing of building facades. This is understandable—street sweepings of litter and of indigents who will suddenly find warm beds inside for the night. All of this is acceptable for a city wanting to put its best foot forward."

Inga and Sarah, positioned on either side of him as he sat at the head of the table, simultaneously each took one of his hands in theirs, and then Sarah continued speaking. "What my father is explaining now is that he would not allow us near the games or the grounds—to support the Olympics in any way. These feelings were the same throughout the Jewish community—none of my friends or their families would be counted in the numbers who supported the event . . ."

"It was a sham," Emanuel interrupted, and would have continued, but Inga abruptly stood to direct them to the front room for dessert and coffee. Taylor wanted to say that he couldn't possibly eat more, but knew that would be impolite.

The living room was a garden bouquet of yellow and green grandeur that took full advantage of the huge front Venetian windows streaming sunshine through tall plates of glass divided into fifteen individual panes and an elaborate half circle crown. The white molding theme continued with a wainscot boasting an intricate square sculptured detail running the perimeter of the room. There were three layers of crown molding at the ceiling, and an ornate white marble columned mantle surrounding the fireplace. Rectangular inlays on each section of the walls presented themselves as enormous frames, and sometimes outlined beautiful paintings or gilded mirrors.

There were high-backed wing chairs with needle-point pillows in the creams and greens with touches of orange. Two overstuffed sofas with thick golden fringe at the base faced each other, and in between were coordinating tufted ottomans on which heavy books of antiques and world maps rested, as if to discourage visitors from placing their feet on the light-toned fabric.

The room bespoke a world where beauty and culture were valued, but the plush furnishings made it more welcoming than intimidating. Sarah sat first on one of the couches and motioned for Taylor to sit next to her. Inga took the nearby chair, but Emanuel seemed too preoccupied to sit. He placed his hands on the back frame of her seat. Although, perhaps, his wife would have liked to transition into a more agreeable topic for conversation, he took up where he left off.

"Taylor, you will walk the streets during your stay, and of course, we all knew that I had no intention of depriving you of that activity, and you will see the beauty of Berlin, but also things that will shock you. What you saw in Paris will seem as nothing to you now. If we walk on Koernerstrasse, you will see store windows defiled with white paint, saying 'Jude' with the Star of David. That—you will have no trouble reading. But there will be signs that you will need translated also. When the National Socialists came in to power, immediately they began with their boycotts.

"Hitler's men—they stood in front of Michalski and Striemer Department store—right after he took over. They held placards—"*Deutschen verteidigen Sie sich gegen jüdische Gräueltat Propaganda. Nur in Deutsch-Shops kaufen!*—Germans defend yourselves against Jewish atrocity propaganda. Buy only at German shops!"

Emanuel stopped talking and paced the room for a moment while the others watched, and then he went to the front window and looked out, as if being reenergized by the streaming sun.

Then Inga stood and took Sarah's hand, raising her from the couch. She led her toward a polished walnut piano angling from the far corner of the room, and together they played a classical duet.

For the next few days, Taylor followed Emanuel through the routines of his workday. With his mentor's permission, he was taking notes as they made the rounds of his two plants. Taylor observed him working hands-on with employees in the boots factory, Emanuel even getting grease on his fingertips, as he helped to make an adjustment on a hole punching machine. Taylor watched as he recalculated the pressure on another piece of equipment that was overheating by fractions of a degree. And then Taylor accompanied him to various scheduled and impromptu meetings with other businessmen.

Naturally, when Emanuel conversed with colleagues and workers, Taylor's understanding was compromised by a language barrier. And though Emanuel was a capable interpreter, his English was wrapped in such a thick German accent that Taylor had to concentrate intently to recognize when he transitioned into it. Eventually, even Emanuel was aware of Taylor's difficulty following him, and so he reminded himself to say Taylor's name first when he began speaking in English.

"I'm so impressed by your father's knowledge of every aspect of the industry," Taylor told Sarah the third evening, as they stood alone in the dining room waiting to be seated when her parents would enter. "I want to be like him. I mean, don't misunderstand me—I am in awe of my own father's business acumen and I feel incredibly lucky to be taking my place in a great business. But I think sometimes my father relies too heavily on managers in each area."

Sarah smiled up at him proudly. "Well, you are right about my father. Perhaps you have already seen the diploma in his office, his engineering degree from Munich University?"

"No, I didn't see it, but that's what I mean—I'm impressed—but not surprised from what I saw, how he conducted himself. I mean, my degree is in the liberal arts, as was my father's, but if I were an engineer, as well—imagine the respect that would generate. Well—I know I don't have that kind of science mind—but you should know I am impressed."

"And you should know that makes me like you even more." Sarah paused for a second, hesitating to offer her next remark. "Then you probably will find this fact even more impressive. My father knows Albert Einstein well."

It took a second to register with Taylor. "You're kidding," he said. "I know who Einstein is—the Nobel Prize winner—the wild hair—that is remarkable. He's always in the news. The theory of relativity. He's something of a celebrity."

"Actually, Mama and Papa dined with him on several occasions. Papa had attended some of his lectures at The University of Zurich and then they made a closer, more personal connection when he was a research assistant for him on a technical project."

"Your father must be incredibly smart to even be able to converse with Einstein," Taylor said, just as Emanuel and Inga entered the dining room. Turning to him, Taylor continued, "Sir, please tell me about your conversations with Einstein."

"I must be honest," Emanuel answered, with a slight laugh, "conversing with Einstein? I'm not so sure about that. You won't believe this, but some people even slept in his lectures; they were not so easy to follow. He noticed me because I was listening so intently, I think. But understanding? . . . I just used to give him patronizing nods. Wait, let me ask Inga." And now he turned to his wife. "Inga, did we ever understand Albert Einstein and his theories?"

"For me," she said, "I was lost after hello."

"There, you see, and my wife is the one with the high IQ."

After dinner, Taylor told Sarah, "I just love your parents. Honestly, I feel so comfortable with them. And they have such a respect for each other. That is what I want in my marriage."

While Taylor had thought he would have had to struggle to continue the pretense that he had had come to Germany to broaden his international business exposure and was eager to spend his days by Herr Emanuel Berger's side, in reality, he did value the time spent with him. But as the weekend approached, he was excited to finally concentrate on his true Berlin interest, the heavenly Miss Sarah Berger.

Finally, it was Sarah's turn to escort Taylor around the city. Like any guide introducing a group to Berlin, Sarah brought him first to the main boulevard, Unter den Linden, and they began their tour in front of the historic Brandenburg Gate. Suddenly, however, it seemed as if Sarah had been drained of her youthful enthusiasm and she just stood and shook her head as Emanuel had on their first day back.

"There it is, the Brandenburg Gate, the most famous entry to our city from 1791. We came as schoolchildren to learn the story. It was designed to be like the entrance to the Acropolis in Athens. When I was younger, we would look at these gates to the city, and that was how we learned about architecture—the massive Doric columns. And our eyes would be drawn to the Quadriga of Victory at the top—the beautiful bronze horse-drawn chariot, with Victoria, the goddess of victory at the reins." As she spoke, Taylor remained behind her, with his hands resting at the tops of her shoulders, intensifying the shared point of view, the experience of sight and emotion as she narrated. He had an idea what she was going to say next. "But now our eyes are drawn to those red Nazi banners—we don't see the classical beauty— we see the hideous black swastika in its white circle. My father said it; Hitler defiles everything. He changes our future and he tarnishes our past. From so far below, you cannot even understand the intricacies of the design or even the dimensions of the sculpture. Napoleon came through in the early 1800s, claimed the Quadriga as a prize, and took it back to Paris with his victory."

"And this is a copy now?"

"No, Germany recaptured it, and then that Prussian symbol, the Iron Cross, was added. But now, I'd rather Napoleon kept it. Instead, people flock here to see it and it is one more chance for the Nazis to shine."

They continued a walking tour for the rest of the day. On the boulevards, he saw the preponderance of the Nazi flags, the posters, the military presence, but she chose now to point out only her favorite shops and galleries, and he chose to treasure each minute by her side, holding tightly on to her hand or putting his arm around her small waist. When she led him through the parks and fountains of the Tiergarten, they were able to be lost in the beauty of the surroundings and they stopped twice in the brief period to enjoy the delicacies of the cafés.

That evening, when her parents entered the room for dinner, Sarah and Taylor were each standing behind their own chairs, and then they all sat down together as if on cue.

Sarah's mother held a familiar envelope. "Taylor Woodmere," she said, as she handed it to him.

"Again?" he questioned.

"Yes, Taylor," Inga began with a sympathetic look, "I have not opened it, but my guess is that your father is once more cabling for you to return to your Chicago."

Sarah looked up incredulously. "What is this about? You are being called home? Your father is telling you to leave? You didn't say anything about that." She stood and moved quickly to his chair.

Taylor was reading the cable, his forehead showing the contemplative wrinkling that indicates mental calculations.

"I am to board the *Queen Mary* for its next western sailing. We have three days left together and then I will have to leave."

Overnight, Sarah had devised a plan to maximize their time together and presented it to him at break-

fast the next morning. "We will take the train to Potsdam for a day trip. My aunt and uncle have a country
estate nearby and my mother has said that if they will
come to meet us for lunch, she will allow me to go. I'd
love to take you to Munich—to show you the Bavarian
Alps—but we'd spend too much time on the train and
not enough walking around. Potsdam is the perfect distance to be able to experience the countryside."

And just after dawn the next morning, they were
boarding the train. "Here—you sit by the window, Taylor. I want you to enjoy the view," she said as they were
negotiating their seats. But after the train departed the
station, Taylor wedged his light jacket at the top of his
seat bordering the window and used it as a pillow to
lean on while he looked only at her.

"Taylor, you are incorrigible. You are to look out
the window and enjoy my countryside." Eventually,
she coaxed him to take the aisle seat. If he must only
look at her, at least the scenery would now be in the
background.

"Sarah, do you know the story *Alice's Adventures
in Wonderland?*" he finally asked after studying her in
silence. "It's by an Englishman, Lewis Carroll. Not one
of your *Grimm's Fairy Tales*, but maybe you know it. It
may also be called *Through the Looking Glass.*"

"Well, yes, I do know it—it was a favorite of my
tutor—I actually learned much English from reading
it."

"Good then—because I've been trying to decide
who you remind me of—and that is it." He was excited
to share this revelation with her.

"Oh—you mean the Cheshire Cat—yes, I do have a snarly, sinister look."

"Of course, you know I do not mean the cat—or the Queen of Hearts for that matter—although you are the queen of mine. No—Alice herself —You are *Alice in Wonderland* come to life."

She gave no response and only bowed her head with the smirk of the Cheshire.

"You've heard this before, I am thinking," Taylor said.

"Well, truthfully, my tutor often called me Alice after he introduced me to the book, and if we were to run into him today even, he'd yell across the street—'Hello, Alice! How are you doing?'—although he would most likely say it in German."

He smiled at the image and then began playing with her hair. "It's a good thing you did not know me when you were younger. You would have had on some sort of Bavarian uniform for school and I would have delighted in pulling your pigtails. I can picture them—tightly braided like Heidi."

"You're ridiculous—that's not how we dressed," she laughed. "We did not look provincial, except on a day like today for a picnic in the country. No, we were sophisticated—blazers and dark pleated skirts, leggings, white collared shirts—like English preparatory school-children. Well, I would have ignored you anyway," she insisted. And with that she turned from him and looked out the window for a few moments and then settled back into the crook of his arm, her head resting on his shoulder.

As with longtime friends, the silences in conversation that mark the normal rhythms of casual discourse did not need to be filled with nervous banter. Instead, the two would begin with just short glances—one pair of eyes searching out and then magnetizing to the other—the connection resulting in the lowering of the chin, the involuntary raising of the shoulders, and the closed-lipped smile that Leonardo da Vinci immortalized with his *Mona Lisa.*

There is always a moment with true lovers when everything from that time on will be indelibly recorded in memory as "before" or "after." It is an instantaneous insight, a perception, an acknowledgement of the ending of one era, the beginning of another. Sometimes this awareness happens in tandem, with the electricity generated from a first look, a first touch, a first kiss. But more often, one partner will sense it, causing the other to feel it in turn. The young lovers will suddenly, separately, and silently acknowledge that previously they were floundering, unsure, measuring time slowly with the completion of tasks, looking forward to subsequent events, checking days off as experiences sought or obstacles conquered with no thought for living in the moment, for taking in the sensory details of the substance of everyday life.

Then, suddenly, there is an emotional maturity with the realization that life is a journey and not a destination, and that they want to enjoy the ride together. And for Sarah and Taylor that moment occurred on the train to Potsdam. Their eyes met and held, and independently and wordlessly, they reaffirmed their desire to be forever connected. Caught by the ebullient glow of Sarah's face, Taylor stroked her hair, twirling a section with his fingers and bringing the strands to his nose, to breathe in her fragrance. Sarah raised her own hand and began to play with the untamed strands from his casually groomed locks, unaware that few women were able to resist that same impulse. Once, twice, she repeated the gesture, and when she finally pulled away, embarrassed, he pulled her back to him. He laced his fingers through the thickness of her full blond hair, and kissed her with an assertive passion that made her glance around, self-consciously. But then Taylor simply and gently closed her eyelids with his fingers and continued with the kiss accompanied by progressively less innocent caresses. And when she pulled away once more, even he understood that their intimacy was approaching a level inappropriate to the setting and he too began to straighten and smooth his garments and to more demurely reposition their seating.

An older couple, situated with a purposeful distance between each other, he awkwardly leafing through the oversized pages of a newspaper, she slowly working with yarn, obviously struggling with dropped rows of knits and purls, kept turning in their direction. The elderly woman, glancing from time to time over the rims of her reading glasses, offered a sweet smile to the younger couple, perhaps thankful for a glimpse back into her own fond memories of a youthful romance. The man, however, sour faced and intermittently scratching his bearded cheek or pulling at the graying hairs protruding from his ears, emitted only disgusting groans every now and then, as if Sarah and Taylor were in some way poisoning his territory.

Finally, Taylor was regaining his composure and modulating his breathing. "Quick," he said. "No thinking—first things that come into your head. Favorite things."

"God, this is too hard." She didn't even question his motives, simply understood that they needed to begin conversing or they would certainly be drawn, once more, to their embraces.

"You're thinking too much," he countered. "You're not being graded, little Miss Teacher's Pet."

"OK—but these are quick thoughts—superficial—last month's favorite things—butterflies, cloudless days, star-filled nights, apple strudel, heated, served with sweet cream . . ."

"My—you are good at this . . ." he returned.

"Books, of course," she continued, "and china collections, mainly tea cups—enameled and embellished."

"Good, good. I am gathering a great picture of you—but what's this about 'last month's favorite things'—have they changed?"

She knew he was being coy, knew she had played right into his script, but she continued pretending to be naïve to his intentions. "But now maybe a man would join that list. Oh, yes—leave room on that list now for an extremely passionate man."

And so it was his turn to feign innocence. "Passionate, you say," and once again he was moving closer to her on the seat.

"Extremely so," she continued, "passionate and talented."

"Talented," he echoed, thinking now that she was recalling his amorous techniques, the soft massage of her throat as he had edged titillatingly close to the mounds of her perfect breasts.

"Oh—yes. A recognized talent."

And now he thought she was referring to his reputation as a ladies' man to which he had alluded.

"Oh, yes—incredibly gifted—gifted hands and an eye for beauty."

"Yes, now. Your favorite thing—a man—his name, please," he coaxed with a self-satisfied expression.

"And you haven't guessed?"

"I want to hear that name from your lips."

And just as his finger reached to touch those lips, she answered. "Henri Lebasque."

"Henri Lebasque?" He was angling away from her again, offering her a confused, doubtful expression . . . until he remembered. "The painting—of course . . . and the painter, now one of your favorite things—my own introduction, and yet I find I am still jealous." He knew that she was just teasing him. But could it really have been less than two weeks ago when he had been captured by the artist's work? Such an entrancing painting, and yet he had discovered it, purchased it, held, and cherished it for the briefest period of time, for too soon he was distracted by his infatuation with Sarah, an Impressionist's model come to life.

And now Taylor took her face in his hands and studied it, as if he were an artist examining his own work, tracing the lines of her high cheek bones with his thumbs, following the curves of her arched brows with his fingers. He shook his head. "You are a fire. You are consuming me. You are hot to my touch. Do you know that? Do you feel it? Don't answer. Back to questions. What makes you scared?" The need to pose this question came to him so suddenly and pointedly that he now understood his own intentions. He needed to know more about Sarah— he needed to know everything about her. He wanted to feel her past, for it to become his past, for that was the only way they could proceed—that her future could become his future—that their destinies would forever be entwined.

The question only confused her. "Of everything there is to know, you ask me this—you ask what scares me?" And he loved that response from her, because it implied that she knew, that she understood, that they did, indeed, need to know everything about each other.

But then she decided not to be obstinate or challenging. "Loud noises. Uncertainty. I am a planner. I have no fear of being lost, because I will always find my way. But I must always know where my mother is—and my father. Bullies at school, I fear—and not for myself, I am tougher than you know—but I hate that powerless feeling of being unable to help others." She lightened the moment again. "Don't laugh, you know I fear being called on and not knowing the answer or sometimes, knowing that the teacher didn't give the right answer and fearing that I will not hold my tongue."

As she completed her list of fears with the almost trite recitation of rodents, and dark, moonless nights, he was unprepared for the direction this innocent game suddenly took. "My greatest fear—again a man tops this list." She paused and looked directly at Taylor. "Hitler—Adolph Hitler."

He put his arm around her and silently, heads leaning into each other and hands clasped together, they traveled on to Potsdam.

Along with droves of tourists, they strolled the picturesque grounds of Frederick the Great's Park Sanssouci. Entering through the Obelisk-Portal and passing the Grosse Fontane, they admired the abundance of ornate gardens, sculptured fountains and classical statues, and then they visited the exquisite rococo country palace, Schloss Sanssouci. Fronted by large, lush terraces of vines and orange trees, the elaborate one-story castle was home to the king's impressive art collection, with many by Rubens, van Dyke, and Caravaggio. They walked the halls and read the accounts of King Frederick entertaining the elite of his era, including his friend Voltaire.

"Sanssouci—coming from French—'without a care,'" Sarah said as they exited, pointing to the sign. "The king sought this town as his country retreat. We are royal then, with the same need to escape."

Taylor thought for a moment. "Or maybe he was just human," he said. "Maybe he was just like us."

Sarah's Aunt Ilse, accompanied by a teenage daughter, Margarete, brought a full picnic array of treats and a large blanket, and they all ate lunch along the shore of the Havel River. The cousin could not stop staring at Taylor and was pulling at Sarah's sweater, urging her to explain about her handsome boyfriend. They stayed only a brief time, as Margarete had an afternoon piano lesson scheduled, but they fulfilled their role as chaperones.

After they left, Sarah and Taylor walked hand in hand along the riverbank, skirting the bikers and watching the boats go by. Taylor was trying to focus only on the carefree beauty of the setting, as that was their purpose in coming to Potsdam. But he was unsettled when a tourist steamer passed with a bold message across its port side, "*Wer beim Juden Kauff stiehlt Voksvermogen.*" When he saw the word "*Juden*," he wanted to know. "I'm sorry . . . Please, tell me. What does it say?"

"The same—we've seen it in many windows in Berlin—'Those who buy from Jews are stealing the people's property.'"

The mood interrupted, they both acknowledged it was time to head for the train station.

Back in Berlin, they made a brief stop at a floral shop, as Taylor was intent on bringing flowers back for Sarah's mother. The store was busy with customers assembling bouquets from the assortments of fresh flowers in large pots and vying for the attention of the proprietor. Taylor saw how the older woman behind the counter was hesitant to wait on certain customers. She seemed to have her eye trained on the door, and overreacted to the clanging of bikes into the metal barriers, as if afraid that brown-shirted storm troopers would be rushing in at any moment.

Taylor had never before understood what a great thing it was to be an American. This was partially because he had never before truly understood geography on a global scale. Just yesterday, in cartography stores on this Berlin street, he sought out maps and Sarah was eager to translate for him. It was dawning on him that nations across continental Europe were like states in his own country. Traveling by train from Paris, France, through Belgium and on to Germany was like heading across the Midwest at home. He never analyzed the literal meaning of the U.S.A. It was the United States of America, and uniting states and keeping them stabilized and secure was certainly not a thing to be taken lightly. Across an ocean, he had not clearly comprehended why countries were always at war, fighting about borders on the pages of his school history books. Suddenly, he understood the proximity of "states" that were nations, without common languages, religions, currencies, ethnicities, or governments. He thought about Wilson's quest for isolation during the last war. He had studied about it, but now he could visualize and verbalize it—these people are far from us and on top of each other. Neutrality, from that perspective, only made sense.

But when you are here and you develop empathy for the people, when you see them as mothers, fathers, shopkeepers . . . and lovers, maybe a great nation like the United States has a moral responsibility to do something. We take for granted that our police and army will protect us against thugs. But what if the police are the thugs? What if your army is armed against you?

"Sarah," he said, when they finally paid for their bouquet and exited the shop, "the Germany of your youth was beautiful, but open your eyes. The climate here is not normal, not acceptable, and not safe. There is tension everywhere; there is a fear."

There. He had said it. "Fear." It was the word that she had kept tucked in a drawer at her home, in her handbag as she strolled, and yet he had articulated the word so easily. "Oh, Taylor, I know you are right," she said, as she bit her lip. "I say these very things to Papa and he tells me it will be all right. But you do not. You are scaring me." They were walking toward her home, where the street lamps were fewer and they had the privacy that they longed for. Taylor turned to Sarah and took her in his arms, lifting her face to his and smoothing back the strands of hair that had escaped her barrettes.

"Darling, you must leave Germany. You and your family. I can feel it—maybe an outsider can see more easily what others cannot." He walked with her for a moment and then he remembered something important. "Even your brilliant Albert Einstein left Germany some time back—and now he lives in the United States. And I think maybe that's where you should be."

She faced him with a sad, scared expression. "I know what you say is true—that my father must consider removing us from Germany—but you worked with him for some days—you must understand his commitment—he cannot bear to abandon his work and his employees. No, I want to find a better phrase. He is passionate about his work—married to his job."

"Sarah, I understand. But I won't be like that. I'm passionate about you and I want you to be safe."

As they turned the corner of her block, he smothered her in his arms and gently laid his cheek on hers. Their eyes met as she raised her face, and when her lips parted, he gave into the sweet intoxication of her breath.

"See, I was right," he continued as if no physical contact had interrupted him midsentence. "Passionate about you . . . married to you. Do you know this? I love you so much."

And she smiled and responded simply, "Yes . . . we are one heart."

While Taylor was eager to present Inga with the flowers and accepted her kiss on the cheek, he was not as quick to broach the topic with Emanuel that had been weighing on him. He waited until the meal was over. The women left the house to deliver a dinner plate to a neighbor who was ill, and so the men moved into the front room and the maid followed them with the coffee service.

Walking by Emanuel's side, Taylor turned to him. "Sir, I thank you for being a part of the most interesting, educational, and pleasurable weeks of my life. You have been generous of your time and your hospitality."

"And, Taylor, I will echo your own words. The pleasure was ours."

This time each of the men chose to sit in the high-backed chairs and Taylor continued. "But I may press that hospitality by approaching you with my feelings now." He paused because he needed courage to continue and he wanted to find the right words. "You can tell, I think, that I love your daughter. And already I love your family."

Emanuel smiled and nodded.

"And you know, I hope, that I have immense respect for you as a businessman, a family man, and from what

I have seen and heard, as a man in the community. If I challenge you now, it is not meant disrespectfully." He didn't look up at Emanuel as he spoke, and so he continued without monitoring his expression. "No, I am not Jewish . . . not German . . . just a man and maybe a young, naïve one at that. But even I can feel, even I know from what I have seen and learned . . . I believe that Germany is not a safe place for you and your family." Now he looked up at Emanuel, "I am sorry, perhaps out of line, but sometimes an outsider can add a fresh perspective. I am scared for you and the family. Have you never considered leaving Berlin?"

As he had on the first night, Emanuel rose and paced the room, this time leaning on the fireplace mantel with his coffee cup in hand. "You remember what I alluded to before, that since Hitler came to power, he has had one main mission, to drive the Jews from Germany." He took a long sip from his drink and then placed it on a small table nearby. "But I did not explain it well enough—that from the moment in 1933 when he became this Reich Chancellor, our Jewish community has worked together to be stronger. This is always the case—people turn to each other when united against a common enemy. Of course, Hitler knows this the best— it was his doing first, targeting the Jews—rallying the support of German workers with this hatred—we are the scapegoats for the sad state of Germany."

Now Emanuel walked back to his chair and sat to have a more intimate distance between them. "Sometimes, we laugh at our own meetings—how disparate opinions have always been among Jews. Often, we were our own worst enemies—arguing among ourselves. But now, he divides us from our Aryan countrymen, and suddenly that unites us. He denies us public schools and suddenly our Jewish schools that were floundering, now cannot accommodate all of our students. The school on Grosse Hamburger Strasse has well over one thousand boys and girls now. He expels our artists, our scholars, our musicians—and we answer. We have made a *Kultur-bund,* our Jewish cultural league. And we organize our own concerts and lectures and museum showings."

At this point Sarah and Inga entered the room and Emanuel rose again and walked over to his daughter and looked at her as he spoke. "As Jews, we will survive, as we always do. I do not fault our friends and neighbors for leaving, but I am determined to stay until this dark era will pass and we will regain our place in society." Then he turned to Taylor. "I cannot leave; I cannot take my family and run. I believe that people look to me for strength and guidance."

Taylor was not sure how to respond. After a few moments, he said only, "I think I understand," although with more of a doubtful tone than one of conviction.

That night, a strong, summer rain pounded the roof of the Berger home, further making sleep impossible on an already restless night. Taylor would be leaving early the next morning to begin the route to meet up with his ship. He had already said his good-byes to Sarah's parents and to Sarah. There had been shared moments for expressing deep gratitude and optimism for a quick reunion, and private moments for embraces and kisses.

But now the loud reverberations of the thunderstorm gave Taylor the idea that he could have one last farewell, and he went to Sarah's room as quietly as possible, using the piercing cracks of the severe weather to veil his footsteps.

She was waiting for him, having read his heart and mind. She was unconsciously flipping through the pages of a book, and when he entered her room, he was once more enraptured by the golden streaks of blond hair softly framing her beautiful face, illuminated by the bedside lamp. Without a word, he moved the covers aside, lay down next to her, and switched off the light. For a long while, he held her as close as possible and barely let their lips separate. Briefly, they fell asleep in each other's arms, and when they awoke with a start, fearful that it was already morning, they were relieved to find it was barely 4:00 a.m. He began to slip out as silently as he had entered, but at the last moment, his hand on the doorknob already, he spoke.

"I have left it for you. You will find it by the entry hall. I will count the days until you both find a home with me in America."

In the morning when she woke up with the first light of day, she knew it was long after his 5:00 a.m. departure, yet she ran down the stairs, nonetheless. She was not looking for him. She wanted confirmation that the night had been real and not a dream. And she cried when she saw it leaning against the wall, the beautiful painting, *Jeune Fille à la Plage*.

Taylor

Atlantic Crossing

August 1937

The Grand Salon of the RMS *Queen Mary*, the new flagship of the merged Cunard and White Star Lines, served also as the first-class dining room and had the two-story columned look of an Art Deco masterpiece. Only a little over a year earlier, the ocean liner had been launched. It was meant to rival the *Normandie*, which had been the ship to transport Taylor on his initial trip east across the Atlantic, but whose return ticket he had abandoned.

Taylor had thought that his passage back to the States would have given him ample solitary time for absorbing all that had happened to him, for formulating a plan, but he soon found himself falling into the entertainment routines of shipboard life in order to maintain his sanity. Surprisingly, he suffered from a bit of seasickness. Although he hadn't felt this way on the trip over, it seemed that the currents were stronger this voyage. He found that if he simply relaxed in his suite there was nothing to concentrate on but the ebb and flow of the waves. As a sailor, it caught him off guard. He had often borne the strong currents on a thirty-foot sailboat on Lake Michigan, and so it would seem that the motion of a large ocean liner would not bother him. But, perhaps, he was especially vulnerable now—his stomach queasy from both the sea and from love.

At dinner the first evening, he found himself at a well-placed table of ten.

"'Mr. Taylor Woodmere of Chicago.' Pardon me for perusing the place cards before dinner." The speaker was a full-bosomed woman who offered her exquisite, but rather gauche, jewelry as if on a display shelf on her décolletage.

"I am wondering if it is possible that you are related to Addison—I believe it was Addison Woodmere, Jr., who my husband and I were friends with during the men's Yale years."

"Why yes, my father is Addison—my grandfather, still quite alive, is Addison Senior." Taylor was happy to feel the familiarity of American camaraderie.

"Well, allow me to introduce myself. I am Mrs. Newland Pritchard, of Scarsdale, New York, and please," at this point she shoved a somewhat masculine, more than timid, girl into his sight. "This is my daughter, Katherine. Katherine Pritchard. She is twenty years old. You must be?"

"Ma'am, I am twenty-two."

"Oh," and she nodded to her daughter, who was embarrassed to the point of blushing. "How wonderful, a dance partner for the duration."

Taylor would have been maddened by the woman's forwardness, if she were not such an almost comical character, if the mortified Katherine had not given him such a look of desperation, saying with her eyes, *Just be happy you don't have to live with this.*

Later, as they walked together along the deck after dinner, Katherine said, "I know how embarrassing this is and I apologize for my mother. Believe me, this is not a new situation for me. Aside from the fact that I am twenty and practically an old maid in her eyes, I have a boyfriend who she will not acknowledge, who she looks down her nose at."

Taylor was surprised. Katherine was not a particularly pretty girl; his first impression was that she was awkward and shy, actually a little tomboyish. She seemed extremely uncomfortable in the evening gown that he now realized was certainly of her mother's choosing, and she was constantly rearranging her shawl to obscure that same feminine feature that her mother was thrusting at strangers.

"Actually, I'm in love," she continued. "And even this European trip—my God, we met two lords and a prince—is not going to make me love Edgar less."

"Well, little Miss Surprising Lady, we may just have a wonderful time on this sailing, as I too am in love. Only I have a major dilemma and I might benefit from some advice."

"That might cost you a bit," Katherine retorted. "If we can just entertain each other and play a role like we are somewhat interested, we could both benefit."

"I see what you mean." Taylor was actually quick at assessing social situations. "If I monopolize your time, your mother will leave you alone, at least for the voyage."

"Yes," Katherine was nodding, "You get it. And, now don't get more of a swelled head than you probably already possess, but you will have dozens of other mother-daughter combinations trying to grab you, if you don't already appear taken."

"Katherine," he said, nodding his head as he spoke, "I am thinking this Edgar is one lucky guy. You are quite a little character."

Within the first few days of the cruise, Taylor recognized that he had made a wonderful friend in Katherine. For the first time in his life, he felt he had met a different kind of soul mate, as if he had found a sibling. And for an only child, that is as precious a gift as is offered.

And as they became further acquainted, walking the decks, participating in competitive games of shuffleboard, looking for sea animals off the side of the ship, he felt comfortable sharing his complicated story with her, seriously seeking her advice on what to do next.

It was actually Katherine's idea to go together to the ship's head purser, Mr. Anthony Bailey, who they found to be an amazing confidante. He was eager to help Taylor in his attempt to secure passage on any future voyages for the family of Sarah Berger. But the well-informed purser was explaining to him the difficulties that affluent businessmen were finding in leaving Germany with their holdings and investments.

Taylor's situation gave Katherine a new perspective on her own romantic troubles and all of a sudden her problem seemed easy and quite solvable. She was in love with a young man, an apprentice in a bicycle shop. They had met when she brought in her bicycle, a birthday gift from her parents, for a minor repair and an adjustment to the handlebars. It seemed to her initially that he never even acknowledged her, his work cap covering his eyes. She could only focus on his greasy fingers as he adjusted the bars, while she straddled the bike as he had requested. Again, seemingly without looking at her, he suggested he accompany her on a ride to test out his work.

After they had ridden down the block and turned by the grocery store, he raised his head up at her, moved back his cap, and smiled.

"My name is Edgar Spinner."

"Oh," was all she could answer initially. She was surprised at the familiarity of his demeanor and its accompanying smile. Then finally she thought to return, "I'm Katherine."

"I know. I sold the bicycle to your father. He said it was for your birthday and that is how I know we are the same age." And then, after a brief pause, he added, "You look like your father."

"Yes, I am told that often—I'm never quite sure how to take that."

"Well," Edgar Spinner said, hesitating, "I like your looks a lot."

And with that they began sharing afternoon rides and eventually sharing dreams. And many of those conversations she was now sharing with her new friend, Taylor Woodmere.

"His name is Edgar Spinner," Katherine offered, "and when he started to decide on a profession, he thought that he was drawn to cycling because of his name. He had a dream of opening his own store, maybe many, maybe employing Mr. Ford's assembly line technique and building bikes. His shingle would read, 'Spinner's Cyclery—Our Name and Our Destiny.'"

Taylor was impressed by the passion with which Katherine told Edgar's story and knew that she would be a strong force behind his future success in business. And as it would turn out, in the recurring theme of life he was experiencing when meeting people, being in the right place at the right time, in the not too distant future, Spinner's Cyclery would be the first of many businesses Taylor would invest in as a silent partner and it would do him well. And aside from his financial gain, he would count the future Mr. and Mrs. Edgar Spinner among his closest friends.

Taylor

New York

August 1937

When he finally arrived in New York, Taylor decided not to book a train to Chicago right away. He needed to unwind from the trip, needed to reflect on his situation—to devise a plan to move his life ahead in the new direction to which he had committed himself.

For this brief period of time he stayed at the beautiful and posh Waldorf=Astoria Hotel on Park Avenue. Despite having been christened in 1931 during the height of the ongoing Great Depression, it presented itself as the largest and tallest hotel in the world and it actually filled an entire city block. This Art Deco structure was the vision of two cousins, William Waldorf Astor and John Jacob Astor, who previously each owned hotels adjacent to one another, with none other than the Empire State Building constructed on their combined lots. Almost immediately, the new hotel became the favored destination of the rich and famous.

Perusing the hotel lobby and corridors as he entered, Taylor saw an impressive display of pictures documenting the history of the hotel, including a photo of former president Herbert Hoover delivering a radio address at the opening—an optimistic high point of that new decade.

After registering, Taylor continued his tour. Walking toward the Park Avenue foyer, his eyes were immediately drawn upward toward the top of the dozen or so imposing columns, where six clusters of enormous and multicolored balloons were decorating the ceiling. He overheard a bellman explaining to another visitor that the decorations were remaining from a children's charity ball held the night before in the adjacent ballroom. Still, his innate sense of style, which was yet one more impressive inheritance from both of his parents' lineage and had been enhanced by his new European exposure to art, immediately found these an offensive addition to the exquisite hotel décor. He knew that perhaps if he had been an attendee at the event, which undoubtedly sported complementary centerpieces, chairs decked with ribbons and bows, and a fanciful backdrop behind the orchestra stage, that he might have appreciated the context of the floating helium balls. But now he found them only frivolous objects. Was this to be his fate, he wondered, to find fault in everything, to walk into the largest and most beautiful hotel in the world and find only details to criticize? Had he gained sensitivity only to lose sensibility? And as if to prove to himself that he was able to remain sane, he focused now on the intricate pebbled tile work—the Art Deco lines, the gold leaf on the ceiling, the silver leaf images of plants and animals . . .

The following day he had full audience to the preparations for an elite society wedding and he soaked in every detail like the most appreciative guest. In fact, he was so endearing to the wedding party as they gathered early in the lobby to take their photographs, so helpful to the elderly grandparents, and a spirited playmate occupying the time of the energetic mix of junior bridesmaids, groomsmen, the ring bearer, and flower girl—that more than once someone asked to which side of the wedding couple he was connected. When it was understood that he was merely a guest at the hotel, he was not shooed away as any ordinary interloper would be, but he was invited to attend the celebration after the dinner, with more than one of the bridesmaids offering him a position on her figurative dance card.

Before he left the group, they let him take an early glimpse into the ballroom set up for the ceremony. At the end of the long aisle, where in a church would be an altar or at least a podium, stood an ornately decorated canopy. From a distance, it seemed to be a broadly arched wooden structure of branches and leaves and garlands of flowers. The grandfather, peering in the room alongside Taylor and hearing him remark on its beauty, told him, "It is a *chuppah*, a beautiful part of our Jewish tradition. And for your interest, young man,' he continued, "I will tell you the most wonderful part of our Jewish ceremony. At the end, after the couple is pronounced man and wife, a glass wrapped in a napkin will be placed beneath the groom's foot and when he stomps down and breaks it, the guests will shout 'Mazel Tov,' which means congratulations and good luck."

Taylor was thinking now of the property at his Kenilworth home, how the backyard was landscaped in a park-like setting overlooking Lake Michigan, how his father had constructed the most intricately arched gazebo, a wooden latticework edifice, and he could picture Sarah's eyes light up when he showed it to her. Perhaps he could walk away now from this crowd of celebrants and try to sustain positive thoughts for his own future.

And then he saw her. She was seated halfway across the extensive lobby, and although most of her back was to him, when she turned her head slightly, a glimpse of her distinctive profile and her shock of blond hair made his heart race. How could this be that she actually made it to America before him? Had she returned on the speedier *Normandie*? He supposed that it was possible, that her father may have come to his senses more quickly than even Taylor had anticipated. And although it would be a coincidence that she would be here at the Waldorf=Astoria, since he had not formulated and certainly had not articulated any such plans, this would be the natural choice for a family such as the Bergers when traveling to New York. All of these thoughts delayed him half a minute in approaching her, and just as she was within his reach, one or two more seconds and his arm would have circled her waist, she rose and approached another man almost in a run. And now that man was experiencing the bliss of her embrace, his ecstatic face in Taylor's full view, his hands resting on that very portion of the small of her back that he had been targeting. He was confused. Who was this—a relative she had never mentioned—another family friend or business associate? But it could not be either, holding her like that, kissing her with his same passion and then twirling her. Twirling her. Thank God, twirling her. For then he saw she was not Sarah at all. She was yet another blond young woman, not even really as soft and pretty as his girl.

Immediately he searched for the picture. Although he knew he had been keeping it close on his person, he was flustered and couldn't locate the right pocket—outside jacket, right and then left, pants empty except for change, but then, of course, closest to his heart in his inside jacket pocket—the photograph with her at the Paris Exposition. He was glad he had insisted that they take advantage of one of the most popular kiosks at the fair, even though it meant waiting in a fairly long line. When it was finally their turn, the photographer had put them in their proper places at a predetermined distance from the camera and from each other, and then went about fidgeting with the mechanics of the process. They stood in a stilted pose as the assistant adjusted the height of the white bulb on its metal stand and then stepped down from his ladder and arranged Taylor's position so that his hat was hanging down from his left fingertips. The photographer, still unsatisfied with the artistry of the shot, placed a flower in Sarah's right hand for symmetry. And now Taylor remembered the moment it was shot, when he looked at her instead of the camera. Despite the impropriety of the bold move to be recorded, he reached out quickly and connected their free hands. He could swear there was a shot of electricity in her touch, and he refused to be sensible and attribute it to the dryness in the air.

Over the years it would be the music of the era that would reignite his feelings of emptiness and longing for Sarah. As it was, foreign songs did not have any consistent play on American airways; that would have been unbearable. Of course, they never shared a song, had "our song." It was just the collective music of the times that would catch his ear and then his heart. So he created memories from these first days back in America, with the first songs he heard. And the most powerful one was from a new musical that had just become popular, *The Lullaby of Broadway*. As he rested and contemplated his future, it reverberated through every corridor, echoed as he passed any dance lounge of the Waldorf=Astoria Hotel.

Taylor

Chicago

August 1937

Finally, his sojourn to and from Europe had gone full circle. The trip that would define his entire being for the rest of his life had come to an end. When the train made its final approach into Union Station in Chicago and Taylor exited down the metal steps of the Pullman car following the porter with his luggage, he took only a cursory glance to see if Emily was there and was neither surprised nor disappointed that she was not.

But then, just down the concrete walkway, skirting people and steel beams, struggling to catch his attention with extended waves of his arms, was a very welcome and familiar face. It was Gregory, his closest contemporary among the house staff, who greeted him warmly, with more of a hug then a handshake.

"Sir, it's good to have you back. I will be happy to update you on anything at home. You look well, but . . ."

They were walking at a lively pace, with Gregory now leading the porter toward the automobile, though continuing the conversation as he glanced back over his shoulder.

"But," Gregory continued, "I want to say . . . distracted . . . I know, of course, you are looking for Miss Emily. So I regret to be the one to tell you some disappointing news. You see, she was called back to Newport earlier in the week. She was beside herself to have to go home just days before you were finally returning."

"Really, Gregory? Is everything OK?"

"Mr. Taylor, I believe that her father suffered a serious injury."

"Oh, my God. And Emily can be so fragile with bad news—How did she take it?"

"I confess that much of what I know about her father's condition I overheard. But I was called upon to help her pack up her things and escort her to the train."

"That must have been a big job," he said wryly.

"Again, I must confess that there were three of us packing." He looked at Taylor with a sideways smirk and they both burst out laughing.

"Oh, I'm so sorry, Mr. Taylor. It is not my business to judge."

"It's OK, Gregory. I obviously know exactly what you must have gone through. I'm not sorry I missed it—although I should have been there for her."

"Well, your mother and father did their best to comfort her before she left—but she does have a way."

"Can you tell me what happened?

"It seems like a freak combination of illness and accident. It appears Mr. Kendall was sailing—they say he might have blacked out from exposure or had a heart attack. He let go of some lines, the boom whipped around and knocked him before one of his sons could react. When he was brought ashore, he was unconscious. I'm not sure if he is still hospitalized or convalescing at home."

"My God, that does sound serious," Taylor responded. "I'm glad she went immediately and didn't wait for my return." Taylor felt guilty thinking that the timing of this event had worked well for him. He would have an opportunity now to gain perspective on all that he had experienced in Europe. He would have additional time to decide how to proceed with plans that he had been formulating on the voyage home.

Emily Kendall

Newport

August 1937

The most striking feature of Emily Kendall, the reason why people were drawn to her for immediate second glances, was the contrast of her whitish skin against her thick, dark auburn hair. Her features were perfect and petite, the small nose—the almond-shaped eyes with dark brown pupils and lids domed with high-arched dark brows. Though her perfectly manicured hands were thin and almost child-sized, her frame was slim, but not short. Simply, she looked like a porcelain doll come to life. And it should have been no surprise that her spoiled and entitled manner was a result, undoubtedly, of a mother who had enjoyed dressing that doll from birth through adolescence in the most stylish and expensive garments—accessorizing with little mink muffs and pearls from the time she was a toddler. Trips to New

York throughout her childhood included overnights at the Plaza Hotel and a suite filled with clothes from Saks Fifth Avenue. Following an afternoon of shopping, sometimes the five- or seven-year-old Emily would fall asleep on the big tufted chairs of the exquisite Palm Court Restaurant, in the midst of drinking a root beer float, her black patent leather shoes dangling off her feet, as her mother sat with friends and sipped tea.

As a young adult, Emily held herself in a straight, regal manner, and when she waved to friends across the campus lawn, she used just the slight twist of the wrist motion that royalty employed on long parade routes. She was one of those beautiful young women that seemed snobbish and unapproachable, and yet made you wonder if she was actually teeming with the same insecurities and angst as any girl her age.

She was not. Emily had been pampered and coddled first by parents and adoring grandparents and then by a court of three older brothers, who playfully tormented and teased her, but protected her like knights in armor and put her firmly in place on her pedestal.

Initially, all that Emily Kendall could concern herself with was the inconvenience of her father's infirmary. She had just spent an extended period of time in the Chicago area, occupying herself with the gracious hospitality of her circle of friends, as well as the Woodmere family. She knew she was wearing on them all and had actually been thinking of returning home soon, but certainly not until after the next weekend with its full schedule of garden parties and with two new dresses waiting in her wardrobe for their debut. But, in truth, if she had known Taylor would have extended his stay abroad, she would have enjoyed the time back at Newport, Rhode Island, with her brothers and her friends, attending the whirlwind of summer parties there that continued, but certainly more limited due to the current economic conditions.

Actually, it hadn't been her idea to stay with the Woodmeres for more than a few weeks that summer, and certainly not to remain there once Taylor left for Europe. But her mother had insisted.

"Emily, you just stay in Kenilworth and establish yourself as his intended," she had instructed her. If this conversation had been in person, not on the phone, her mother would have witnessed the familiar pouty sulk of her twenty-one-year-old daughter.

"Mother, there are so many other girls I know who are my age and not yet brides."

"Then believe me, my dear," her mother continued, "they have mothers just like me scouting out prospects. Or maybe they have no concerns for their futures. But honestly, as my only daughter, I want to know you will be set and secure. Lord knows I will worry how the boys will establish themselves, but I have less control over that."

Her mother's last statement caused Emily to pause and quizzically wrinkle her forehead. What did those words mean? Her father had said he would always take care of her—and her brothers—all of them. Why was her mother speaking so strangely now, she wondered, but she set aside those thoughts to challenge her mother's instructions to remain. "I know you are already equating me with your spinster sister, Aunt Ella, but I think your concerns are unfounded," Emily said, as she reminded her mother that before Taylor, even when she first started seeing Taylor, she always had a following of boys interested in her at school and at Newport.

"Well, the same was true with Aunt Ella," her mother continued. "You know that, Emily—pretty as you are today, when Ella was young she was a dazzling figure in the new fashion of dresses that were so slim and figure flattering after decades of puffy ornamentation. My God, when we were younger, I was so jealous of her—she could have had her pick of any of the boys. I would keep my boyfriends from coming home when she was around, as she would intoxicate them just by walking into the room. Well—you see what happened to her—she let her moment pass and then her debutante years—and then the next years. And here she is alone without a man because she let her prime slip away."

"Mother, you are truly exhausting," Emily returned, picturing her smart, exotic aunt, usually dressed replete with a stylish hat and black netting covering one eye. She was always a commanding presence with her skirt suits and textured hose—and thick high heels that accentuated the curves of her calves. "Aunt Ella is not alone and you know it. Aunt Ella—well—she has a girlfriend. You know it, although you won't say it; she is in a lesbian relationship."

"Now, I have told you not to speak like that ever, and especially not to me. You know how those kinds of rumors get started at girls' boarding schools. They are vicious and unfounded lies. My sister shares an apartment in Manhattan with another female associate at her design firm and you need not read more into it. And if she had acted sooner on her many choices, she would not have found herself the subject of such malicious and unreasonable gossip that, frankly, I find at this time too unnerving to continue to discuss."

"Oh, Mother—you don't become a lesbian because you kept turning down men—you turn down men because you want women."

"Emily—I am hanging up now. You just stay in Chicago and wait for Taylor to return."

And with that, Emily heard only the final slam of the phone on the receiver.

But now that conversation was weeks in the past and Emily had been called back to Rhode Island before Taylor finished the final leg of his trip home by land from New York to Chicago. It was as if she was a young child again and could not or refused to comprehend the severity of the situation with her father. But perhaps this worked well for her, as she had a long, solitary trip back to Newport and would travel best if she were not in a distraught state.

The news at home was not good, and so Charles, their chauffeur, chose to drive in silence from the Boston train station to the compound at Newport. This was not something that Emily had registered as unusual, as she always found him remotely proper (and he found her to be a snobbish brat). He had actually begun a conversation inquiring as to her health, but, as usual, she returned no such salutation, and so he let the silence fill the air.

Taylor

Newport

October 1937

It was only a few months after Taylor returned back to Chicago from Europe and his stop in New York that he received the desperate call from Emily and knew he was expected to be with her in Newport. In those months, Taylor had tried not to act distracted at home or at work, but had thought of nothing but being reunited with Sarah. They wrote letters with a far greater efficiency than either postal system could manage, and Taylor surprised himself with a talent for composing love sonnets. Although he had given his parents detailed accounts of his experiences abroad, they were mainly limited to business interactions. He struggled with admitting his feelings toward Sarah until he could resolve the situation with Emily. But with this call, he knew he could no longer simply maintain a phone relationship with her on the pretense that he was giving her time alone to be with her family.

"Taylor, I thought you'd never come." Emily glided toward him, smiling and holding out her arms, as he stood at the opened front door of her home. Watching her advance, he felt a turning pitch in his stomach. What was he doing here? He shouldn't be here. But now that he was, he knew he should be meeting her approach halfway. He was willing his feet to move forward, willing his hands to reach for hers. But his brain was no longer controlling his actions—his heart was. And his heart was still with Sarah Berger of Berlin.

Luckily when Emily fell into his arms, she buried her head into his broad chest and did not search out his eyes.

"Don't even look at me. I'm a pitiful mess," she said. "Please, say you won't go away. Please say you won't leave me. Papa is gone. I am alone."

"You'll be OK. You'll be OK," he said, gently smoothing the fullness of her hair—but he made her no promises—though at this point that did not register with her. He had come to her immediately upon news of the death of her father, as it would be his perceived duty to be with her during the mourning period. But as much as he would have liked to have told her the truth right away and lift the burden from his shoulders, it was not about him feeling comfortable; it was about comforting her. It would be cruel to be totally forthcoming about his new relationship right now.

"Emily, you know I am so sorry about your losing your father—I've said it on the phone—but I am glad I can say it to you now face to face. I know that is something we both valued—closeness with our fathers."

When Emily finally withdrew from Taylor's arms, she still kept her head directed away from him, for it was memories of her father that were her focus now.

"You know, Taylor," she began, barely audible through short breaths and sniffles. She was leading him to sit with her on the front veranda. "It doesn't seem that long ago that I was at my Presentation Ball. We did the Father-Daughter dance—and even then I was remembering backward in time—dancing on his patent leather formal shoes at my older cousin's wedding when I was about eight years old. Always looking up at him—always envying my mother for her handsome husband. Wishing someday I would be as fortunate. Do you know what my dad said to me at the debutante dance? In the middle of our dance, he told me I was even more beautiful than my mother. For so many years I kept that a secret—I didn't want to hurt Mother's feelings. But I knew how immature I could be and that one day when she was controlling me and I wanted to wound her that I would toss it in her face.

"And you know what—I did. We were fighting over some silly thing—probably a dress I wanted to buy—and I was frustrated by her—criticizing the fit—and so I let go of the trump card I had been holding. 'You're jealous,' I said, 'because father said I was more beautiful than you.'"

Emily paused now, finally looking up at Taylor. "And you know what she said?"

"Was she hurt?" he asked.

"Oh, no. She had her answer as quick as a split. 'Poor dear, don't you know that all fathers say that to their daughters. Silly girl—so vain.'"

Despite his determination to withhold overt affection from her, so as not to mislead her, he felt the great compassion for her that connects all human beings and he had no heart to withhold a hug. He put his arm around her, lay his cheek on hers, and smoothed back her hair. This was not about them—their relationship. This was about consoling someone at the time of a devastating loss.

Again, Emily was sobbing softly. "As she said it, my eyes grew wide and my chest heaved, and then, just like she had hoped, my whole body deflated like a balloon that had a slow leak." This Emily explained without looking up, and then she raised her head once more. "And now I am abandoned by the parent from whom there was nothing but unconditional love and left to 'parent' the remaining immature one."

"No," Taylor insisted, "I know your mother adores you—I have seen that—she was always negotiating what was best for you."

"Best for her," Emily shot back. "And one more thing—and this is what my father said next as I curtsied and he bowed at the end of the debutante dance—'One day I will dance with you at the Father-Daughter dance at your wedding' . . . But it won't be so—he will never see us wed—and one of my brothers will be recruited to take his place—oh, nothing is as it should be. I feel like Alice in the book—*Alice's Adventures in Wonderland*—where nothing is normal and you have to adjust to a new reality."

His head jolted immediately and he snapped at her in response. "What did you say?"

She did not understand his sudden hostility and so she repeated cautiously, "I just meant it's like I'm Alice shrinking in the rabbit's house—or maybe boys aren't familiar with that story."

He became hardened to her again. "You are not like her. You are not like Alice." And there was a coldness in his eyes that she had been hearing in his voice these last weeks.

"OK," she said. "I don't know what I said that disturbed you. I'm sorry." And she ran back into the house, reiterating in a soft cry under her breath, "Everything is wrong."

He silently berated himself. Certainly, her comment was innocent and did not deserve his strong retort. But he knew for sure that he now needed distance between them. At this point he was envisioning no such future with Emily—no wedding—no brothers walking her down the aisle. He had eyes only for Sarah, and in his dreams it was always Sarah walking toward him in a white dress, and it was her father, Emanuel Berger, to whom he returned a slight bow as he "gave away" his daughter in marriage.

Finally, the next day, he decided to tell Emily about the Berger family of Berlin and his fears for them, explaining that he was especially concerned for their daughter, Sarah.

"Oh, how sad, a young child," Emily responded, seeming empathetic and forgetting for one moment her own cares. "How old is the girl?"

"Well, I believe she is seventeen or eighteen," Taylor said cautiously.

And then Emily changed her body language to a more posturing pose and a wary look came to her eyes, as she leaned back and looked directly at his face. "Is there more that you are not telling me? Is this why you stayed longer in Europe? Is this behind your new coldness?"

Again, Taylor was too harsh. "Emily, there is a big world out there, not just your little existence. This is about terror and the plight of persecuted people."

Again, Emily cried. At this point, Taylor recognized that his presence was not serving the needs of either of them, and at the end of the mourning period, he packed his bags to return home to Chicago. But he still did not have the courage to be totally honest with Emily, and he hated himself for that.

Taylor

Kenilworth, 1938

Almost weekly, letters were exchanged between Sarah and Taylor, although sometimes what seemed like an interminable amount of time would pass and then three letters might be delivered in a bunch as a welcome surprise. They were careful to exclude specifics of any future plans, cautious that censors or spies might be editing their words and reporting to superiors. So they were only able to write freely of feelings, emotions, and dreams, as if they were simply forlorn lovers like Romeo and Juliet, separated by warring families, not national ideologies.

And then suddenly there was no communication. In the first weeks of desperation, he would make lists, resources he could use to track her down. Embassies, the Red Cross, the HIAS Jewish Agency he had learned about through his research. He would search newspapers, place cables to contacts in Switzerland and all over Europe. It was as if she had simply vanished into thin air. He was nervous even about his efforts to find her—

could it hurt her in some way? Would he be opening a hornet's nest if she was using her status as part Christian to disappear into the countryside, to masquerade as a pure Aryan?

Sarah Berger

Germany

1938–1939

For the Berger family, luck and time were running out. It seemed almost a distant memory now to eighteen-year-old Sarah—the sweet words, caresses and dreams she had shared with her American love. In the year following Taylor's departure, Sarah's family slowly began making arrangements to leave Germany, as laws against Jewish business owners became stricter. Communications with Taylor were extremely difficult, but he worked from his end to facilitate their transition to America, postponing commitments to Emily, covering his actions as humanitarian efforts. And then the unimaginable happened. Whether from lack of strong motivation on Emanuel's part to leave the business or an inability to arrange their departure from Berlin, the Berger family was caught in the horrific devastation of Kristallnacht.

It had been one more night of chill to add to the
calendar that November, and the chill was not just a
product of the cool temperature and the brisk breeze
of the late fall, but it was the chill that Taylor had per-
ceptively described in midsummer almost a year and a
half before. Sarah called it the shadow, the disruptive,
unsettling feeling that had become part of her very existence. The shadow had eclipsed her immediate world.
Her parents reflected a pall of fear; the young school-
children, no longer interacting in spirited outdoor play,
were becoming increasingly thin and anemic looking,
and were one by one escaping the cloud with their
families.

Sarah and her mother were on a mission that evening. Their elderly neighbor, Hanna Sagan, barely able
to climb the stairs to her second-floor apartment, had
been wracked by the weather with arthritic bouts. And
so, the Bergers scraped the pots and pans of their more
than ample dinner so that they could offer her nourish-
ment along with company.

On the way, they passed Officer Miller who was standing at the corner once again, but he no longer had his
nonchalant pose of boredom and seemed rather to be
pacing to and fro in an agitated manner. They walked
past him quickly, careful not to catch his eye, keeping
their heads down, Inga holding the dinner cache with
a firm hand on the lid, so that none of the pleasing
aromas would invite him nearer. Wilhelm Miller was
more than aware of their obvious shunning, and, surprisingly, it was hurtful to him. When he was a policeman in ordinary times, he always felt he was a favorite

of Sarah and her friends. He was adored; there were smiles all around. But now he understood that he was perceived as a conduit of the SS. Now that his uniform markings were more boldly offensive to the residents of his district, things had changed. Others in his patrol had risen to the occasion and they wore their elevated status proudly, taking pleasure in executing any new orders sent from the headquarters of the Third Reich. But Wilhelm was different. He was wounded by the loss of the melody of Sarah's giggles, by the denial of her mother's captivating greeting and her succulent strudel treats. He wished he could say, *This is not my doing.* He wished he could recapture the elegant Mrs. Berger's favor. But, especially in front of his colleagues, he knew he must appear distant and even offensive, and he would try to present facial expressions to the residents that would mimic the return of an unfavorable gift of spoiled meat. Eventually, he was no longer surprised by their rude demeanor. From the charming young Sarah and the beautiful Mrs. Berger, he knew to expect only piteous looks of betrayal and scorn.

All that may change on this night, though, he was thinking. With the onset of evening, he would try one last act to redeem himself in their eyes, and to cautiously distance himself from his post. He would warn them of what was ahead. He knew where and when his fellow officers were gathering to begin a marauding night of destruction to the Jews—where they lived, where they worked, where they prayed. He saw the directives; there would be intensified roundups for the work camps. Inside the police station only hours before, there was a party atmosphere as orders were dispersed along with so many wooden batons and metal bars. Outwardly, he had joined in the rally, but in his mind he was actually formulating treasonous thoughts. Oh yes, he whistled along with the others who were singing the songs of the motherland; he raised his arms in victory yelps and supportive salutes.

But he knew that he was not quite like the others, and he took a certain pride in his independence, although he feared that eventually it would cost him dearly. He only hoped to protect the simple pleasures of his daily routines. Those pleasures, although they had faded, had far surpassed the burdensome weight of his evenings at home, where he was greeted by the chipmunk pouch face of his wife, a square-shaped woman, almost as wide as she was tall, who had long since redistributed the appealing swell of her breasts to meld with her corpulent midsection. And to add further insult to the injury of his bridal choice, the gravity of years had pulled on the once alluring charm of her smile, settling it firmly into a permanent scowl. Constantly, he berated himself for succumbing to the lure of her father's connections with officials in the police department in asking for her hand . . . not that his choices would ever have been grand. He knew that his impoverished background and the ungraceful presentation of his own physical attributes would never have prompted someone like the elegant Mrs. Berger to have looked his way. No, this woman, a Christian like himself, who would never have considered him for a suitor, had actually chosen a Jew for a husband. And yet, he admitted, he always respected the very affable Herr Berger. Many times, this man, whose work hours were long and whose home hosted a parade of important visitors, would take the time to talk to him, even offering him a specially made insert for his walking boots, when he noticed an uncharacteristic limp in the officer's gait.

And so on that night, although he knew that he alone could do nothing to stop the tidal wave that would strike, he was waiting for Mrs. Berger and her daughter when they came back down the stairs. He planned to stop them with a dissonant "halt," if need be.

"Darling," Inga cried, rushing back into the house, shouting "Emanuel" once—and then a second time with a stronger urgency—that finally brought her husband from the kitchen with his glass of tea. She ran to him and grabbed it from him, the sway of the movement swishing the hot drink so that it scalded her hand, but she waved away his efforts of comfort.

"Oh, darling. Something big, something bad will be happening tonight. It has already started." She had been thinking that that fool policeman Miller had finally proven himself a useful civil servant, and now, even in her state of anxiety, she reconsidered her assessment of him and decided to be more generous with her words. "That policeman—Miller—the one who stalks our corner . . . I'm not sure why . . . but he just did something kind. He warned us just now. He warned us to go home immediately. And to stay inside—away from the windows, he said, and specifically—away from the synagogue. He actually accosted us so that we were scared of what he

might do—and yet he wanted to make sure we understood that there will be terror in our streets tonight."

Emanuel backed away from her and looked straight
into her eyes. He moved his head from side to side,
seemingly as one would before revealing a secret, and
then he nodded to his daughter who had been standing
by the door so that she knew that he wanted to address
her, as well. "A pogrom," Emanuel said. "The curse of
our generations. A pogrom now on these very streets."
And they huddled together for many minutes, sharing the same questions—would something happen on
signal or would a pulsation build from street to street?
They discussed ways to warn more of the neighbors, as
Sarah had immediately rushed back up the stairs and
cautioned Mrs. Sagan to remain quiet in her house,
away from the windows.

And then they wondered how to protect their beautiful Neue Synagogue. It was only five years before, with
the opening of the Jewish museum next door on Ora-
neinburger Strasse, that they had donated kiddush cups
and silver Shabbat candelabras from Emanuel's mother's family. They fretted about all of the precious arti-
facts from their family and others that would be at risk,
but knew they were of no significance compared to the
sacred Torah scrolls that would be in jeopardy. And so
they set their route toward that very destination, donning once again the coats and hats and gloves they had
just removed, hoping to give a timely warning to the
rabbi and the caretakers of what was ahead, spreading
the word from building to building before they settled
back at their own residence.

They did not spend that evening listening to the usual pattern of alternating recordings of Brahms and Tchaikovsky symphonies or playing their own much more meager interpretations on the piano. Instead, they paced the house and peered outside and listened through the slivers of open windows on the second floor, reacting to each shout and crash and scream outside with a cupping of their mouths, a chorus of "Oh my Gods," and anguished visual exchanges.

And then there was a knock on the door, so light at first that only Sarah, with the acute hearing of youth, noticed it, until they all reacted to the growing intensity of the pounds. They had inched down the stairs, but no one moved toward the front room. Instead, they huddled by the kitchen door.

"Emanuel—open up."

It was a familiar voice, but none of the three recognized it immediately until they heard, "It's me. It's Jacob—Jacob Dritz."

At that point they separated quickly, as if vying to be the first to receive the man, and when the door was unlocked and opened, he practically fell into the room and into the net of their arms. There was a steady stream of blood winding down from an open cut on his forehead and snaking past his right eye and his cheek, ending in a shocking pool of red broadening on his white collar. With the slightest nod from Inga, Sarah ran to dampen a cloth at the sink and when she quickly returned, she relinquished it to her mother who held it to Jacob's wound with a steady pressure.

Like Emanuel, Jacob was well known, not just in the Jewish community, but in all of Berlin. He and his brother, Joseph, owned two of the premier department stores in the city, one on Unter den Linden and the other on Koernerstrasse. After the first round of boycotts of Jewish businesses in 1933, Joseph had left the country, his wife inconsolable over fears for their four small children. But the elder Jacob, able to send his married daughters and their husbands on to relatives already in New York, had been holding out through the waves of economic Aryanization.

Although they had wanted him to lay still and recover, at his insistence, the Bergers wrapped him with a blanket and Emanuel cautiously moved him through the seclusion of three adjacent backyards, to be reunited with his wife, Ruth, already in a desperate state.

On November 9, 1938, this "Night of Broken Glass," echoed throughout Berlin and other cities of Nazi Germany. Store windows were smashed and contents were looted and destroyed; synagogues were set afire and decimated, and countless Jews were attacked. And the next morning brought no relief, as many of the remaining Jewish men, often those so prominent that they ignored the first emigration waves, were rounded up.

When they came for Emanuel Berger, he let them take him without any resistance. His bowed countenance revealed a pathetic resignation that came with the understanding that he was foolish for ignoring the warning signs of what was coming. His stubbornness to remain in Berlin to protect his factory, despite pleas from his wife and daughter and his daughter's new young American suitor, had placed his family in great peril. He was so overcome with guilt that his body had no further place to store the emotion of fear. As the front door reverberated from the smashed glass forced entry of the Gestapo, he simply stacked up papers he was working on that would delineate his holdings and passed them surreptitiously to Inga. He asked them as politely as one would ask a valet at a restaurant if he might get his hat and coat. He knew that above all, he did not want to leave his house being dragged like a victim—he wanted to proceed in dignity, to minimize the distress to his beloved women.

As it turned out, initially, he was taken no farther than the local police station, where he was jailed. When Inga had briefly glimpsed him through the window bars on a second floor cell, she had seen desperation and maybe resignation in his eyes, a look that would continue to haunt her. She stood outside his jail for a week, protesting with the other Aryan wives that their husbands should be exempt from the Jewish statutes. On the eighth day, she could see him motion to her from a window. She barely recognized him, his nose askew and face bruised.

He was urging her to leave with side nods of his head. She was beginning to understand. Her protests were having a negative effect. They were disruptive to the jail warden who needed to squelch such activity quickly. He wanted to eliminate any incidents that reflected negatively on his position. He knew the Nazi officers sought and valued order and discipline and so he retaliated on those arrested when he was made to look bad.

When Inga returned a final time to the prison, now under hooded cover, the news was bleaker than ever—Emanuel was gone—transferred, they said. They had moved his group during the night in a truck convoy of prisoners. They would not provide more information—but most likely he would be taken by train to a more remote location, perhaps to one of those rumored camps.

It was months later that Sarah and her mother came upon yet one more inn, as they wearily walked the countryside with one horse and a small cart with their bags.

"My husband has been taken as a soldier. He was not good with money ever, and our food could not sustain us. We are good workers. I have been employed for years at a tavern. That's where he met me. A customer—a good one—I should have known he'd be a bigger drinker as time went along. But I have no regrets. I have my lovely daughter here, partially thanks to him. And here I offer my child as a worker. She'll serve you well as a maid. Knows her linens and toilette routines. But she is bright too, could even be a hostess—picked up on languages at some of the big houses where she's gotten experience."

Sarah was shocked by her mother's verbal litany. She even managed a lower-class accent and demeanor. Sarah had no idea how skilled Mama was in thinking quickly on her feet.

She knew that she and her mother would not have to be like other friends and neighbors who had fled the city—where persecution of the Jews was becoming epidemic. The two of them would not have to hide in attics or barns. They could pass as pure Christians fleeing poverty and abandonment, thinking the countryside would offer more shelter and resources would be more plentiful—they would claim that they could not take the physical hunger of the city. At an inn they could clean, cook, and serve, whatever was asked of them, for a simple roof over their heads, a soft bed, and a couple of meals a day. Sarah's mother, who had tried for more children—now understood God's plan that her only child would be a blond, bobbed nosed double of herself at that age and not a boy—who could be betrayed by the mohel's cut of his circumcision.

There were country homes they could have rented— lived more in a style they were accustomed to—but there were rumors of neighbors turning in Jews—even half Jews. No—Inga wanted her daughter to be totally safe, and she knew the best chance was to have her reunited with Taylor in America. And she had a plan to make their way to Hamburg, where ships were leaving for overseas.

Though it would have seemed most logical that they try to lodge with Inga's family outside of Berlin, she knew that even there she would never really feel Sarah was safe from "friends" who might knowingly or unknowingly expose her. Instead, they left quietly and in the night from their Berlin residence, with only a few suitcases of precious items and, of course, Sarah's cherished painting. They stored their possessions in the neglected carriage house of a summer cottage they often rented, they negotiated for a horse and cart, and then they continued further into the countryside, where they would not be recognized. Inga would return biweekly to that location, where she would be met with communications from trusted agents of her family who were working clandestinely to secure papers and passage for the trip to America. They both imagined that letters from Taylor remained unopened at their Berlin address.

After two or three unsuccessful attempts to find employment, when they had been circling the countryside for more than two days, they happened upon a fairly large inn with a neighborhood tavern attached and this was where she had been telling her tale.

One previous innkeeper had immediately shown an interest in hiring the pair, but Sarah's mother was wise to his motives.

"In fact," he had said, "I have two lovely rooms available—too little for guests, but each of you could have one. Let me show you to yours first," he had said to Inga, "and then I will take Young Liesel." They had changed Sarah's name so that it would have no Semitic resonance and, ironically, as if to validate her insight, within the next year, among the many laws against the Jews that would be passed, was the edict that each Jewish woman was to take a new middle name—Sarah.

"I'm thinking perhaps that your husband in his drinking also beat you," the man continued. "You are a sexual thing; perhaps he accused you of straying—perhaps you did."

Many retorts ran through Inga's mind at this point, but her aim was to remain as inconspicuous as possible.

She had assessed their situation and was not being conceited, only realistic. They were two beautiful, desirable women alone in the German countryside—they may have more immediate fears than the Nazi campaign.

And so, understanding the motives of this particular proprietor whose strategy was, obviously, to divide and conquer, she made excuses for them to move on. Inga wondered if her daughter had noticed that among the valuables she was hiding was a shiny kitchen knife and she would not be afraid to use it for more than cutting vegetables.

And it was finally at just this next inn where they knew they had found safe refuge. Here they were greeted at the door by the large and imposing wife, literally blocking her thin and timid husband, who could barely be noticed wiping down pitchers and glasses behind her. She was almost grandmotherly; she told them immediately that she would be so happy to have such sweet faces in her establishment, as it was populated nightly by an increasingly rowdy crowd.

"I understand your plight," she had told them. "Left the city myself some years ago, 'cause I couldn't take the factory smoke—breathing is much easier out here." But she warned that she couldn't host slouchers; there'd be plenty of work for them in their busy establishment.

"Got one room left—two beds—heat's not great there at night 'cause it's low in the house, kind of a cellar, but I got some fine blankets."

"Thank you, Frau," Inga responded quickly, shaking the woman's hand, as if extreme gratitude for the simplest acts of benevolence and charity had been an ingrained part of her upbringing. This woman would never have pictured that just twelve months ago Inga had been the mistress of a home that employed up to four workers at one time, and this just to maintain the residence of her small family, not as staff for an inn.

That first night Sarah crawled from her own bed in their small room and lay down next to her mother, sharing just the edge of a wonderfully plump and soft pillow. For the first time, she noticed the gray strands that were multiplying in her mother's hair, distinguishing it from her own. She stroked that hair now, wishing she could be giving more comfort to this amazing woman, but knowing that, in her own case, circumstances were actually rendering her less mature, more needy. Soon she turned, and when she cuddled against her mother she was facing away from her. Knees tightly bent and tucked to her chest, encircled by her clasped hands, she had unconsciously maneuvered herself into a fetal position, as if she could retreat into the protection of her mother's womb once more.

"Mama—I think the world is a mystery to me. I don't think I understand anything anymore." Her mother was surprised to hear her speak now, thinking her slow rhythmic breathing had indicated that she was finally asleep.

"My darling, my sweet Sarah," her mother answered with a very slight ironic laugh, "we are not meant to understand it."

"Don't say that, Mama. Say that I will understand it when I am older." Sarah stretched her body abruptly and turned to face her mother. "Say that when you were my age you posed that same question to your mother and she told you that you would understand one day."

"But it isn't true." She put her hand under Sarah's chin and gazed directly into her eyes. "Look at me. I am older now, my hair is graying prematurely, and I do not understand still. The world changes. You can learn the rules, but then the rules change."

There was only a slight silence, and then Sarah spoke again. "Mathematics doesn't change. You always said that to my incessant questioning. You said I would understand more when I was older. Like when I was frustrated after I learned addition and subtraction, and I only wanted to continue on and learn multiplication and division. And I did learn it soon enough. And then you told me to be patient once I discovered there was algebra and then geometry and eventually, like you said, I learned that as well."

"Yes," her mother agreed now, as she stroked the back of Sarah's head and breathed in the familiar scent of her daughter's skin.

"And, Mother—what about love? Do you understand how that works?" Lately, she had been tortured by the memory of what it was like feeling Taylor's arms holding her firmly, then his hands so lightly tracing her skin, skimming just the tops of her breasts, awakening unfamiliar sensations in her, sensations that were new to her, that caused her to have some sort of warm, stirring feeling that she wanted to recapture. Often at night, she wouldn't just think of their conversations and replay them in her head, but she would recreate the feeling of his body pressing against her as they lingered with kisses in the dark front portico.

She was embarrassed to share with her mother the real questions she had wanted to ask. She could never articulate the physical desires prompting this dialogue. In this tumultuous year of changes, she had also made passage from eighteen to nineteen years old. But there had been no opportunity to discuss the natural changes of her burgeoning sexuality. And so again she repeated only the question about love to her mother, because she was not sure what, if anything, she had said aloud and what she had just thought. "I wish I had loved Taylor more when I was with him—I didn't know that he'd be gone so soon—that we would be gone ourselves—that our world would be gone and I would have no chance to really love him. I need to know, Mama, if you understand love."

"For sure not love," she said, though she knew that would frustrate Sarah even more.

"But it can't be true that you understand physics, and yet you do not understand love."

"Darling," her mother said, smirking now because she knew she could finally lighten the moment, "even the brilliant Albert Einstein got divorced."

"Mama," Sarah finally whispered, "will we ever feel safe again?"

"Sleep—my sweet child—we may only feel safe in dreams. Awake—I can promise only one thing—we will survive."

With those words, Sarah retreated to her own bed. But her mother was wrong already. There were no sweet dreams. She was plagued once again with memories of the nightmarish rifle butt entrance of the police in their Berlin home—them rushing into their parlor and attempting to grab her father as he sat working with papers. She was impressed and proud of his handling of the police bullies, his leading them himself out of the house, so you would barely observe him as a prisoner.

Rachel

New York

February 1975

By the time Rusty was five years old, Rachel had been in a two-and-a-half-year relationship with Richard Stone. It was one that was more than just comfortable; it was tender and sweet and loving and passionate.

During her years in New York, she had continued to live with Aunt Ida, and then as a threesome with Rusty, but she remained very close to her parents. It seemed that twice a year they made the trip out East and at least that often she brought Rusty to Chicago. There were many friends and relatives so accepting and eager to see the pair. And there were museums to explore. Rusty was probably no older than three when she made sure he had an outing to her beloved Art Institute of Chicago and then farther south to the Museum of Science and Industry to watch the incubators with the baby chicks hatching and to go down in the coal mine and ride the train. She had a wonderful bank of cherished childhood memories and she wanted them to be a part of Rusty's history as well.

But she wasn't ready to move back yet. Though times were considerably more liberal than in past decades, she still enjoyed the nonjudgmental anonymity of New York. She was a Chicago girl at heart and wanted to return to raise Rusty there, but maybe not until she was "husband in hand," maybe not until she finally accepted Richard's proposal.

The first time he came to her on bended knee she was not really surprised. He was too predictable. It was their dating anniversary and they were at Tavern on the Green Restaurant, where there were probably at least five or six engagements on an average weekend. But she had not exactly said yes yet. It was, by no means, the Sharon Lee Stein fiasco, although Rachel did joke with him about the ring.

"Don't even try to give me that old, rejected one," she had said when she laughed off his first proposal.

"Rachel," Richard began, trying to make light of her noncommittal answer, "the sale of that ring financed a portion of my MBA at NYU, so you can just thank Sharon Lee Stein that my debt level is low."

This time he did not hold forth for her an exquisite marquis cut diamond. For her, he was smart now. He came only with words. When she would say "yes," they would go to Uncle Chal at the diamond exchange and together they would choose a stone she would want to wear forever.

"Richard, you have been more than patient," she had finally said to him some months later. "And I am going to ask you to indulge me just a little longer. I need to go to Chicago one more time and I need to call on Court Woodmere. I have his address in Kenilworth or at least his parents' address, so maybe they can lead me to him. I just want to talk to him once. It has been over five years since I had that last awful encounter, and once I talk to him I will be ready to begin a life together with you."

Richard, of course, heard nothing past the words "call on Court Woodmere," and that was why Rachel had not told her neurotic boyfriend what her plans were months ago when she made them. She waited until two days before her planned trip home and to Kenilworth, in an effort to reduce to days what she knew might be a difficult time for Richard.

She had actually booked this weekend around her demanding work schedule at *Young Miss Magazine*. After graduating the year before, with highest honors and distinction, she had immediately secured a sought-after junior editing position there. But she was often tied to the hectic schedule of fashion openings in the city and feature layout shoots elsewhere, ever appreciative for her wonderful babysitter, Aunt Ida. Finally, Rachel had found a weekend to schedule herself out of any work commitments and to return to the Midwest with Rusty.

Rachel

Kenilworth

February 1975

On Saturday afternoon, as she left from her parents' home in Rogers Park on the North Side of Chicago and wound her way along the beautiful, peaceful, elegant route of Sheridan Road to Court Woodmere's home, she was silently reviewing her motivation.

She didn't want anything from him. But she wanted to be fair to him. Maybe he had grown up, matured. Maybe he suffered emotional ramifications for what he thought he had made her do. She convinced herself that she was coming this day for his benefit. Rachel knew that eventually she would be moving back to the area. She did not want to run into Court on the street one day, while she held her precious boy's hand, and when he saw them, he would be tormented, or worse, maddened, that he was excluded, that he never really knew. And so today, for the first time in a long time, she followed Sheridan beyond Chicago's limits, leaving behind the mixture of apartment buildings, storefronts, and small diners that lined its route, and entering the realm of the upscale suburban residences. In the spring and summer months, the extensive foliage of the mature landscaping fronting the houses on either side of Sheridan and bordering the intermittent parks of the lakefront to the east would actually camouflage the resplendent character of the area. But now, through thin, bare branches, she was astonished at the size of the homes and could barely keep the car aligned to the curves of the winding road, as she searched for the address of his parents' house, in a town where addresses were not even needed for those in the know.

She had no preparation, however, for the grandeur that would meet her. Over five years ago she had met a boy, a "college hippie" like herself, dressed shabbily in worn jeans and a T-shirt, driving in what, she initially thought, was a friend's new red Mustang. Even when he said it was his, no bells went off. In her world, yes, such a car was the mark of indulgence of middle- or upper-middle-class parents, but it was not reserved for the wealthy only or the upper-wealthy—whatever this house would portend.

Although Rachel had originally planned to park on the street in front of the home in Kenilworth, the wide expanse of the half moon driveway was so elongated that parking anywhere else would have required an extremely long walk just to reach the front door. And since the open position of the entry gates, decorated with the filigree monogram detailing of an iron master, was actually more inviting than intimidating, she decided to follow the curve of the brick pavers with her automobile and actually park inside the property, right in front of the steps leading to the impressive portico. After exiting from the driver's side, she moved around the car and opened the door for Rusty who was easing himself out of his position in the backseat. Closing the door behind him, the two of them just stood there, visibly awestruck, and took in the exterior of the Woodmere residence.

Impressive and imposing, but not at all garish, the white stone edifice presented itself. On either side of the five broad steps leading to the entrance, four marble columns accentuated the grandeur of the structure, gleaming with a polished finish that was enhanced by the beams of the midday sun. And it brought the observer to understand not just the mansion's towering presence with its surprising height, but the tremendous width of its footprint on the lot. For once the eye followed the columns in each direction, right and left, it became apparent that the home had north and south wings that jutted back out toward the driveway, stretching for four more sets of windows on either side, like broad shoulders protecting the more ornate middle section.

Holding Rusty's hand, Rachel continued up the steps, edging closer to her destination, but still moving slowly, in a somewhat nervous, guarded manner. Glass windows on either side of the huge wooden doors allowed them to peer through the whole depth of the home and Rachel now saw that beyond the backyard was a panorama of Lake Michigan. She envisioned that the astute architect when drafting the orientation of the blueprint had maximized the number of rooms that could boast views of the bustling waves of the dark blue water.

Once she self-consciously wiped Rusty's small prints from the beveled glass pane he had been fingering, she began searching for the doorbell. Her son, however, found the huge pair of lion head metal door knockers irresistible and he was jumping up to try to reach them. His childlike enthusiasm helped her to refocus on her mission, and so when she found the appropriately camouflaged heavy plastic rectangle she was seeking, she held Rusty up so he could be the one to ring it.

As the front door was opened and the interior was revealed, it was all she could do to keep herself from releasing an audible "Oh . . . wow," yet the words resonated so clearly in her ears, that it took her a moment to realize that that exact phrase had come instead from her young son by her side. The enormous foyer had such a broad diagonal pattern alternating black and white heavily grained marble squares, and the formally attired butler stood so rigid in his black uniform, that she felt she was stepping on to a giant sized game board and was greeted by a chess piece. And then her eye was drawn upward in the same manner as the outside columns had led her gaze skyward, but this time she followed the lines of an exquisite ebony, iron, and gold winding staircase that led to a second-floor landing and encircled a magnificent multilayered crystal chandelier.

In their brief period of togetherness, except for the words Court had spoken at the end that wounded her, she had no indication of his background. She laughed now. When someone in her world said that three generations were living together in the same home, it usually meant a third-floor walk-up apartment. But now she understood—this is where he grew up—this impressive mansion—these were his roots.

Although she had not really been cognizant of his social standing, she acknowledged to herself that part of his draw had been due to prestige. But it was that he must have been bright to be attending Northwestern University, not a city college like so many of the boys pursuing her in the restaurant. In her family, in her circle, education was what was valued. True, education that would lead to a respected career was always best; mothers spoke with highest pride when sons were doctors, lawyers, or accountants. Northwestern University—that had been her dream. But its private tuition made it unattainable at the time. Maybe graduate school, she had always thought, at the Medill School of Journalism.

What Rachel had not known at the time was that Court had actually been accepted at Northwestern because of his family's donations and not his own accomplishments. Although the two generations of men before him had attended the same Eastern Ivy League school, they wanted to contribute to Northwestern's acceptance as an upper-echelon institute, as they were dedicated to the Chicago area. And what Rachel would never have imagined, clouded by her love and infatuation of the summer of 1968, was that Courtland

Woodmere would never be an NU graduate. She could never have known that after his sophomore year, he would do poorly or do nothing in enough courses that his father, Taylor Woodmere, would be called by a college dean to consider finding an early place for Court in the family business.

Yes, Rachel was a smart girl, but not street smart—more book smart, less worldly.

The Woodmere Estate

Kenilworth

February 1975

Taylor Woodmere had been enjoying the customary Saturday morning time in his library he reserved for interactions with Sylvie, his precocious four-year-old granddaughter. Although he was extremely busy at his company, often traveling for weeks at a time, he knew the importance of bonding with Sylvie, knew he was her strongest father figure. He had been showing Sylvie something on the globe, pointing out to her his latest international destination, when the lyrical doorbell rang. But he did not move to answer it, as those in his position have been conditioned to let others respond to such tasks.

It was then that he had heard the lovely, almost timid, voice of a young woman explaining that she was trying to locate Court Woodmere. And Taylor had actually left his cushioned leather desk chair when he heard surprise in her tone when she continued, "Oh, he is home here—well, that is good—very good. May I see him?"

The houseman, Reed, knowing that Court was, as usual, just milling around on the upper lounge and pleased to send him any interesting visitor, directed her to the second floor, indicating he was to the left of the reception hall. He had only meant to tell her that he would get Court—but she was following his gesture quickly up the stairs, as if, with a moment's hesitation, she might change her mind.

"Now Rusty, you wait here, please," she admonished the little boy who accompanied her to the home and who remained in the foyer as she made her way. And she nodded to the butler so that he might watch that the child stayed put.

It was actually Sylvie, emerging from her grand-father's library shyly at first, who spotted the little boy and then with a burst of energy darted to this stranger. "Hi, I'm Sylvie," she said, grabbing his hand.

Taylor's immediate reaction was that it was gratifying to watch Sylvie happy and playing with another child. Her personality, already so engaging with adults, seemed a magnet to the young boy. Taylor had glimpsed him just briefly as the two ran up to the playroom, the boy ignoring his young mother's words to wait at the door. Something had compelled Taylor to watch the jubilant bobbing of their heads on the steps, and he noticed that this little boy had the same dark auburn hair reminiscent of Sylvie's locks, and of Court's.

As the pair ascended, Taylor witnessed the boy stopping at his own favorite painting, pointing to Sylvie and saying something. Apparently the little boy had asked Sylvie if it was her in the painting.

"I don't know. I never looked at it," was her answer. Watching closely over them, his houseman, Reed, responded laughing. "No, young man, that is a significant Impressionist work painted in Europe by a famous artist, Henri Lebasque, generations before little Sylvie. I am not totally sure of its provenance." The young children looked at each other quizzically, not really understanding what Reed had said, and, giggling, continued on their way up the stairs.

The grand scale of this child's playroom was not lost on young Rusty. A native New Yorker, he had spent more than one Saturday afternoon as a wide-eyed, enthusiastic shopper at a dazzling FAO Schwartz store, and so he half expected a ringing cash register to be situated somewhere near the double door entry. He imagined Sylvie oftentimes cuddling herself within the paws and claws and hoofs of the menagerie of giant stuffed animals that greeted him to the right, or literally straddling the backs of the life-sized ponies or the four-foot-tall elephant and companion zebra. He thought she must have a great many siblings of all ages and both sexes to warrant the purchase of this assemblage of toys. Rusty was a bright child with an intense eye for details, and though perhaps he could not properly articulate this concept at his young age, he easily summed up his intuitive assessment by simply asking Sylvie where her brothers were.

"No one else, just me . . ." she said quite easily, as if this was not the first time this question was posed by a visitor to this fantasy domain. "And now you," she continued. "What's your name?"

"Rusty. I'm five, almost six," he said without looking at her, darting a quick path to a train station table that miniaturized an entire Midwest village from the 1950s, full of "miles" of train tracks, every imaginable train car from a pricey HO set, and a collection of bridges and turntables, built-to-scale stores, a post office, school, and hospital. Eagerly, he ran his fingers over the fake green grass, easing himself to the prize of the control mechanisms, but found them to be just out of his reach. And then, once again, Sylvie led him by the hand, but this time to the area where an appropriately preschool-sized kitchen revealed itself. "You sit there," she insisted, directing him to the blue chair at the little table. "Today we are serving tea and cakes and I will be cooking. Do you want sugar and milk in your tea?"

For one moment only he sat as commanded, facing the colorful metal set of a refrigerator and matching stove. But after Sylvie opened the doors of the appliances and he saw the model foods within, the wooden milk and juice cartons, the plastic ketchup and mustard bottles, the lifelike eggs, he immediately raced for a scaled-down shopping cart and was briskly filling it with the inventory and then racing around with it in a most disruptive manner. Instead of being dismayed by his disobedience, as might have been expected by this seemingly prim little girl who at that time was distracted as she donned her Betty Crocker apron, Sylvie reached for a second cart nearby and yelled "race you." Quickly, she caught up to him with a crash by the building block, Lego, and puzzle area, and shouted, "Hide-and-seek, this room only, you count to ten." And it actually took him another two minutes to find her hiding in an enormous wooden playhouse structure near the rear wall of the room. She was sitting camouflaged behind a shelving unit hosting a collection of thirty or so exquisite dolls, representing countries around the globe, and when he found her they both screamed, leaving the highest tones of childhood delight to shake up the solid, formidable bones of the mansion.

Initially, Taylor had been intrigued watching his granddaughter and this little boy, first tracing their climb up the stairs, and then briefly spying on their nursery play, but once on the upper landing, he was drawn instead to the dialogue of the young adults. He heard his son, Court, who had been resting in the game room (resting from what he was used to thinking) and responding to his visitor.

"Yeah," Court said, eyeing Rachel approvingly, yet cautiously. "I—remember you—great summer of fun—I was still in school then—as brief as that was. Name? Place?—It's not coming to me."

She was shocked at his appearance; it was as if he was in a time warp. What in the year 1968 was the accepted mode of dress for a college student, now had deteriorated into the appearance of a disheveled miscreant.

She almost whispered her name, "Rachel."

"Yeah, that's right," he returned with the constantly nodding head of a person with a slow pattern of word retrieval.

In a sense, his disappointing demeanor and attitude actually made it easier for her. If he seemed receptive, she was going to tell him the truth about Rusty, tell him that she knew he would be proud once he met his little boy . . . tell him that she actually bore no grudge because her little boy was a blessing to her.

She had come prepared to tell him that she had not taken his money for an abortion, but used it to travel to New York to stay with her Aunt Ida during her pregnancy. That she knew he had been unprepared for fatherhood at the time and she grew to understand that his harsh words were just immaturity speaking. That how could she have hated him if she nicknamed her son "Rusty," as a term of endearment, reminding her of the rusty-colored hair of him, her first love?

She had planned to make sure he understood that she wanted nothing from him. Her life had taken an unexpected turn—but as it turned out—not an unwelcomed one. She just felt she owed it to herself and to Rusty to call on Court and have some sort of closure with the past before she ventured any further into the future, before she accepted Richard Stone's proposal.

But now, seeing Court again, she felt sickened. He did not know that she had his baby—and now he never would. She simply shook her head while looking at him, her mouth forming the involuntary downturn of a frown acknowledging his pathetic deportment, and only his words brought her back to reality.

"So what's the story? How come you looked me up?" Court spoke finally and approached her, as she was actually backing up toward the door.

"Well, to be honest . . . no reason, a mistake. Sorry, I have to go." She had made a split-second decision, but immediately felt it an empowering and easy choice. And then as quickly as she entered the room, she exited. She looked down the stairs and did not see her young son in the foyer, but before she could become frantic, she heard his voice in the playroom on the same level.

"Rusty—we're leaving—now," she said. And as her son peeked out from the room, she grasped his hand firmly, and quickly, but carefully, retraced her steps down the stairs and out the door.

Taylor Woodmere and his houseman Reed were as intrigued by these events as was Court, who actually emerged from his lounge and looked over the railing after she had disappeared. "Hey, did she really leave already?" he called down to Reed.

But his father answered him, "Yes, they went. (Court never picked up on the 'they'). Who was she?"

"Oh just some girl I knew some summers ago. Rachel, I think it was Rachel Gold. She was pretty, but, well . . . never mind, it ended badly."

The story of his life, thought Taylor about his son. And then it was as if a light went on in his head. The conversation he had overheard the summer before

Court left school and eventually married the pregnant Lilly. Way before Sylvie, before the accident. Taylor had once again overheard Court—but this time he was asking his mother Emily for money—"a problem with a girl—Jewish." That was all he heard. And now this little boy in his home. It was not hard to figure out this scenario. Taylor would make it his business to understand what had happened.

Occasionally in the past, Taylor had used the services of a private detective agency. Business investigative needs, especially when dealing with large government contracts, usually entailed guarding against industrial espionage. They most often involved installing security devices, which was much less dramatic than catching masterminds. And more and more he was finding the need to facilitate background checks on employees, as there had been a disturbing surge in false representations of educational records and work experience due to the competitiveness of the marketplace.

In the movies, there would always be the weathered-looking, gray-suited, gun-toting detective nosing around for the task. And his experiences had borne out the stereotype, although if there was gun toting, it was well hidden.

So now, as he overheard this unsettling interaction between Court and the young woman, as he saw her almost run from the house with this precious auburn-haired boy who reminded him of a young Court, he was thinking to call upon the services of Metropolitan Security once again.

It was more than a desire to protect his family or to skirt trouble. It was, surprisingly, that when he saw the little boy, he had that renewed feeling of optimism and joy for the future that he held when Court was small and innocent like him.

Three weeks later, retired police lieutenant Phil Roberts, now with Metropolitan Security, reported his finding.

Rachel Gold, originally from Chicago, left the University of Illinois after her first year. She moved to New York City where she lives with Ida Lieber, a relative or family friend, a Jewish immigrant following World War II. Rachel, a single woman, had a child, a boy, in 1969. She completed her education at NYU, funded partially by scholarship, and she graduated with honors. She works at *Young Miss Magazine*. She appears to be in a serious relationship with a man, Richard Stone, also Jewish and an MBA graduate from NYU, now with the Goldman Brown Trust firm. There is no confirmation of an engagement at this point.

Rachel

New York, 1975

Sunday evening Rachel returned to New York with Jason, consciously deciding that she would no longer enable his nickname "Rusty" to surface. She was actually as eager to see Richard as he was to meet with her. But with a late arrival and a potentially sleeping boy to contend with, she knew it was only prudent to postpone the reunion until dinner the next day.

She phoned Richard from Chicago's O'Hare Airport before her plane took off—and his heart raced and stomach tossed with anxiety when he heard her voice.

"No, don't meet me at the gate," she said, "I can't really talk in the car. Tomorrow evening. Alone, without Jason."

Everything he feared was materializing. He was thinking that no one needs to sit down for good news. And he was further confused by her use of the name Jason, instead of Rusty.

"I know what I want to do for the rest of my life," she was saying, "and I found it from visiting the Woodmere home. But I will tell you everything tomorrow."

Now he was sure he could not continue breathing. He was not sure that he wished to live until tomorrow.

When he met her at Mario's Little Italy, one of their favorite intimate eateries, not pricey, but with a chic candlelit look, he seemed as white as the tablecloth, like he hadn't slept and barely shaved.

"Richard, what is wrong with you? You're scaring me."

He looked at her eyes across the table and gently took her hands, fearful that she might pull away. "It's because you're scaring me. I couldn't sleep. Just say quickly what you have to say. And if my heart stops suddenly after you dump me—please respect my Do Not Resuscitate order."

"Richard, you are so overly dramatic. I only wanted to tell you that I know what I want to do with the rest of my life."

"Oh, just that, you're right—no big deal—doesn't affect me."

"Richard, please," she said, becoming exasperated by him. "Not my love life—my professional life—well, in a way, my love life. I am going to combine my two **professional** loves—writing and interior design—and try to write for interior design magazines. I want to gain access to the most beautiful homes of the world. And I want to share their grandeur and excitement with middle-class America."

"I don't understand," answered Richard. "You said you came to a decision after visiting the Woodmeres; I thought you were returning to Court Woodmere, father of your child. Are you telling me you're not? Are you telling me that my last will and testament will not be read by week's end?"

"Richard, my God, I had no idea you were even thinking something like that. I told you I went to see Court to decide if I would tell him about Jason. This didn't have to do with you and me—I love you—you nut.

"It's just that when we do marry, I want to be a real family, and I know you do too. I wanted one chance to see if Court had changed, had matured, had become someone Jason could identify with for a dad and be proud of."

"And what did you find? I bet he went insane when he saw how beautiful you were and you told him the truth."

She took time to consider her response. "Let's just say he seemed insane and he will never know the truth." She began the sentence with a disgusted, annoyed tone and ended with a slight laugh and satisfied smile. And then she sat back in her chair, finally realizing that she was not disappointed, but thoroughly relieved to have that chapter closed. She knew she would no longer look back at Court, and so with her full attention, she looked directly at Richard. "I know now for sure—I can totally move on from that part of my life now. I hope one day you will want to adopt Jason as you have intimated."

"Rachel, I would adopt Rusty . . . ah, Jason, tomorrow, even before you agree to marry me." Richard was no longer sitting across the table from her, but had moved next to her on the booth bench seat to sit side by side and put his arm around her. He was starting to breathe normally and his appetite had returned. And now he was not just concentrating on the wondrous smell of her hair, but on the flavorful aromas of the Italian cuisine.

"I'm starved," he said. "Ready to order?"

"You order for me," she answered, because she knew he would get it just right.

Working at *Young Miss Magazine* had been an extraordinary experience. Any of her contemporaries would have considered it a dream job. But, of course, though the experience was great, the pay was low. And just looking around it was understood that just as with real dreams, eventually you wake up. Everyone in the office, except the small number of senior editors, was around her age. In other words, this type of job had a limited run; it could only be a resume builder for all but a few of the staff. You were not just marketing to the society of youth, but you were working in an environment that valued youth excessively.

Unlike most of her young colleagues at work who were eyeing future positions at *Vogue*, carrying around copies, like bibles, at lunch breaks, she set her sights on *Architecture Today*. She loved immersing herself in the glossy feel of its pages. And the ads were as attractive as the articles. She especially loved the fabric manufacturers' spreads of prints and patterns in complementary shades. She had begun to envision a career shift—thought about being a decorator. She was drawn much more to the form and textures of furniture, than of fashion. It wasn't that she felt fashion was just fluff, but the very essence of the fashion business was counterintuitive to her own values. The point of fashion, what made clothing designers continue to thrive and magazines to sell, was that each season brought new trends and discarded old ones. No—she loved the timelessness of decorating. Certainly, there were trends in the field, but they lasted years, even decades, even centuries.

At the Woodmere home, it was like everything came together for her. Realistically, she knew that she did not have the training or talent to create the vision of elegance and taste she had been briefly introduced to. But she did have the training and talent to describe what she had seen. She would feel so much more fulfilled writing about this exquisite eighteenth-century carpet or that marble fireplace imported from a chateau neighboring the Palace of Versailles. Of course, she was not naïve. She understood there would be a whole new field to learn about, knew that she would need some classes in the history of furniture, would need to spend time roaming antique shops instead of Bloomingdale's or Macy's. But now she would have direction.

Her high school district had many pockets of upscale neighborhoods, and she had grown up exposed to the plastic-covered sofas of the forbidden-from-use living rooms. Wealthy people that she knew were what "old money" would call "nouveau riche," and their homes would have beautiful interiors from local furniture stores or Chicago's Merchandise Mart. But even the most elegant homes that she had been to had what was referred to as "sofa art," pictures that matched the décor, often very lovely and pricey originals, but not on the scale she glimpsed briefly in Kenilworth, not works of art that would weather the time test of fads and generations—museum-quality art.

Stepping inside the foyer only at the Woodmere Estate, she was struck that the decorating was like no house that she had ever visited, except on a tour. She remembered the summer homes, the "cottages" of Newport, Rhode Island, which had amazed her on a family trip years ago. These were the mansions of the Vanderbilts and their crowd during the Gilded Age, built in the late 1800s, when the scions of industry were true multimillionaires, before tax structures. And visiting them, no one would say they needed redecorating, that they were too traditional and old-fashioned.

Within weeks of her self-discovery, Rachel had approached a senior editor at her magazine for a letter of introduction to *Architecture Today*. Elliot Willis had taken an interest in Rachel from her first day on the job, and eventually Rachel understood that she reminded him of a daughter lost to the Hari Krishnas for the past few years. Elliot was always seeking her out, in a fatherly manner, to compliment her work, offer encouragement, and help to see that her editors were giving her prime assignments.

As he also served as a vice president of the publishing firm that held both magazines, he was in a position to authorize her freelancing for *Architecture Today*. And he had actually been conducting business in the staffing office the week following Rachel's return to New

York, when a representative of Taylor Woodmere called to make inquiries regarding the career of Rachel Gold.

This had set into motion what would appear to be just a series of coincidences and incredible good luck for Rachel, the true definition of "luck" being "when preparation meets opportunity." Within weeks, Mrs. Regina Palmer, of the esteemed Chicago family, would call to tell *Architecture Today* that she would open her home for their cameras if they used a local Chicago-born writer, not a New Yorker. Her experience with Eastern writers was that they had appeared condescending to Midwesterners in the final copy. And this call occurred as the features editor of the design magazine had on his desk at that very time the resume of one, Rachel Gold, from Chicago.

Sarah

Germany, 1939

Contrary to her usual demeanor, Sarah had become depressed in her new situation. Her time with Taylor had taken on a dreamlike quality and occasionally she questioned if it had, literally, been a dream. Between their separation, the imprisonment and disappearance of her beloved father, and the many months she and her mother had already spent in the countryside, she had not felt safe and coveted and loved in what seemed like an eternity. While she marveled at her mother's resilience and optimism under their present conditions, Sarah had a harder time. Day by day, she was losing the innocent and youthful glow to her skin—skin that had now taken on an ashen pallor. Her personality, once so vibrant and self-confident, became insecure and subdued.

Though in the past she had never acted spoiled and entitled, she had been privileged, and she had been complacent in that privileged world. A generous and sweet soul, at their Berlin residence she had befriended each housemaid and loved helping with the folded corners in the bedrooms; the cook was forever worried she would chop off a finger or overturn a boiling pot in her insistence to be of assistance.

So she was incredulous at first, and then sad, and then resentful, and finally fearful, when valued employees started turning on the family. It began with missing items of value. Questions to the staff, not even accusations, were turned back on the Berger family. "Yes, it would be like Jews to count every piece of silver. But maybe your counting is not as precise as you imagine." She was horrified when one of her favorites of the domestics, Bella, who always took tremendous pride in the perfection of her ironed linens, told her that she would be leaving, as "the Fuhrer" thought it unnatural that pure Aryans would work for Jews. Even hearing that word "Fuhrer" in her home, with the accompanying idolization present in Bella's delivery, was like a slap to Sarah's face.

And now months later, Sarah, who was the domestic, making beds, cleaning toilets, and preparing food, understood that she had taken her status for granted. She was reevaluating her past relationships with her "friends" on the household staff. How they must have resented her behind her back—and even if they began as being just moderately jealous of her good fortune of birth—the rhetoric of a man such as Hitler would feed that jealousy until it became a diseased growth that would swell and spread. And her home was just a microcosm for the current German homeland. Hitler had made a scapegoat of the Jews, blaming them for the depressed economic situation and the diminished German status in the world following the Great War. And people in droves were nodding their heads in agreement that yes, the Jews were responsible for all ills of their once glorious society, and so they were signing on to this philosophy of hate.

Rachel

New York, 1976

Three months after her return from Chicago, without the fanfare of a romantic dinner at an expensive restaurant, actually while sharing a hot dog at a street stand and wiping mustard from the corners of Richard's mouth, Rachel searched out his eyes and simply said, "I'm ready." Immediately he knew what she meant, interpreted the coyly innocent bow of her head as his invitation to raise her chin for the sweetest kiss of his life.

Unable to contain his burst of delight, he turned back to the street merchant. "Hey, I'm getting married. This is my finest moment. I've been waiting for this forever. What is in those hot dogs anyway?"

The vendor, a barely shaven, burly man, who looked like he had eaten more than his share of inventory, actually humanized with a smile. "Well, congratulations. What a nice story to tell my wife."

Rachel and Richard exchanged glances and burst out laughing. Clutching each other as they thanked him and walked away, they gestured in unison, "Who'd have thought?" Neither was expecting such a sweet reprise from the man.

And then it was the usual pre-wedding whirlwind—calls to parents choked with emotion (he had asked her dad over a year ago for her hand)—the much anticipated visit to Uncle Chal at the Jewelry Mart—engagement dinners, showers, fittings for a sophisticated dress, and, of course, a darling little tux for the proud and beaming Jason. In her professional life, by the time of the ceremony some ten months later, Rachel had two major features, one a cover article, in *Architecture Today*, and was ready to transition from a freelancer to a staff member, resigning from *Young Miss*. Her new position would commence following the honeymoon.

Although Richard offered her a vacation in Mexico, Europe, or even the moon—as it seemed to be the premier destination in the news—Rachel, not surprisingly, knew what she wanted.

"I know it sounds boring to someone like you, a native New Yorker, but in all honesty, and we've never discussed this before, my dream is to stay at the Plaza Hotel. As a little girl, I had a passion for the book *Eloise at the Plaza*. You probably don't even know it. It's about a little girl who lived on the top floor and had full run of the hotel while her wealthy parents traveled."

"You know we could go there anytime," he responded, confused.

"I know. But you see, if I'm going, I don't want just any room. I want to live for a long weekend like Eloise, in a magnificent suite. Honestly, it's not about hesitating to leave Jason for a trip—I want to do that. I've started traveling a little for my assignments—and I would love to see Paris and Rome. I promise you I won't be a home-body. But I just have this silly dream."

"Then the Plaza Hotel it shall be! But you must show me the book, so I can make sure we don't miss any of her adventures."

"Well, she did wind up sliding down the laundry chute quite often, so I will only ask you to use discretion with the choices—but we must experience drinks in the Oak Room and tea in the Palm Court."

Sarah

Hamburg, 1939

Finally, by spring, 1939, as they continued working at the inn with the robust wife and the lean husband, Inga received word that passage had been arranged on the ship, the *MS St. Louis*, which would leave out of Hamburg, Germany, in mid-May, with Cuba as the destination. In truth, Sarah had started thinking that this day would never come. The ship was part of the Hamburg-American Line (Hapag). Multitudes of Jewish people from Germany were desperately seeking safe harbor, especially in the United States. The American Jewish Committee was working feverishly from their end, but governments everywhere, even the government of the United States offered only roadblocks. With the complicated regulations regarding visas and the reduced quotas for immigrants abroad, it was not easy, or inexpensive, to place the wandering refugees. It was felt that reaching Cuba would be a close step to reaching the U.S., and people jumped at the chance.

It was such a ridiculous thing that Sarah worried about as they approached the ship on Saturday, May 13, she admitted to herself later. She was cognizant that her beautiful, elegant mother, who had always carried herself like royalty in Berlin, now looked drawn and disheveled. No longer did she shine above the throng. She blended inconspicuously into the crowds of people from all classes of life, men and women, all in suits and hats, all waiting to embark. A carpenter or painter or butcher, who worked only with his hands, could not be separated from an upper-class professional when he presented in his Saturday *Shabbas* suit and proper hat. But differences the long voyage ahead would unveil would be that one class came dressed each evening with the same one or two outfits, which would be threadbare on the closest examination, while another class, especially those lucky enough to have left directly from their own homes, would have a wealth of fashionable attire and some exquisite pieces of jewelry. Later, Sarah would berate herself for her shallowness, for pitying also the sparseness of her own wardrobe and jewelry collection, as time and circumstances had allowed her to transport so little.

As the passengers congregated in the dock area for the signal to board the luxury ship, they sat on trunks and valises, at first exchanging only the simplest of nods and the briefest of salutations. And they watched as each new passenger approached the liner, just as they had—initially with a look of relief that there might be hope and a future ahead, only to see that facial expression change to one of alarm and trepidation as they recognized the hated Nazi flag flying from the mast.

Each would have his or her own tale of a stressful flight from a treasured home. At this point, none would imagine that Captain Gustav Schroeder of the *St. Louis* would possess an extreme empathy for his charges and be the staunchest advocate for them to reach their goal of safety. Prior to the sailing, he had warned his German staff to treat these Jewish people with dignity and respect, and later he would be working feverishly to deliver them as promised.

But as they waited to board, they knew only that they were entering one more threshold bearing the despised emblem, the swastika. And though they were leery of being pulled by the magnetic draw of the luxury liner, they were tired and they viewed this passage as their best hope.

Throughout the morning, passengers would speak softly in their own family groups and listen intently to nearby conversations. Here or there would be a familiar name, and a representative would run to an adjacent conversation circle and say, "Did I hear you mention Hyman Polk or Lawrence Teitel?—Do you know where they are?—Are they all right?" And more often than not, it was not the same name; it was Hershel Folk or Lawrence Sytell that they had referred to. But sometimes it was the person and there would be cries of anguish or embraces of relief as these stories unfolded.

It was in just such a manner that Inga Berger overheard a gaunt and solitary Maxwell Selig explain how he had been rounded up on the horrific night of November 9, and eventually sent to Sachsenhausen Concentration Camp. One day, to his surprise, the warden came to him and a few others of those who had been large business owners and said they would be released if they promised to leave Germany, without their holdings, within two weeks. Maxwell had literally run back to his home, put his things in order (composing well-documented inventories, in case he should be able to return one day to claim his possessions) and secured passage on the *St. Louis.*

"Excuse me," Inga said. "I have overheard your story and I must ask you something," she addressed Maxwell, her voice quivering. "Is it possible that in Sachsenhausen you came across another group of Jewish men from Berlin—does the name Emanuel Berger have any familiarity to you?"

Maxwell Selig looked at this beautiful, desperate woman and it gave him the greatest pleasure to be able to give her a ray of hope. "Was Emanuel Berger your husband?"

"Yes, yes he was. You are making me think that you spoke to him."

"Yes, my dear, I did. And I can understand now his strong will to live through the blows the Nazis dealt him, as you are as beautiful as he described." He was not flirting with her—he had no strength of desire of that sort left in him at this point. But he knew he was giving her some encouraging news and that was stirring in him the simple human emotion of pleasure that had abandoned him the past months.

"Emanuel was at Sachsenhausen when I left. I am sorry that I cannot assure you that he received the same 'generous' offer that the Nazis handed me, but I can assure you that he was alive in Sachsenhausen just a month ago."

"Thank you, sir. Thank you, thank you," and with the third repetition of gratitude she broke down in such a torrent of tears that Maxwell searched his pockets for a handkerchief, and Sarah, still yards away and almost out of hearing, ran to her overcome mother. As Sarah tried to console her, Maxwell introduced himself and repeated their brief conversation. And then Sarah could not hold back her own sobs and sought the comfort of the man's emaciated frame, wrapping her arms around his waist, leaning her head on the stranger's shoulder.

When Inga regained her composure, she did so with a startling resilience and stoic form. "Sarah," she said, "I have made a decision and you must obey me and you must be strong."

"Yes, Mother, what is it?" Sarah questioned. Over the past months of fear and insecurity, her one source of sanity had been the new reverence she had for her mother's strength and ingenuity. And now she knew her mother was trying to empower her in that same manner.

"My daughter—I must ask you to take the next step out of your childhood and adolescence and overnight become a woman. Forgive my obvious metaphor, but we know it is easier to survive adrift in tumultuous seas when you are holding on to a life raft. I can no longer be your raft, but with your own inner strength, and you are my daughter with that strength, you will always have your own life vest on."

Now Inga moved them to a more private area and sat Sarah on a vacated wooden bench. Inga stood in front of her to continue, so that her daughter had to raise her head to follow her words and expressions, and they both knew that this manipulation of stance had been purposeful. "You know already that you have become Liesel Schultz as we traveled, although on this ship's voyage, reserved for Jewish émigrés, you will be resuming your true identity. I cannot accompany you now. Our news now is that Papa may be alive, may have been allowed to depart the country. At this point I can travel alone as a Christian woman with more flexibility and I must find my husband, now that I envision I have led you to safety."

Sarah was listening and nodding through her muffled sobs.

"Now, you know love. And you know what you would do to be together—think of the letters from Taylor that we received before going into hiding. Think of his desire to work to arrange for your reunion. That is me and I must find Papa now that I have renewed hope from this man who was with him at Sachsenhausen— that he is still alive."

"You mean I will go on this ship alone, don't you?"

At this point, Inga took Sarah's hands and raised her to match her own height. "Yes, I do—I will introduce you to a family that is traveling with young children and see if they might not allow you to mingle with their table, under their protection, in exchange for your skills as an English tutor to their children."

With these words Sarah was suddenly beginning to wonder if this had truly been a plan long in formation and not a spur-of-the-moment decision. She was realizing that her mother had never planned to board the ship with her—that she had no intention of leaving Germany without knowledge of her beloved husband.

And so now Sarah furtively looked into the boarding packet that she possessed and saw that it had always held only one ticket—just for her. And though there were two passports in the packet, each described the same nineteen-year-old girl—but one said the name Sarah Berger—one said Liesel Schultz.

It was inconceivable to Sarah that within a brief period of time her heart could be torn apart by separation from a loved one, not once, not twice, but now a third time, as her mother "abandoned" her at the pier. How long ago was it that she had fallen in love with Taylor, her handsome American, who surprisingly appeared to her one day, and truly captured her heart with one look? Maybe he never truly knew that—maybe he thought he had to win her over with his complimentary words and tender kisses—but they were never necessary. She knew immediately. He was her *beshert*. It was a Jewish term—her soul mate—the one meant for her. Naturally, it was supposed to apply to a Jewish match—but Taylor immediately had said he would never reject her religion—he had that intuitiveness about him—that he knew it would be important to her.

And how about his generosity? "Keep the painting until you return with it to be with me in Chicago." That had been the note he had attached to the carefully wrapped artwork that he had left with her in the summer of 1937. The night before, it had stood against the suitcases for his early morning departure, but when she awoke, it was the surprise that remained.

It was another of their connections—this love of art. In the first weeks after he left, she became obsessed with the beautiful Henri Lebasque oil, *Jeune Fille à la Plage*. She examined every intricate dab of paint from a close view and then again from the far perspective that made the Impressionists' works so noted.

She could barely believe that her suitor, Taylor Woodmere, had possessed the taste and foresight to purchase from this artist, known as an illuminator of art and light, well known among art aficionados, but to the general public not as familiar as Renoir or Monet. Imagine that this artist died within months of the purchase of that original piece.

Sarah thought of Taylor's acquisition as amazingly wonderful and brilliant, but not because she understood the business of art, that paintings escalated in value upon an artist's death. What she was so pleased about was that she possessed one of his works when no more would be created. She was not thinking in monetary terms; it was the vibrant colors of the painting, not the currency, that mesmerized her.

She also could not believe the coincidence that she had come upon another painting by the same artist the following summer at a distinguished Berlin private gallery. This one was entitled, *Fille de l'été*, "Girl in the Summer," and Sarah wondered if the model was not the same little girl of *Jeune Fille à la Plage*. In the true Impressionist style, you could barely visualize the young child facing you, her back to the rolling waves, bending down to collect a seashell to add to the treasures in her small bucket. Only on a close view you saw that her tiny fingers sought to choose the perfect one for her collection, and her lips were slightly separated by her tongue, as an expression of deep contemplation. She was meant to be a surprise to the viewer, as she was off to the side, placed between the last two of a row of seven vacant beach chairs. On the low-slung wooden seating closest to her, a beach towel was draped as if it had just been used for a quick drying, and a wide-brimmed adult-sized hat rested atop it, as if reassuring anyone that the child was not abandoned, but her mother was presumed to be just out of vision. And so the observer can enjoy the beauty of this little brunette with her hair shooting off reddish rays of light from strands shimmering in the sun. She was wearing a swimsuit, appropriate to the turn of the century, a little sailor suit in two colors of blue horizontal stripes, which pantalooned at her legs.

The bottom third of the painting held the beach in perspective against the azure sea and then the light blue horizon. The artist mixed the beige and gray particles that make up the sand of the Mediterranean beach by applying tiny brush strokes reminiscent of the dots of Pointillism. Here and there a green bush took form out of the sand and a triangle of color emerging from the bottom left corner erupted with tall green and brown shoots of wildflowers ranging in colors from deep blue to purple to yellow. Balance in the work was achieved by the yellow gold of the wildflowers in the lower left and the rising sun in the upper right.

But despite the artist's resplendent rendering of nature, it is the innocent face of *la jeune fille* that the viewer is drawn to once it is evident that she is more complicated than a dab of color.

The gallery owner explained that Lebasque had actually been friends with many of the most famous painters of the era who often lounged together interpreting the ponds and lakes and beaches and landscapes of Southern France. Influences of shading techniques similar to those of his friend Georges Seurat were present in this work, as if the artist himself was sitting with an easel next to Lebasque and allowed him to borrow the colors from his own palette. But, however beautiful a painting *Fille de l'été* was, it did not possess the entrancing storytelling quality of *Jeune Fille à la Plage.*

In the weeks following Taylor's departure, Sarah would unwrap and rewrap her painting, challenging herself to discover a new secret of its surface. Finally, her mother had encouraged her to hang it in the hallway above the vestibule table.

"Well, let's just all enjoy it while we arrange our departure. It will calm us, as we wait. Father is still slow in his plans—I know he feels he has a special status because of having a Christian wife. He fears leaving the factory and abandoning what he has built. There are so many concerns, my dear Sarah. We must trust in your father—that he will do what is right for us.

"Let's put it here," her mother continued. And as quickly as she said it, she popped an old family portrait of five scary and subdued-faced ancestors out of its frame and pushed in the Lebasque until all the corners fit snugly into place. Again, *beshert*. This new uplifting painting and that old frame—a perfect fit—meant for each other. And so the painting held a prominent spot in the front entrance of the Berger home in Berlin. And now Sarah not only studied the intricacies of the painting, but also the craftsmanship and artwork of the handcrafted mahogany and gold leaf frame that previously she had ignored, but now she embraced so lovingly.

The painting would hang in that position until November 11, 1938—a few days after Kristallnacht—when any valuables became fair game to be smashed, destroyed, or looted. Sarah packed it up—without the frame now—one last time, and when she would eventually board the ship that she thought would bring her to freedom and to Taylor, she marked it prominently with his address and had it placed in the cargo hold. She actually wrapped two small bedroom quilts she had carted from her home around the piece to protect it from careless handling and even the elements of moisture or mold that undoubtedly would accompany it in the bowels of the ship.

Releasing this precious cargo to the ship's porters was like replaying her good-bye to Taylor. She caressed it with her hands, and blew it a finger wave kiss, as an understanding mate carried it gingerly up the ramp and out of her sight.

After comforting Sarah, her mother left their belongings in a pile and took her hand as she surveyed the surrounding clusters of groups awaiting permission to board the *St. Louis*. As she had anticipated, it was not hard to find a young family that needed an adult helping hand. They were both drawn immediately to a handsomely dressed couple, looking somewhat over-whelmed, as they corralled their three children, the youngest one a newly walking toddler. Just as Inga had been aggressive in addressing Maxwell Selig when she sought information from him, she was determined to talk to these people. Again, Inga acted in such an offi-cious manner that Sarah could hardly believe her plan to remain in Germany was newly formulated.

"Good morning," she said to them in German, as she scooped up and returned to their circle the oldest child, a boy probably six or seven, who was dashing away from his exhausted father and edging too close to the water.

"Thank you so much," the father offered quickly.

"As you can see we are in need of more hands," the mother added, juggling a diaper and bottle while hold-ing the active baby by his suspenders.

Quiet and trying to be helpful was the middle child, a girl around five years old.

"I'm a big help, Mama," she said defensively, with eyes hungry for her mother's attention and praise.

"Yes, my sweet Madeline. You are Mama's big helper."

Inga gave the parents a sympathetic look and a warm smile. "My dears," she directed her words to both adults. "I would like to introduce myself—I am Inga Berger and this is my daughter, Sarah."

At that point Sarah stepped forward and acknowledged the parents and then took a moment to recognize each child in turn with a "pleased to meet you" and a handshake. "I know you are Madeline," she said to the girl, "and I would be pleased if you would tell me your brothers' names."

Madeline warmed to her immediately. "The baby is Berthold, but we call him Berty, and that wild man is Willy."

The parents felt an immediate respite from chasing the youngsters and introduced themselves as Cecile and Alfred Blumberg.

Inga shook their hands and added, "We are Berliners—or were."

"And we are from outside of Dresden—but we presume also to be on our way to be Americans, or at least Cubans," she said with a light, quizzical nuance, signifying no true knowledge of Cuba.

"Well, it will be an adventure—no matter what. And if you would not think me forward, I have a proposition for you. My daughter has her passage booked and I find now that I cannot accompany her. For my own peace of mind, I would like to know that she would have a family to identify with—so she will not feel so lonely.

"As you can see," she continued, nodding her head in Sarah's direction as her daughter had already managed to gather the three youngsters in a semicircle and was passing a ball among them, "Sarah has a gift with children—and she knows English well. She could tutor the little ones, and even both of you, if you are not already fluent in English."

"What a wonderful idea," the mother answered. "And our needs in those areas are great. But, unfortunately, we cannot pay—we used the last of our money to purchase our tickets. Perhaps another family could afford her services."

"Oh, my dear, I am so sorry," Inga responded, embarrassed that she had not been clear. "Oh no—I am not asking for pay for her—just some companionship so I will know she won't be alone—a dinner table at which to sit. No—you misunderstand—for that she will pay you with help and tutoring."

Once more the parents turned from Inga to view Sarah with their children. Already Madeline was on Sarah's lap, as the older girl was retying the bows on their daughter's braids.

"Mrs. Berger, we are privileged to do so little for you in return for so much."

"No, it is not too much for my peace of mind. You see—I have just received reason to hope that I might be reunited with my husband. If there is any chance, however small, I must pursue it. Sarah's final destination will be to meet a young man in Chicago. I need her safely off this continent."

"Yes, we all need that," the father interjected solemnly.

Again, Sarah's mother had made a bright and resourceful move. Giving her the companionship of the Blumberg family gave her five souls to hug as the ship pulled from the harbor and she stood there, tearfully waving and throwing kisses.

Once the sailing was underway, the tugboats having released their lines, the passengers drifted from the rails and moved inside the vessel. And Inga could walk away from the dock knowing that she had done the right thing for all concerned. Her daughter would be on her way to safety and a new life—and she would be free to find her husband—and together, with the will of God—they could work toward reuniting the family someday soon.

The purser was able to relocate Sarah's room adjacent to the Blumbergs and adjust her dining assignment to their table. While Inga may have recognized that Sarah possessed a natural way with children, what she probably did not anticipate was the endearing relationship that she would form with the mother, Cecile Blumberg. As it was, Cecile was only eight years older than Sarah, and they would wind up bonding tightly with each other.

Before dinner the first night, Sarah knocked on the Blumbergs' door to see if she might be of assistance in dressing the children. She would not have disturbed their privacy, but she had just passed Alfred Blumberg with young Willy in the corridor on their way to stroll the deck.

When Cecile slowly opened the door, Sarah could tell she had been crying.

"Oh, Mrs. Blumberg," she began.

"No, we are 'Cecile' and 'Alfred,' please."

"Oh, Cecile. What is wrong? Why are you crying? Here you have been comforting me and I've thought nothing of your own story." As she spoke, she saw a cluster of family photos that Cecile was holding in her free hand.

"I'm trying to be strong—I am the mother—I cannot be weak—but I, too, am a daughter—I am a sister. But my family—they were taken from their home—we don't know where they are—I don't even know if I did the right thing by escaping and maybe leaving them in harm's way."

For the first time in months, Sarah felt the passion of strength that she must have inherited from her mother. Until now, her mother had enabled her to be weak, and now she was ready (and prepared from Inga's example) to be strong. She put her arms around Cecile.

"For now, **we** will be sisters," she simply said, as they clung to each other. Then, after another moment, she added, "Please show me your pictures."

Cecile let the dozen photos splay along the nearby vanity top. "This is me with my sister, Estelle—I'd say we are about twelve and eight. We are visiting our grandparents' summer home and our mother has dressed us in matching outfits." She allowed herself a slight laugh. "I was so mad. You remember that age, almost a teenager. I was mortified to be dressed like an eight-year-old. Look closely, there; her ribbon is askew because I had been pulling her hair in an adolescent tantrum." She looked up at Sarah, grateful for the audience, for the opportunity to open up about her family.

"And here—this was a year ago—see how much Madeline has grown just since then." In this picture, she held her daughter in her arms as Cecile stood between her own sister and her mother. The three women were all young looking; you could hardly put them in age order. "We had to take three poses of this picture before Madeline would face the camera. It was worth it now, I know, this waiting for the right shot."

Later there would be photos taken from this voyage of the *St. Louis*—similarly smiling photos of well-dressed men, women, and children, leaning on railings, relaxing on deck lounges, looking up from dinner tables . . . people who let their troubles of a past distant shore escape them for moments here and there, who allowed themselves to be lulled into the security of their old lives of friends and food and laughter. These pictures spoke a cruel irony in later years when they were used to document that historic voyage—a part of family albums or museum archives memorializing so many lives that were lost in the Holocaust.

Rachel

New York, 1976

It was surprising with all she had on her plate, a demanding position at the fashion magazine, freelancing for the design magazine and preparing for a wedding, that Rachel still had the time and the desire to pursue one more project. Although she loved the warmth and security that Ida's small Greenwich Village two-bedroom apartment had offered her and Jason, she envisioned simple redecorating that would brighten up the interiors and maybe shine more light on its longtime resident.

She wanted to do this as a gift to Ida for her tremendous hospitality. Though Rachel had a limited budget, she had an unlimited creative flair, a natural ability in the field. Ida met Rachel's proposal to make a few changes in the apartment with something between approval and enthusiasm, and insisted on extending an ample monetary contribution.

Rachel's first purchase was a vintage mirror that was calling to her from Sally's Resale, a dusty old storefront she passed daily that had been rediscovered in the past few years by Park Avenue decorators. Sally confided in Rachel that she knew they were snatching up her items, including the costume jewelry, and offering them to clients at hugely marked-up prices, promoting them as "*tres chic*" additions to rooms or wardrobes.

"What do I care? It's win-win for me," Sally confessed. "I just run back to the flea market sellers and restock."

One thing Rachel splurged on, however, was a scrumptious new bedding set for Ida from Bloomingdales.

After less than a month of preparation, while warehousing all of her purchases in the basement storage area of a friend nearby, Rachel was ready to present the make-over to Ida. She persuaded her to spend two nights at a co-worker's apartment, and then with the painting help of a gentlemanly neighbor, she was ready for Ida to return to the surprise of the new look. With moderate expense, Rachel accomplished her vision of making the rooms come alive with colors. She integrated the popular earth tones of the era—painting most of the space a light cream, and then adding a rust accent wall in the dining room and a cocoa-colored one behind the living room couch. She placed an area rug under the coffee table and found a fantastic paisley fabric to recover a chair.

Ida walked into the apartment and glanced around. She walked from room to room without really saying anything. For a moment, she bent her head as if her breath had escaped her and she couldn't take another step. Rachel had a brief thought that maybe she should not have insisted on redecorating, that maybe she had insulted Ida. And then Ida lifted her head and smiled and nodded with gracious approval to Rachel. Ida then took Rachel's hand and led her back to the kitchen table and motioned for her to pour some hot water and find a tea bag. And then she pointed once again for Rachel to sit down.

"My room when I was young was yellow," Ida began slowly. "It was one of the few meaningful choices in life I was allowed to make. I chose yellow because I loved the outdoors, especially the warm months. We lived in a town in Hungary. Our springs and summers were extended and they could be glorious. Fields of wildflowers surrounded our home. For me, though, the warm season always ended too quickly and the bleakness of winter remained too long. So I wanted to bring the summer sunshine inside all year round.

"That is why I became an artist," she continued. This was a surprise to Rachel; she had no idea that Aunt Ida was an artist. There had been no evidence in this apartment of any such inclination.

"I don't know if you are born with that talent or if you can will yourself to develop that creativity out of necessity," Ida continued. "But, for me, I believe it was the latter. It was not like today," and she took Rachel's hand and walked with her quickly back to the hall bathroom. "You see here—how you put up this simple, but beautiful Picasso print—this colorful bouquet of flowers. Well,

I envisioned walls of paintings like this, although I had never seen such work. So bright and beautiful—but you could not go to a store to buy them. Not when you lived in a village. And even in the bigger cities—there was no such thing as inexpensive art available to the masses—of art reproductions for everyday people. That is a modern thing.

"I was a lucky girl in many respects. My brother and I did not share a room, and that was unusual in that time and place. But we were not poor people in the village and we were not a family with six or eight or even ten children, as was common. So my mother indulged me in this one thing after months of begging—to freshen up my drab room.

"Ever since I was very young, in the summer, I would sketch the flowers that were blooming along the roads and in the fields. And now my mother said that for my fourteenth birthday Papa would take me to the city and I could purchase some paints and brushes. This was a shock—Papa was so conservative in everything he did—and our community was very religious, although we were only moderately observant. One more thing—Papa had the son of a learned rabbi in mind for my marriage match—a realistic dream, since Papa was a wealthier man in the village. So it seemed out of character that he would chance having me perceived as a girl of independent thought, who might not be an acceptable bride. But, you must understand, above all he loved making me happy, seeing me smile. I could kiss his cheek for the simplest reason and he would be searching his pockets for candies for me."

Rachel could not help the soft "oh" that escaped her lips. She was trying to respect Ida's body language indicating that she could tell her story best slowly and uninterrupted. But Rachel wanted her to know that she was there for her, that she was devouring each memory laid in front of her, as she had been hungry to understand Ida for so long, hoping to bring support to this woman who had helped her so much.

"By this time, over the past few years and continuing on, my friends would be leaving the town with their families—something between relocating and running away. Most of them wanted to follow relatives to America. When they did go, they would be leaving behind items they could not carry. We would never pilfer from an abandoned property—that was not our way—and, as I said, we were not a needy family. But friends would continually offer us furniture or clothing or fabrics or some cherished item that they could not feasibly transport.

"But, no matter how beautiful an item and how adoringly I cherished it—integrated it into my wardrobe or my room—I would rather have had my friend return to reclaim it."

At this point Ida paused, as if the words of her memories had actually transported her back in time and she was not sitting in a New York apartment, but was truly in the bedroom of her youth in Hungary. For a few moments, she wanted to savor the pleasant images that were surfacing. And then, she took a deep breath and continued. "In particular, I remember wanting to see Raizel once more, with her plump cheeks and full skirts; I wanted to hear her infectious laugh. I wanted her to sit on her floral ottoman that was now my vanity chair. I wanted her to come through the door and say I am so sorry but we didn't go far, so might I retrieve this or that."

Ida took Rachel's hand once again and brought her to sit in her bedroom on the new comforter that Rachel had purchased. Like a child, she bounced a few times on the mattress and patted the pillows.

"My first big project was making a patchwork quilt of all the fabrics that we had inherited from these neighbors. But I chose only the bright colors to make up my bedspread. And then, right on the walls, not on canvasses to hang, I would reproduce the flowers of my sketches and those in my memory. I had a mural of a field. I was terrific in recreating the fern-like green leaves with tiny white blooms and that was what bordered my whole room like an indoor hedge. And then I had the idea to draw a gate opening in that field. Later, in America, when I learned a little more about art just by walking through galleries, I understood my technique was *trompe l'oleil*, a technique for making a flat piece appear three-dimensional to 'fool the eye.'"

"Aunt Ida," Rachel said and then paused for a lengthy time, now being the one to grasp her aunt's hands and search her eyes. "Why don't I know any of this? Why have I never seen any evidence of your artwork? Honestly," and now she was trying to lighten the moment, "I don't even see you doodling on phone pads."

"There is a reason." She spoke now so softly, with her head bowed once again, so that Rachel had to listen intently to her. "Rachel, you see . . . and this is hard for me to speak of . . ."

At this point Rachel could have backed off, insisted she had not meant to upset her, but she felt maybe it was time for Ida to have a cathartic moment—she knew that she could lend an empathetic ear to her story, so she encouraged her to continue.

"This which you call a 'talent'—was a blessing—and a curse. When the Nazis rounded up our small family, after mutilating our Torah and setting fire to our synagogue, and then moving business by business, house by house until they felt they had one more town empty of Jews, they loaded us onto trucks, like cattle, for a short distance to the train station. This was already 1944, and I was seventeen years old. We had heard rumors of this— heard how they orchestrated the pretense of peacefully relocating families with their belongings, but then they confiscated everything and loaded them on trains to detention or extermination camps. But for us there was no pretense. How they handled us—by the time they came for us—again it was later in the war—we were not fools to their motives—we were fools to have remained. With each family you were first driven from your house and then told to go back in and pack one small suitcase. On this count, these people were smart—this way **we** selected items of greatest value **for** them. They didn't have to waste time rummaging through our drawers.

"And these horrid intruders, many of them conscripted to the army from local farms, were often faces familiar to us, as customers at our father's store. Did this give them a heightened sensitivity toward our plight?

No, this gave them an outlet to vent against perceived injustices. We were the scapegoats for all their ills. 'Yes, this Jew overcharged me on my tools or this Jew put his finger on the scale when weighing my purchase,' when the reality was the storekeeper . . . for sure I know my father did . . . often extended credit to these boys' families or added candy here or there when a hungry child stood eyeing the counter.

"On each transport, the truck and then the train, my family remained huddled together, as did the others. As you can imagine, we were exposed to all the indignities of loss of privacy for our physical needs. We did have room to sit, unlike other packed cars where I know people could only stand." And then, as if an aside, she looked up at Rachel, saying, "You must understand that much of what I tell you, I learned after the war."

And then she looked once more into space. "We each found something to focus on to occupy our time. For me, it was my sketching. Papa would use the time to instruct young Jacob on history, mathematics, and astronomy, as if we were on a family vacation in the summer and he wanted him prepared for the new school term the next week. Many of the others listened intently to the words of my father, a truly self-taught man. But another father, a rabbi, berated my own—'Only Torah—only Torah—do not waste energy with words of the secular world.' We knew the answer that would be coming from Papa—'So, Rebbe—where is God now? Tell me—where is our God now?' And the rebbe and his family circle turned their backs on us and shunned us. It was good for me because I could laugh to myself, 'There goes my match.'

"But I ask God still—where was he when we emerged from our railway car at our final destination? A phrase greeted us on the gates, '*Arbeit Macht Frei*,' 'Work Will Set You Free.' Yes, we had arrived at Auschwitz."

The words slammed into Rachel like a brick. Spontaneously, she moved closer to Ida and gently rubbed her back.

"The men and women were separated immediately; somehow we knew that would happen. I had initially retained a certain strength of spirit knowing I would remain with my mother. I had been watching the selection process intently. First, they would look through the valises—remove a few items for the bins—and then throw them on a large wagon and point for the people to follow an established line delineated by gender.

"They smiled at my mother's haul—a few modest pieces of gold jewelry—some in the town had none— some coins and paper money—good—then the photographs of life—that would be trash.

"And now my bag was opened to them. And you know what it was—paintings and sketches—so many that they knew immediately they were not purchased. As I began to say before, during the transport, everyone occupied their time differently—I drew more. Without even being aware of it, I had begun documenting the Holocaust.

"Roughly, they pulled me aside. I thought they would kill me immediately. I screamed—I did not want to be separated from my mother." Again a long pause, "I never saw her again. I never saw any of my family again, unless you count the smoke of the furnaces." By this time, Rachel had grasped Ida's hands so that she could hold and comfort her. But Ida had no tears, as if all those emotions had been spent long before Rachel arrived in New York.

"Allow me to be brief here. I was taken to one of the officers of the camp who the guards knew would appreciate their singling out someone with my ability—they felt they would be rewarded for their find—and I believe they were. For my time in the camp, I would be drawing constantly. But they tore my pictures documenting the horror of the trains. They wanted sketches of the officers in their uniforms and then naked sketches of the women they were using as their whores. Innocent Jewish women, like me. On this, please, I can say no more." And again there was an extended silence that Rachel did not breach.

"Just before the camp was liberated and there was a mad rush to escalate the extermination, my main officer fled, simply allowing me to hide, as if that act would make me thankful to him. So you see—my art—my talent—was a blessing and a curse. Yes, it allowed me to skirt death. But, you know, because now they are starting to write more about those times– it is called 'survivor's guilt.'

"If my talent had been the violin, I might have been one of the pretty girls in skirts playing tunes like 'The Merry Widow' as the prisoners followed the path to the 'delousing area,' which was really the gas chamber. That memory might have even been worse."

And now Rachel was the one to stare blankly and search for her voice following the emotional narrative.

"But, Aunt Ida, maybe you are looking at this wrong—punishing yourself for nurturing a talent—maybe the moral is that we all need a talent—something that will distinguish us and make us valued. Something that will save us . . ."

Ida would hear none of it—while Rachel thought only of the word "survivor," she could focus only on the word "guilt."

Rachel

Chicago, 1976

Only weeks before her wedding, Rachel was kissing her two men good-bye and was returning to a prestigious suburb near her Chicago hometown for her first permanent staff assignment at her new magazine. When she entered the home of Blaise McCormick, she was overwhelmed on two levels. First was that she should have the good fortune not only to tour such a fabulous property, but also to get paid for it. And second was that instead of pandering to the whims and wants of the Twiggy-thin models, she was being pandered to by residents, proud and humbled that *Architecture Today* had chosen their property. "Would you like some coffee or tea? Perhaps should I move this vase? What can I get for you, dear? Are your accommodations satisfactory or would you care to stay in one of the guest bedrooms?" Now **this** was a dream job. A few times at these beginning assignments on Chicago's North Shore, she was baffled by an owner's mention of their friends, the Woodmere family,

as if Rachel should know them, but she smiled noncom-
mittally and offered no reply.

On the grounds of the McCormick property, in the
expanse of back lawn that bluffed gently to the magnificent Lake Michigan, were seven distinct planting
areas, a private botanical garden. Had Mrs. McCormick
herself not been an amateur horticulturist with a vast
knowledge of her grounds, Rachel would have felt thoroughly ill equipped to conduct the interview. But Blaise
McCormick offered a wealth of knowledge about each
annual and perennial and the European gardens on
which her designs were based.

Over the two days of her assignment, Rachel became
increasingly enamored not only with the landscaping,
but with the lyrical narration of the owner, with her captivating and eclectic dress style. And then a further idea
came to Rachel. What if she convinced *Architecture Today*
to expand to a new media and produce a television
special on Great Homes and Great Owners. Ideas were
developing in her mind that she would let remain at
this point on the back burner. Who was she to pretend
that she had enough experience in the field? How naïve
she was to think that she didn't need a great deal more
tutelage in all related fields before she was qualified to
even make the proposal.

It was her work personality, with its wizened nods
and "of courses," and "oh yes, I am familiar with that,"
that helped her to bluff her way through this initial
amazing assignment. And such a loquacious socialite
as Blaise McCormick was most comfortable and would

be most forthcoming when she had no competition for knowledge, just a responsive ear like Rachel's. In the future, though, she would be better prepared, because she knew she should be more the one in control, knew the traps journalists fall into when they are in too much awe of their subjects.

And these were all things that Rachel would come to understand in her new field. The subject could be as much the homeowner as the home—each with a distinct personality, most often in a tandem mold. But most magazines missed the opportunity to feature this. The totally traditional mansion—with no painting dating past 1907, for instance, was most often hosted by a soft-spoken, modestly dressed couple, who needed to be prodded with each description.

In the most contemporary homes—where horizontal lines, multi-levels of glass windows and leather furniture in black and white would present themselves, there would be similarly dressed owners in all-black or all-white linen fabrics, wrinkling at the photo shoots. Black-rimmed clear lenses and blacked-out sunglasses identified the interchangeable residents. Rachel didn't seek out those assignments, though, for she found the homes so minimalist that she was often struck with "writer's block."

It was actually on her honeymoon at the Plaza Hotel that she expanded her professional vision. But first, on that sacred, romantic weekend, she fell even more in love with Richard than she could have believed. In the morning, emerging from the movie setting of the magnificent bed, she walked over and pushed the drapes aside to reveal the horse carriage lines fronting Central Park. Richard awoke almost simultaneously from her stirring and took his place behind her. He put his hand around her waist and once more began to lower the straps of her nightgown so he could gently caress her shoulder and kiss her neck.

"Good morning, Mrs. Stone," he whispered in her ear, as he slightly nibbled it.

"Good morning, husband," she returned. They had never been so truly alone, feeling the luxury of waking up together, knowing that no one was wanting them right now—that the only people needing them that morning were each other. And so with just the slyest of smiles, they returned to the bed and replayed the scenes from the night before.

But later, when Richard had left the room to grab a newspaper and wait for her at the restaurant for breakfast, after she had time to luxuriate in a morning bath in the opulent suite, she called her editor and said simply, "We're doing hotels too."

Her first such assignment was the Drake Hotel in Chicago, boasting the city's premier location as gateway to the Magnificent Mile of Michigan Avenue. It was one more assignment that would prove a magnet to her, pulling her back to her hometown, to the comfort of her roots.

Rachel would introduce the property by pointing out important historical notes. "In the palatial Italian

Renaissance style, the Drake was built in 1920 at a cost of $10,000,000. The vision of the flamboyant architect Ben Marshall, working for the Drake family of hoteliers—he not only designed the impressive exterior, but was extolled for his interior shopping arcade, destination restaurant, the Cape Cod Room, and magnificent ballroom, the Gold Coast Room. Over the years, the guest registry would include such notables as England's Queen Elizabeth and Prince Philip and Winston Churchill, U.S. presidents Herbert Hoover and Dwight Eisenhower, and even Walt Disney."

The management treated Rachel royally, offering her a magnificent corner suite. Out one window and the shopping mecca of Michigan Avenue presented itself. Out another window, and you were overlooking Oak Street Beach on Lake Michigan, as the steady parade of cars on Lake Shore Drive swung into view. There was no conflict of interest in her accepting luxury accommodations like this, as it might have been had she been a journalist writing a review. When you do an assignment spread in a pictorial magazine, it is already assumed that a positive, even exuberant write-up will follow.

She was even allowed a discreet peek at the guest list of the Drake, which revealed, for that weekend alone, among the guests—one rock star with a six-room entourage of band members, stagehands, light and sound coordinators, managers, and possibly some female groupies. The hotel management intimated that a security deposit of several thousand dollars had been required, as past entertainers in that particular field had done everything from stealing towels and lamps to trashing rooms.

Elsewhere in the hotel, a senator from a neighboring state was enjoying the Chicago summer with his family, although rumors were floating that when they went off on their museum explorations, he went off to a room on a lower floor, also charged to his Capitol Hill account.

And seven members of a major national sports figure's family, whose team was in the off-season, were seen frequenting the lobby and lounges of the hotel. The football player, his wife, parents, and children were actually mannerly and quiet people, but all of such an enormous stature that housekeeping had already been in their rooms with three times the normal complement of towels and it had been necessary to repair sagging bed frames and replace a broken toilet seat.

Sarah

The St. Louis, 1939

Finally, her third night on the ship, Sarah did not immediately cave into the physical and emotional exhaustion of the journey and fall quickly to sleep. Now she stayed awake in bed and welcomed the solitude of her own reflections. It had been almost six months since she had to end her communications with Taylor. Inga, in her obsessive desire to protect both her and her daughter, would not even allow trusted contacts to notify Taylor as to their whereabouts. By the time they arrived in Hamburg, it had been almost two years since she had been enveloped in his embrace.

But even now, among this multitude of passengers aboard the *St. Louis*, every masculine silhouette of his approximate height and exhibiting his same general posture and broad shoulders would remind her of Taylor. The simplest imitation of his hand gestures or the echo of his inclusive laugh or the hint of his freshly groomed scent would transport her back into a dream state. She would be with him in Paris or Berlin or Potsdam, holding his hand or wiping croissant crumbs from his lips. Sometimes she thought she heard, not just remembered, the way he spoke, how his American-accented attempts at French or German made her cover her face so that he would not see the pathetic look it reflected. "OK, I have no gift for languages—I don't want to be too perfect," he would shoot back at her in his defense.

What a cruel trick that life was playing on her now. Two years ago, she had been a contented, fairly self-absorbed adolescent, not yet truly aware of the passionate secrets the adult world would unveil to her, certainly not yet fully aware of her own sexuality. When young men had leered and whistled as she passed by, she had never taken it seriously, had accepted it as a tease, almost a joke, not understanding the physical power of her presence. And now how ironic—that one wonderful man had changed her small world's perception of love at the same time that one evil man had heightened the larger world's perception of hate. On so many counts her naiveté and innocence were visibly diminished, but her dreams had not yet vanished; her optimism was reduced, but not depleted.

Now understanding more about love and life, she tried to be strong, to buy into her mother's philosophy that if they survived their ordeal then the future would work itself out. In fact, she was wondering if her unexpected relationship with Taylor had actually been part of some master plan, that all that writing to him had given her a certain proficiency in English that would serve her well now, as if it had been her preparation for her new role on the ship.

When her mother had first presented her as an English tutor for the young family, she wasn't even confident that she had the necessary skills for keeping children's attention. She had always prided herself on being very adult. At school, she made friends easily and tried never to act intellectually snobbish. But she would always much prefer lingering behind in the classroom with the teachers at the lunch hour, continuing the discussion of a book or challenging herself with one more math problem, instead of wasting time gossiping with her classmates or experimenting with makeup.

As an only child, Sarah had never been required to babysit, to even watch young children for five minutes while their mother or nanny was otherwise occupied. She was not in an extended family with younger cousins living nearby and her older cousins were not yet bringing around babies. She could recall now just one young neighbor, Gerta, who was often at her house, always wanting her attention. Sarah was remembering how Gerta immediately noticed the Lebasque painting when it replaced the old one in the foyer of her home.

"I like that painting and that little girl in it. I never liked those frowning people that used to be on your wall," little Gerta had said. Of course, Sarah never told Gerta how the painting had appeared there, and now she felt guilty knowing how she had always ignored her, thinking she was too babyish to comprehend affairs of the heart, and missing the opportunity to nurture the interest in art they both shared.

Before the latest edicts forbidding Jews to attend college and dismissing Jewish instructors, Sarah was contemplating a future teaching at a university, certainly not babysitting at a nursery school. So it was a surprise even to her that on this ship she slipped into this nanny-type role easily and felt comfortable and fulfilled immediately.

Sarah had become a type of Pied Piper for a large group of children on the *St. Louis*—ages about three through ten, who began by tagging along with her and the Blumberg family. She taught them all English with activities such as putting them in lines and counting off and telling ages. On the trip west toward Cuba, she found that she had no trouble keeping them occupied from her memory vault of games she was recalling from her youth. But she would always think of a twist to help transition the children to English—for instance, saying, "Ready or not, here I come," in English now.

But this sailing to freedom aboard the *St. Louis* would not turn out as any of the passengers had envisioned. As the ship broke through the first strong Atlantic waves and the salt water mist sprayed the views of the lower portholes, the majority of travelers had been busy unpacking their suitcases and feeling their anxieties would find a short reprieve aboard the cruise. Captain Schroeder and many of those on an ad hoc passenger committee, however, had been aware almost as soon as the ship left Hamburg that trouble might be brewing for them at their destination. The Cuban authorities were not going to honor the immigration documents of all but a small group of the passengers. It would be a combination of circumstances, ranging from blatant anti-Semitism to a general hostile environment for immigrants, from corrupt Cuban officials peddling false papers and demanding bribes, to the miscalculations of representatives of the Jewish Joint Distribution Committee that would keep the *St. Louis* from finding safe harbor once it finally arrived in Cuban waters.

For days after their arrival, the ship lingered at the port awaiting word that intense negotiations would be successful in allowing them to dock. While they floated under Cuban guard, dozens of small private boats filled with friends and relatives of the arriving refugees surrounded the large ocean liner and audible cries of longing, pleas to reunite with loved ones, filled the air. A desperate Arnold Schuman gazed with a visible hunger at his two brothers signaling to him from their small craft below and it was only the strong arms of nearby passengers that kept him from jumping overboard. And this scenario played itself out again and again at many positions along the rail.

Finally, Captain Schroeder ordered that the ship follow a northerly path along the American coast, hoping for word that a United States disembarkation would be allowed for the *St. Louis*. For this stint, U.S. vessels closely shadowed her every move, and many of the passengers swore at their crews, assuming that they were guarding against any unauthorized attempts to land. Later there would be rumors, however, that Secretary of the Treasury Henry Morgenthau, from a prominent German Jewish family himself, was interested in monitoring the path of the ocean liner to ensure a rapid response should President Franklin Roosevelt acquiesce and grant them U.S. entry. But President Roosevelt could not be persuaded to fight the unsympathetic, isolationist mood of the United States. And so, despite the monumental efforts of the ship's captain and others, eventually the *St. Louis* was commanded to return to an eastern crossing of the Atlantic.

Two or three deep standing along the rail, the entirety of passengers looked longingly at the lights of the American shore blinking to them like the teasing eyes of a flirt. Here, a young teenage boy turned to his mother. "But what will we do? Papa will be waiting. Papa will be heartbroken." Not even understanding the repercussions of their return, he ached for his father's loss. "You and me and Julia—we'll have each other. Papa will still write how lonely he is."

Another boy in his late teens assumed the stance of the mature man he needed to become. He comforted his distraught mother and said pointedly to his innocent, young siblings surrounding her, "Understand now that I will be in charge and please do not cry anymore."

When the ship made its final definitive turn back east toward the European continent, the adults were busy in anguished meetings discussing their plight. At this point, Sarah organized a group of children to draw pictures of their favorite things, houses or flowers or animals or the big ship, pictures they would let fly off the side of the vessel. She explained that maybe when they returned to Cuba or the United States that they would find their artwork washed up on the shore. Of course, it didn't make sense and a few of the older children were voicing their skepticism—"The colors will wash away . . . The papers will sink . . . Fish will eat them . . . Maybe they will be washed on a different beach." But none of them challenged that they would return to freedom, and therefore Sarah knew she had succeeded in alleviating, if even for a brief time, the children's fears, while their parents dealt emotionally with the harsh reality that the ship was leaving still waters and heading into a maelstrom.

In the late afternoons, when the children were napping, Sarah allowed herself time to be alone, time to lose herself in her own reflections, to create a positive scenario with fairy tale happy endings and dramatic reunions with friends and family. This was the one that worked best for her and kept her hopeful and directed:

Finally the St. Louis, as it headed sadly back across the Atlantic to Europe, would be called to turn west one more time and would be welcomed at the Port of New York. Cuba's rejection of the passengers, though frightening and aggravating, actually brought her closer to her chosen destination. When the president of the United States of America, Franklin Roosevelt, finally acknowledged the need and admitted the German refugees, he would be there personally to greet them and hear their stories. He would be so horrified by the accounts of the passengers that he would directly order an assault on Nazi Germany. All those in the jails would be freed, all those interned in the camps would be released, and medical professionals would attend to any needs.

Hitler himself would be captured and hung in full view of the country. This would be a deterrent for any others dream-

ing and plotting to be dictators, scheming to destroy the Jewish people.

At his home outside of Chicago, Taylor, who would have been desperately looking for her, would read about the plight of the St. Louis. Finding her name in newspaper accounts of the passengers, he would be ecstatic with the most glorious emotions of love and relief and would board a train immediately for New York. By the time they had been processed and she was emerging finally from the customs port to the harbor deck, he would be waiting for her with a luscious kiss and a bouquet of flowers. She would motion for a porter to personally hand him the Lebasque painting, Jeune Fille à la Plage, the painting that she had lovingly wrapped in her quilts and securely packaged, and that was bearing the address of the Woodmere residence, as a precaution—in case she was separated from it.

And then to complete the dream, her parents, who had their home, business, and possessions all reinstated, were able to join them in beautiful Kenilworth, Illinois, for a spectacular wedding on the back lawn of the estate he had described overlooking Lake Michigan.

She was not alone on the ship in imagining a future with happy endings. In the evenings, as the Blumbergs put their children to sleep with bedtime stories, Sarah began to wander from one discussion group to another and found that there were many perspectives on their dilemma. There was a palpable division in thought among the passengers and divisions among the divisions. First, were the true optimists, usually those closest to her age—on the brink of adulthood and understanding all of its promise, and though even to be on the ship they had to have had frightening experiences, they still maintained a cushioning naiveté.

Then there were the verbal optimists—those were mainly the young parents, those who had to bolster the spirits of their dependents. But at night, they shared fears with their spouses, fought back tears, and worked to have alternative methods of survival.

That second night on the return voyage she overheard the raucous voices emanating from one lounge and it was to this third group that she was drawn. Here were young men and women, mainly in their twenties and thirties, the single crowd and the young married couples she had watched interacting on the ship. They were the realists, daily becoming hardened to the futility of their plight. Even if the United States would eventually accept them, some of them now knew that they would never truly feel safe. And they no longer wished that they could recreate their old lives in the cities they fled, as some of their elderly relatives hoped, even if that were somehow possible. No, they were now talking about the Resistance Movement and they were talking about Zionism. They began holding small group meetings centered on their desire to protect fellow Jews from the Nazis now, and then to establish a nation for the Jewish people. And daily those meetings were drawing more and more interest from the general disenfranchised population of the ship.

"I think we have all been duped," one voice rose above the others. "We were easily allowed to 'escape' on this Nazi ship as part of Hitler's plan." Some of the others looked at the speaker skeptically, while many of the group immediately began nodding their heads in total agreement. "Think about it. Hitler has now shown to the world that no one believes we are in real jeopardy in our homeland—and he has proven that no one wants the Jews. This is the best scenario he could have imagined and it didn't happen by chance—he orchestrated it. Imagine, even the great United States does not want more Jews."

And he was more than correct. Though at the time he could not have been aware of it, Hitler had actually sent an envoy ahead to stir up Cuban unrest over their own unemployment problems in an effort to ensure they would not want to accept any ship full of refugees vying for their jobs.

So around the ship, while most passengers just wanted to find another way to get back to freedom anywhere in America and they would be brainstorming with those of similar inclination, there were these others who knew there would be no safety until they had established a Jewish homeland in Palestine.

A second speaker took his place at the front of the crowd and extended a handshake and then a strong hug to the first, who willingly relinquished his spot and sat down. This second man was obviously familiar to most of the group and projected an undeniable charisma. His voice was strong and people quieted immediately when he began. "Friends. No, that is not right. 'Friends' I would have addressed you only days ago—had we met at dinner. Had we by chance been seated together in the main dining room or struck up conversations on the lounge chairs enjoying the warmth of the midday sun. Had we played the game of finding connections between our home towns, our places of work, our schools, our synagogues; enjoyed the discussions that have been our heritage through the years; understood that our cousins knew each other, that our rabbis were brothers, that we had attended the same lectures, shared professors without even knowing it."

He stopped and looked up momentarily. Further energized by the multitude of nods, he continued. "But now I will call you 'brothers and sisters,' because 'friends' is now a word too impersonal. 'Comrades,' I might have said to some of you—some of you, yes, some of us who had been drawn to the Socialist principles, who had been trying to come to terms with ideologies and weigh them against theologies, and live in a world where we were deluded into dreaming that we even had a choice of such a freedom of thought. Yes, now, I address you as 'brothers and sisters,' because now we are closer than friends; we are family. And we know, and I will shock some of you with this veracity, we must know that if Hitler has his way, we may be the only family we have.

"Should I say to you, 'Thank you for coming to this room tonight'? I cannot say that, because again, that would be acknowledging a nonexistent freedom of choice, freedom of action. No, my friends, my family, you had no such freedom. Our Lord, Hashem, has directed you here. Do you not see, once again, our Biblical lessons come to life, the testing of our people? This is the price that we pay to be Jews, to have been Chosen, to have received the Covenant. And this group, in particular, this handsome and healthy and strong and hopeful and pathetically naïve gathering of young people is here as part of His design. Hashem creates and destroys at will. On our High Holidays, on Rosh Hashanah and Yom Kippur, we read the words, we recite the prayers. It is His will. 'Who shall live and who shall die . . .' But we take the words of the prayer book, the Bible, the Torah, as allegory, as an antiquated reality or maybe even fantasy. The Plagues, the smiting, the cruel hand of the all powerful Pharaoh, are stories from an age gone by. We have lived in Germany, in an epicenter of advanced thinking and progress and culture. Oh yes, Jews have always had troubles, had to be more careful, even in our modern times. But now we have proven ourselves. We are more than accepted. We are so thoroughly assimilated into the society that it could not function without us. We are recognized as leaders in thought, in business, in medicine, and science. Finally, finally in our modern age, Hashem has watched over his Chosen people.

"Oh, yes, this is what you thought. Why not? We can only believe what we are taught, what our parents taught us. Whose parents here were not good people? Fathers making a living, mothers making a home. And it was their goal to make us feel comfortable and protected, to spoil us even. Yes, of course, a little religion, lighting Shabbas candles, keeping alive the stories of the Passover Hagaddah in the spring when the Goyim had Easter and the tales of the Maccabees in the winter, when they had Christmas. We needed to know we were Jews, to know our heritage. This would ground us and give us our sense that we would have challenges, but that we were special—again, the Chosen people.

"But now the world has come to life from the pages of a biblical history that repeats itself continuously over a five-thousand-year span, a history that we never really took literally. And we think we can make sense from this? That we can deliberate on plans of action, as if there is a plan other than the plan of Hashem. Well, yes. I surprise you now, I suppose. You can tell now, I am sure . . . because my speech is so confusing, perplexing . . . that I am the son of a rabbi. But I have been that rebel son from the Hagaddah. I have been the son searching for answers, asking questions, the wise son and the simple son all in one, because I know that the more I find out about the world, the greater my need for understanding. So I will accept some religion, because, again, you are what your parents have molded you to be. But I will take charge of destiny if I can, and if I need to, to gain your confidence, I will say that we must be here for a reason. By here, I mean literally. Not just here on earth, but here in this room, at this time. How many of you came upon this ship with a certain guilt? Now I ask you—I will be done speaking soon. So I ask you about yourselves. Raise your hands to answer. Who among you has had the Nazi terror reach into your lives? Who has had a close friend or relative dismissed from a job or denied schooling, accosted or beaten, perhaps taken for questioning, or, perhaps even disappear?" There was a stir among the audience, whispers between people, and then the slow, almost mournful raising of hands in a rhythmic wave beginning at the front seats and continuing through the rear.

"And I knew it, although I dreaded it. Not a hand among yours is down. And so you came aboard this ship feeling as I did, I am sure. Grateful and yet bewildered at the puzzle of life. Why is it me? Why should I have this opportunity and yet my brother will not, my father will not, the entire neighbor's family gone in the night, with no explanation, and not by their own design—no, taken. And then when this ship was turned back, yes, with you, my initial reaction was rage—rage with frustration and sadness and fear. And then, within hours, my emotions changed—'acceptance,' you may say, but I say 'relief.' The answer to the question posed—the 'Why was I spared so far, why my new wife—and not the others we knew?' Because . . . and now you must listen to me as you have not yet listened—you must listen to me without hearing the calls of your loved ones interfering with your comprehension. And this is the answer—so that you would be here in this room at this moment with these people to hear this speech—to be moved to your calling—to meet your destiny. We must take our place with the movements that have already started and we must be leaders. Some of you—already young mothers and fathers—I will give you a single goal—I will not demand that you recognize a calling to fight—I will insist that you accept the Zionist vision and proceed with the greatest speed to reclaim the land of our forefathers. There you will go and you will work to build our own society—and you will keep your children safe and you will have more children to populate the land. If Hitler has plans against the Jews, who knows how many thousands may pay for his insanity before he is stopped. But you cannot stop him, for you have precious cargo and I beseech you, the young parents, to consider not finding passage on another ship, not going on to America, but going on in the opposite direction—go to your new home due east. And wait for us . . . prepare the land for us. Because this remaining group I will shape into freedom fighters first, and then Zionists."

Three or four times during his monologue, the speaker paused to acknowledge the young woman by his side. Although his words were visibly energizing the audience, a selected assembly having interrupted now and then with the affirmations of "Yes, yes . . . say the words," reminiscent of an Evangelical rally, his waifish wife remained only silent and somber faced. Often, when he did not need to use them to gesture, his hands would be stroking the back of her head or clasping the tips of her fingers, as if his own musculature could give her strength.

When he finished speaking, the audience rose with a swell of applause and gathered around him and his wife. During a ten-minute period in which the speaker was both praised enthusiastically and respectfully challenged by an equally intellectual crowd of his peers, his wife was comforted and coddled by many of the women in attendance, and brought a cup of tea by an especially empathetic friend. Then someone waved a short stack of papers above the huddle and encouraged them all to move to a large round table so they could exchange names and cabin numbers and formulate initiatives for further action.

Only Sarah remained seated, drawn to a final embrace by the leader and his wife who had not moved with the others to the rear of the room. She was unable to ignore the soft, sweetness of the moment, and it awakened in her once more a strong longing for Taylor's embrace. She watched intently as the man planted a kiss on his wife's forehead and then raised his head to survey the room, obviously pleased that his efforts had resulted in an enthusiastic participation around the table. And as he continued to survey the room, his eyes were drawn to the beautiful young woman who was yet to leave her seat. He spoke softly into his wife's ear, and then he grasped her shoulders and gently lifted her to a standing position, encouraging her to join the others. She rose and nodded her head; regaining any lost composure, she walked toward the rest of the group.

And then he looked straight at Sarah and began to approach her. Sarah, however, turned to look around, unaware at first that she had been targeted, that no others were left seated behind her. And when she realized that he was walking toward her, she self-consciously began to gather her belongings, hoping to inconspicuously join the others or slip from the room.

"Wait, wait," he said. "Don't be in such a hurry to go just now. Stay, please, to talk with me. Do not worry. Nothing is demanded of you. I come only to introduce myself." He held out a hand disproportionately large for his frame, and gave her a firm and powerful handshake. "My name is Joseph Levin. I apologize that I spoke so strongly that I am scaring you away. This is not my intent." She looked up at him, and before she could respond, he continued, "How do you do?"

"Well," she stammered. "Thank you. I am well," she continued, and then she realized that this last phrase from him—the words of this simple question—were the only words that he had spoken all evening that were in English, not German. And likewise, her response came out automatically in English.

But now he was transitioning back to German. "Please, miss, let's talk for a moment," and he motioned for her to sit down once more, to share the small table setting with him. "Aha," he continued. "I knew it. Well, actually my wife, Hannah, first had the idea, but then I thought, as always, she just may be right—you speak English. You see, I know only a few phrases. I can maybe say 'how are you' in four languages, but often the answers will elude me. I have no great linguistic skills. Please, I have introduced myself and now I ask for your name, if you would not mind."

"Sarah. I am Sarah Berger."

"From?"

"From Berlin."

"Aha," he said again. "I thought so. Cosmopolitan. And you've traveled. You are fluent in English, I am presuming, by the natural ease of your response."

"Well, yes. I have had years of instruction."

"And what other languages?'

"Well, French. And I guess Swiss and some Polish, as well."

"Sarah," he paused. "I may call you Sarah, may I not?" he posed rhetorically, waiting for no answer. "We are informal here. Sarah, you saw my wife by my side, did you not?"

"Yes, yes, I did," she said, wondering if he was displeased that she had intruded on their private moment. "You are right. I was watching you both. I will apologize for my poor manners. She seemed so quiet, so sad. You had such tenderness for her, although you had such force for your audience."

"Ah, you are a student of human behavior, as well. What you say is true. She is very sad. But not because this ship has reversed course. She did not even want to leave at Hamburg and I physically had to lead her aboard."

Sarah could envision the scene, perhaps not so different from her own. "It is the guilt. I know it myself. The pain of abandoning loved ones."

"Yes, you are right. Separating from her parents—as well as mine—not knowing if we will see them again—not knowing if they will be safe."

Hearing this admission reawakened her own despair and brought tears to Sarah's eyes, but she held back the sobs that often surfaced during her lonely nights.

"But with Hannah, there is more," Joseph continued. "You see, a month before we secured passage on this ship, we accompanied Hannah's younger sister, Miriam, to the train station, where she began her journey relocating to the French countryside. There was a group— maybe thirty children—and the promise that more will be able to go—to hide out—to become Christian children until the madness ends. In the weeks before she left, she had to be instructed in the most basic of Christian tenets, and we had to impress upon her the need to deny her heritage—explain to her the importance of keeping the secret. For a nine-year-old, this is not an easy assignment. You heard me say it earlier—I am a rabbi's son—and yet I had to tell Miriam to deny her Judaism. And so now she is Mary."

Finally, Joseph looked up at Sarah for a moment, but did not pause for her to comment. "My in-laws could not bear to take her to the train—and so it was Hannah who had to make sure that Miriam took her seat—Hannah who had to wave as the train left the station, her sister racked with convulsive cries through the window." Now Joseph closed his eyes and rubbed his hands on his temples. He swallowed deeply in an effort to control his own emotions. "You have to understand that because of the age difference, because Hannah's parents have become paralyzed by the Nazi rampages, Miriam was more like our own daughter than a sister or sister-in-law. And so Hannah is so incredibly distraught that she cannot even eat. You see how thin she is."

He looked up and saw Sarah nodding slowly. "And yet, and this you will find hard to believe, Hannah is happier now than she has been. There is a relief to her that we are returning. She does not know if she can locate Miriam, and she understands, anyway, that we should not try just now. But she wants to find ways to help with the Resistance herself. And she knows that I too feel the same now. You see, we made a good match. We were *beshert;* we are soul mates. And now that is very important. And these people organizing the evacuation of the children, they are proof that there is humanity among some of the Gentiles. We were lucky in this one respect. God provided our community with a few Church elders who have compassion for our plight, who despise the Germany that Hitler is creating, and so they are helping us. And Hannah believes that we must do more to help ourselves. When she saw you earlier on the ship, before today, she pointed you out to me. 'This is a young woman for our cause,' she said. 'Look how she handles the children, and she does not look Jewish, but I know that she is.' And so I see that my emaciated wife still has energy in her mind. She wanted us to talk to you—to recruit you to the Resistance—and then on to Palestine when we succeed."

Late that next afternoon aboard the *St. Louis*, sitting at a small deck table and grabbing the sun's lingering rays, Sarah composed her letter to Taylor. She had been formulating thoughts in her mind since the voyage had reversed its course, but she kept waiting to put pen to paper, initially still holding out hope. But finally she was facing the truth—the same truth she saw reflected in all of the bleak faces that surrounded her on the lounges of the promenade level. The days of people smiling, laughing, playing games, and even simply conversing were only a memory. They had been swept away with the ocean breezes. And now only a thick, depressive fog was palpable in an ostensibly cloudless sky.

It had been so long since she had written to him that the very act of gathering the stationery materials was overwhelming. Only the previous week, she had been practicing the words she would surprise him with on a telephone call. "It's me—yes—it's Sarah. No, I am not calling from Germany." She didn't know exactly where or how or when the call would be made—but she wanted it to be perfect. She could envision him on the other end, almost dropping the phone in relief. But now there would be no such call. Instead, she had to picture him receiving this letter and she winced when she visualized the reaction it would evoke.

My Dearest Taylor:

Darling, I can only imagine the way you have quickly torn this envelope, ready to devour its contents as a starving man would unwrap a gift of chocolates. Yes, I know you still care for me as I do for you, although I have not been at home to receive or send any correspondence for over six months. But your dreams have reached me, even when your letters could not. In those dreams, I sensed your search for any word from me and my family, and some answers to that are the meager bites I can offer you.

This past year, the terror that you knew was coming managed to strike hard. I have been separated now from both of my parents. My father was arrested and taken away in November of 1938. My mother and I later left Berlin and assumed Christian identities in the countryside until we could find a way to escape to America. But just as you would have expected—you would have understood it even before me—my mother would not leave the country without word of my father.

I have spent these last weeks on a ship that was to bring so many refugees to a safer life across the ocean. But we have been

*denied—we have become a leper ship looking for a port. And
now we are almost back on the continent from which we sailed
in fear. My latest news is that I will leave the boat in Belgium.
I have so much to tell you—and although I know I need you
more now than ever before in my life—I must try to explain to
you briefly why our reunion, which once seemed inevitable, now
seems impossible.*

*So many experiences in my recent past have molded me into
a different person. Even the new person still loves you, still
hopes to be with you someday, but I don't know if that is someday soon. I feel l cannot put my wants and needs first right
now. I cannot be more forthcoming in this letter, as I do not
know whose evil hands may contact it before it reaches your
sweet touch. I only know that I cannot turn my back on my
people now, especially the children, when I am told that I can
be of help. I know none of this makes sense to you—and that
now both of our dreams will be only nightmares. Although I
will pray to be once more in your arms, I cannot ask you to put
your life on hold for me. No matter what the future will bring,
I promise I will always love you, I will never forget you . . . It is
all in God's hands now.*

With all my love,
Sarah

As she sealed the envelope, she could not move
from her chair to deposit it with the purser. She simply
sat back and held it at the end of her fingertips, as if
a postal agent would happen by and collect it on his
rounds. And within only moments, a very trim, blond
young officer, his epaulets possibly signifying a fairly
high rank, and the metal buttons of his impeccable

white uniform glowing with the reflections of the last beams of light, tipped his cap toward her and reached for the letter she seemed to be offering.

"Miss," he said, and then repeated again, for she did not appear to be concentrating on the present and seemed lost in thought. "Please let me take that for you. It would be my pleasure to see that it is on its way to its destination."

She looked up only briefly. He and his fellow officer exchanged knowing glances, immediately sensing her sadness, imagining the story behind this beautiful girl with tears in her eyes. And she had seen the pair before, so alike they could have been twins or, at least brothers, not inconspicuous on the ship, both in their professional roles and outwardly flirting with the female staff.

"Thank you," she said so softly that it was almost inaudible, and then remembering her manners, she gave them an appreciative smile as she released her hold on the letter.

As the pair walked away, she did not follow them with her eyes. And so she was not cognizant of their suddenly cheerful, posturing gait, their jovial discourse. She did not hear their words, as they were approaching the turn at the stern of the ship. "Yes, my dear blond Jewess," one remarked to the other. "I will be sure this letter is properly handled . . . Poor Captain Schroeder. He has not been able to protect his charges like he hoped— and now one more time he has failed." As he spoke, he led his friend closer to the ship's railing and then without the slightest hesitation, he let the letter fall to the water. The two officers watched its slow descent, and then turned toward each other as if on cue. "Heil Hitler," they said in unison.

Only a nine-year-old boy, scouting the ocean horizon for passing ships or hints of land, would bear witness to the fate of the white rectangular object as it floated ever so slowly to the waters below, lingering on wind pockets and drafts of sea water currents, gracefully dancing in the air before it was engulfed by the powerful waves and then disappeared. And he walked away, thinking that one more of his playmates' art projects was making its way back to the very place that he had hoped to be.

Throughout the days of the return voyage, the very brave Captain Schroeder of the *St. Louis* had worked closely with Jewish groups to negotiate with the four European countries that would absorb the passengers so they would not have to return to Hamburg, their port of embarkation in the Third Reich. All of the passengers would leave the ship at Antwerp, Belgium, and then be processed and transported to their assigned locations. And just as Sarah's mother had surprised her by parting from her by the dock of the *St. Louis* when it began what turned out to be its doomed voyage, so Sarah now turned to the Blumberg family to say her farewell.

Once again, in small groups, the passengers were dispersed on a dock area sitting on suitcases, dressed in suits. But there was no hint of hope on their faces this time, only fear and despair for the majority, rebellion for a minority.

"No, Sarah," Alfred had insisted. "You are part of our family now. You are our daughter and our sister all in one. We will proceed into the future together." He was holding her hands tightly and sincerely as he spoke. "Sarah, we all love you," he continued as his wife and the children devoured her in a circle of affection.

"I love you all so much also," Sarah returned. "But I have made a decision that I believe my mother would approve of. No one knows what lies ahead for any of us now, but we know that we have many enemies in this world and few friends. These last evenings I have spent in meetings with our fellow passengers who are not going to try to make their way to America again, but are impassioned now to join the Resistance Movement. They feel I could be of great help to them because of my Christian looks. And I do hold a second passport as Liesel Schultz. I have to admit that I initially met their proposal with reluctance and trepidation. But they insisted that they have been watching me on the ship and they see I have an ability with children. Some of them say they are happy to return because they shared my same guilt of leaving and they plan to become involved in relocating German Jewish children to the French or British countryside. They know there are many displaced young people and many orphans. They not only want to protect them, but include them in a Zionist vision. And now I am telling you that I have signed onto that same philosophy. I know that you are set on making your way to the United States, and believe me, I don't fault you for that. I care so much for you and I pray for you to be settled in safety as soon as is possible. But right now, I feel I must follow this calling. Just please—never forget me—I will never forget any of you."

And then, just as she did when they initially met, she acknowledged each family member separately—but no longer with a handshake—now with a hug and a kiss and tears.

Sarah would disembark at the same port as the Blumbergs in Antwerp, but she would surreptitiously meet up with her new group and would eventually become a resourceful and respected member of the Resistance Movement during the war years. In 1947, she would finally sail to Palestine on one of the ships evading the British blockade. This ship would provide passage for refugees from four centers: Switzerland, Belgium, France, and the Buchenwald Concentration Camp. Even after liberation from Buchenwald, many of the Jews would have wished to return to Poland or Hungary—but the shocking truth spread quickly. They were not wanted back home—there were few, if any, Jews, and anti-Semitism had taken no rest.

The stories they exchanged on the way to the Promised Land were remarkable and followed a distinct pattern—those from the three countries told of years of fear and luck and the aid of decent, moral countrymen. And those from the camp told of the inhumanity of misguided and evil men.

The irony was that in decades ahead, when Yad Vashem, the Jewish Memorial of the State of Israel, began honoring those Gentiles who aided Jews during the Holocaust, the name Liesel Schultz was put forth many times. The grateful sponsors would be shocked when they were assured that Liesel Schultz was actually of Jewish heritage, just like them. In 1993, however, Gustav Schroeder, captain of the *St. Louis,* was recognized posthumously for the Righteous Among Nations honor.

Taylor

Kenilworth

August 1940

"Taylor, dear," his mother said as she uncharacteristically greeted him at the front door and ushered him into the expansive living room.

His day at work had been long and he actually felt gritty and grimy from hours spent in the factory, training with the two foremen on some new machinery.

"Mother, you seem especially welcoming this evening—I don't usually see you downstairs for another hour with your dinner dress preparations completed." The family was still maintaining the formal dining pattern of the previous generation.

"But, darling. You just must see this. The most delightful surprise has come today. I don't know who would have sent it to us, but it appears to have come from abroad. It is so beautiful. I didn't know what it was at first. The doorbell rang and since I was passing the foyer I just answered it myself and this fairly tattered package was dropped off."

"Mother—I haven't seen you so excited like this—actually, maybe ever. I'm not really sure what you are telling me—could you be less cryptic, please?"

At this point she took his hand to lead him farther into the room. Taylor was used to the controlled decorum with which his mother usually presented herself. She was truly a wonderful, warm and supportive mother—a demonstrably loving wife—and he adored that about her. But she was also extremely formal and regimented. Tea time at three o'clock, and then from four to seven, she would have her evening repose, and then appear newly made up and fashionably attired, ready to share a pre-dinner cocktail with her husband, son, and any guests that may have been invited. But now it was well after six and she looked as if she had begun no such ritual preparations.

"I opened the door," she continued, "and a driver brought in a rather large package. It had 'Woodmere Residence' written on the outside—some customs markings—and so I tipped the driver, naturally, and he was on his way. I wasn't even going to open it, but it was a bit torn at the edges and something was protruding."

Although she had been leading Taylor toward the object under discussion, at this point she held him back, wanting to finish her narrative before she revealed her prize. "No Taylor, just wait now. I want to unveil it to you as it was unveiled to me."

"OK, Mother. I am trying to be patient—but I would request you come to the point, as I am in need of major freshening before dinner. Do you see the dirt on my hands?"

"My goodness, Taylor—you are not touching it."

"Yes, I agree—whatever it is, I am not touching it. Go on, please."

"So I start to unwrap the package and I see that it is a blanket—actually some sort of small quilt and then another . . . How odd, I thought, the package had a stiff rectangular shape. And then I realized these were blankets protecting something. I removed the blankets and then I saw the surprise. The most beautiful painting—museum quality—perhaps a French Impressionist work."

At this point Taylor was having fun with his mother, humoring her with a pretense of fascination with her story. "Mother. Are you to tell me it was a Renoir dropped on our doorstep?"

"No, dear—now don't make fun of me. The signature was clear. But I admit no familiarity with the name." And now she finally moved Taylor to the corner of the room where the painting rested on the bridge table. See there—she pointed to the lower right portion of the work—it reads, 'Henri Lebasque.'"

His heart stopped. His senses blurred. He could not hear or see clearly for more than a few seconds. He had the sensation of floating briefly and then of drowning. He was suspended in space and time and he could not will his body to move forward.

"Taylor, dear—are you OK?" His mother looked at him quizzically and he saw her face as one views a person through the distorted peephole of a door.

Although it seemed forever, it probably was a full ten seconds before he regained his composure and was able to focus on the painting.

And there before him, as vibrant and compelling as the day he purchased it, was *Jeune Fille à la Plage*, the beautiful work he had bought originally for Emily Kendall, but shortly after had presented to Sarah Berger. It was the very painting that he had left for Sarah in Berlin until both she and the painting could join him in Chicago. That was in August of 1937, and now it was three years later. Three years of torment, of waiting and searching for Sarah.

He fell to his knees before the painting. But instead of studying each colorful stroke of its canvas, he first wiped his hands on his trousers and then grabbed and caressed the blankets that had lovingly protected their hidden treasure. He brought them to his nose, as if they still held the wonderful fragrance of Sarah's home and maybe of Sarah herself. For, instantly, he had recognized these as the same fabrics that had adorned the family beds during his stay with the Bergers. He held them tightly and then he simply leaned back on his heels and he cried as he had never before allowed himself to cry.

And then he rose abruptly—so quickly that he was dizzy from the sudden change of blood flow. He rushed to the front door, opened it, walked to the edge of the high front stoop and searched forward, then left, then right. Nothing. No one. He had been taken by the moment, hoping that the incomprehensible arrival of this painting was easily explained as that childhood prank when someone rings the doorbell, drops off a package and then hides in the bushes. He was looking for Sarah, seeking his Alice in yet another "adventure in wonderland." But the lawn was empty, the street quiet except for an occasional passing automobile. And once again he was distraught and breathless.

His mother, and now his father who had returned to the estate through the rear entrance, watched incredulously as their son actually ran the long expanse of driveway, which led to the gates bordering Sheridan Road. They looked at each other and then stood arm in arm waiting for him to return to the door and, hopefully, offer an explanation.

Eventually, Taylor made his way back up the drive and into the foyer with a pathetic look of resignation and despair. And then he was once again re-energized, racing toward the wrappings that bore their address, piecing together the puzzle of its origin. It was stamped not only with a Miami seal, but with Spanish words that he finally realized signified a Cuban port. There was a familiarity to the name that was on the markings and custom stamps. The name of a shipping line and then boldly marked words—The *MS St. Louis*. He remembered when the newspapers covered the story—the ship of Jewish German refugees turned back at freedom's gate. At the time he agonized for the passengers and had even sent a cable to President Roosevelt to allow the immigrants safe harbor. He had done this out of his newly formulated empathy for the plight of these people—he had never dreamt that Sarah Berger herself had been on board.

In the year to come, Taylor Woodmere would be an industrious and productive asset to the family business, but his free time would continue to be spent in an obsessive campaign to locate Sarah and the Berger family. He would be among the first in his area to volunteer for the army following the attack on Pearl Harbor, December 7, 1941. With considerations made for a recently diagnosed heart murmur, combined with the important government supply contracts of Woodmere Industries, he would be placed as a director in adjunct services and would remain in Chicago.

Taylor

Newport, 1942

It was one more lead to find Sarah after two years of diligent searching. A contact who had come from Berlin discovered that the people who had sailed on the *St. Louis* had disembarked at Antwerp and been dispersed to England, Belgium, France, and the Netherlands. He made inquiries on Taylor's behalf, but once again the trail led nowhere. The last record of her existence was when she boarded the *St. Louis*. It was as if she never got off. From his investigations, which had been hard and intense, he was aware of at least one suicide attempt among the passengers once the ship was denied entry to both Cuba and the United States, and such a possibility did cross his mind, but it seemed unlikely, as it was unpalatable that Sarah was capable of that act. Of course, he had no idea that she had boarded using her original passport, and after disembarking, became Liesel Schultz again.

And just as Taylor was at his lowest, with his parents extremely concerned for him, proud that he wanted to aid this family, but anxious for his own mental health, that a call came from Emily Kendall.

He had not even spoken to Emily in over three years. Their separation was easier than he ever would have anticipated, for sometimes all of the planning in the world cannot compete with the happenstance of life. In this case, just as he returned from his time with Sarah in Europe, knowing he would have to be forthcoming with Emily, she could hardly face the reality of her father's infirmary and subsequent death. Unable to cope with her new circumstances, she needed an extended time at her home. In her defense, her depression was not just because she understood now that the family finances had actually been depleted, but because she really had loved her father and missed his unconditional love for her. She was like a lost girl. Her mother, who had been her entitlement tutor, was devastated herself. And the boys had proven unable to give her the support that she sought. They could not cope with the neediness of the women and were each escaping the family home. But to their credit, they had moved elsewhere to establish careers and earn livings, until eventually they were called to military duty.

Although Taylor had, of course, been the gentleman, gone to Newport to be there for Emily upon his return to Chicago, and had stayed with her family through the funeral and mourning period, he could not hide that his feelings had changed. He was there for her in many respects, acting concerned and supportive, but certainly not loving and passionate. When he could be alone, he was preoccupied with communications regarding the Berger family. And soon he realized that his short temper with Emily was more hurtful than helpful.

But years had passed and now Taylor sensed immediately that Emily had changed. On the phone, she seemed so sweet, so soft, so vulnerable. In some ways, she was barely reminiscent of the old Emily, the self-confident debutante, the girl who was always placed above the mundane crowd. And it wasn't only her fault. Just as people on seeing Paris for the first time seek the Eiffel Tower before the Louvre, so Emily had been an admired and sought-after object, although previously she was all façade like the renowned landmark and did not offer the depth of richness of the museum.

Now she had simply called him and asked if he might come to Newport to visit her. She knew through friends that he had not shipped abroad like so many of the men, that he had no new girlfriend, hadn't even been seen much socializing with the group. They encouraged her to connect with Taylor as much for his needs as for hers.

Though Taylor accepted Emily's invitation to visit her at Newport, he was careful not to commit to staying at her residence. He didn't want to feel an obligation to her in any way, in case he realized early on that he had made a mistake by going there. On the phone, she had asked about him and his family, and he had found her to be very genuine. Surprisingly, he was drawn to the familiar cadence of her speech, as if their years of separation had been only months. But he was cautious now—he would visit her as a friend, not as an old boyfriend looking to reignite a relationship. He was simply a person in need of a change of scenery, a stateside "soldier" in need of a leave. But he didn't know her motivation, even though she had professed only friendship on the telephone. And so he didn't want to be trapped in an awkward situation from which he could not easily extricate himself. No, he would look for a comfortable, convenient hotel for his stay.

Immediately after he replaced the phone receiver, he was trying to remember the name of a hotel in Newport that a family friend had told him about the first time he had planned to visit there. Although at the time in 1937, Taylor was quick to mention that he would be staying at the Kendall residence, the man continued on about the Hotel Explorer. It was the Woodmeres' neighbor in Kenilworth, Jacques Van Shaw, who offered the history of the hotel and convinced Taylor that "no finer accommodations on the seafaring shores of that state or any adjacent ones existed."

"You know my grandfather, my mother's father," he had told Taylor in 1937, "was a Beaumont. When you visit the area, you will see it—the Beaumont Estate, I mean—well, the current one that is. There were others before it—fires—you know in those times—before the turn of the century when the really big money built their summer homes there—kitchens weren't necessarily part of the main house. There were grand stone edifices built—The Breakers and Marble House—but so many wood structures would easily catch fire. And you don't want a simple kitchen fire to burn the whole house down. Legend has it that the Beaumonts were slow learners and stubborn about that."

Taylor remembered how annoying Jacques was with his almost incoherent soliloquy on Newport, but he had been more than a bit drawn to the history embedded in Jacques' story and he planned to find out more about the alluring destination at a time when his mind would be less preoccupied.

"Yes, sir—that gets me thinking—the Breakers and Marble House," Jacques was continuing, *sans* encouragement. "How pretentious to 'name' your place—as if 'the Vanderbilt Estate' wouldn't be impressive enough. But then again—those in my grandparents' set—they had many homes in many places. When you see them, you won't believe it. Grand mansions. Some used for three months out of the year—some for weeks only—some were vacated for two years at a time, the owners off to Europe or preferring Maine or Cape Cod."

Jacques Van Shaw was not one of a kind on Chicago's North Shore, but possibly, he was one of the wealthiest of the "trust fund babies." At fifty-five—that was still how he referred to himself. And he encouraged people to call him "Sport," further evidence of his childlike demeanor, since he was known for his prowess at all athletic endeavors from ball or racquet games to water activities. He was a little bit Eastern erudite—educated at Harvard with a degree of no practical value. But his father had a fondness for horses and so Jacques had developed a southern accent and even a slow drawl attitude from so much time in the Kentucky Blue Grass region.

"Never worked a day in my life," he would expound proudly within the first hour of any new introduction. He may have often grabbed the ear of Taylor or his father, Addison, when they met on walks along the lake behind their houses, but he never grabbed the respect of either Woodmere. They thought him to be an irritating name-dropper and tried encouraging him to put his time and money to better use, aligning him with some charitable causes.

And now, some years later, Taylor sought out his colorful neighbor to confirm the name of the hotel.

The last time Taylor had been to Newport left him with the almost unbearable memory of Emily's father's funeral and his own poor manners. But already this time was different. This time there was no chauffeur to meet him at the station. Emily had driven herself. She was still beautiful. He studied now the fantastic auburn hues of her hair—noticed once more its striking contrast to the pale tones of her skin. And surprisingly, almost immediately, he felt an urge as never before to revitalize its luster. He was thinking that she hadn't smiled in a long time— that he would receive more pleasure in hearing her infectious laugh than in experiencing a long kiss—for now.

She actually had not protested when he insisted on taking a room at the Hotel Explorer instead of her home. At that point, Taylor had no knowledge that her family compound had already suffered greatly from neglect. She said the Explorer was such a wonderful place and she encouraged him to study all of the pictures lining the walls. She told him that he would be familiar with some of the names of the boarders from industry, politics, and show business.

That first afternoon she was anxious to walk with him on the beach, showing him the boats docked in the marina before he checked in. But by four o'clock, she was evasive. She had somewhere to go.

"I hope you don't mind, but tonight I will need to leave you for a while," Emily said, at first almost mumbling, facing away from him, embarrassed by her own words. But then with a renewed strength she continued, "From five until ten each evening now, I work at the Newport Arms, as a hostess in the restaurant." She still couldn't even look at him when she said it; he was, after all, a wealthy young man who was used to being served. Although he had always been overtly kind to the help, she understood that he did not mingle with them socially.

But he didn't miss a beat. There was no hesitation in his voice to try to absorb this admission. "You are amazing. I am proud of you. You've become a resourceful woman now." With those words, she fell into his arms and cried. She cried as she had never before allowed herself to cry. She cried sad tears for her dead father, for her absent brothers, for her fragile mother, but mostly for her lost innocence. And after Taylor tenderly brushed her tears away, she cried for the welcome and caring touch of a friend.

When she stepped back from him now she was confident and excited to reveal the rest of the evening plans. "If you drop me at work with the car, then you can see where it is and pick me up afterward. I want you to meet all my friends from work. The cook is a total showman and always saves us some of the special dessert to share with us and tonight it should be cherries jubilee. Then we'll go on with that group to a beach get-together. I want you to meet some of the Newport boys, especially Chase and Mac III, who are stationed at the local base and can join us. They are so unbelievably immature. You'll know why I couldn't stop thinking of you."

When Taylor finally did check into the Hotel Explorer, he was more than impressed with his room. It was beautifully furnished in a colonial style and had an enormous four-poster bed. He was not surprised that nestled to one side was a daintily appliquéd step stool, as he could not imagine a petite woman having the ability to easily mount the mattress. The view from his open window stretched far down Bellevue Avenue and offered the most welcoming cool breeze to enjoy the tops of mansions and the ridges of coastline that he was anxious to survey. The hotel name was appropriate to his mission now, although it did not refer to an exploring tourist, but rather to the Scandinavian Vikings who were purported to be the original inhabitants of the region.

Just a short time later, although he was not hungry for a full dinner, he was anxious to enjoy a drink at the bar and peruse a map he had secured from the concierge in the lobby. While studying the outlines of Newport and putting little checks at sights he knew he would want to investigate—mansions, or parks, or churches—one small square caught his eye. Was this correct? In the midst of this white-steepled Presbyterian and Episcopalian enclave was actually a Jewish House of Worship. He looked down at the accompanying map legend—The Touro Synagogue, founded in 1763, was the oldest synagogue in the United States. George Washington himself had sent a letter of good wishes to the congregation.

It was not something that ever would have previously captured his attention—but now he felt a strong need to see it—as if the air within would have some scent of Sarah Berger. And a mezuzah. He thought now of when he asked her about the slanted silver object on so many door frames at her home in Berlin.

"So God will bless our home," she had told him. "There is a sacred paper scroll inside." And then when he looked at her doubtfully, she continued, "Yes, a tiny sheet of prayer."

He might have once again been lost in the past with his thoughts and the subsequent depression of his memories if he had not been interrupted by a booming voice halfway down the bar, interjecting an "Excuse me, sir," in his direction. Taylor lifted his face to see a well-dressed gentleman in his midfifties. The man was so insistent on grabbing his attention that Taylor returned his words with a polite nod.

"You're visiting here—I'm guessing—don't mean to be prying, but the map is a true giveaway. Don't need to be a detective," he said in a most colloquial dialect, although he exuded an extremely sophisticated presence with his navy blue blazer and plaid patterned ascot.

"You are correct, sir," Taylor responded in the encouraging tone of one open to a continuing dialogue.

The gentleman then rose from his stool, martini in hand, and re-sat himself just two seats from Taylor.

"Friends call me Harold," he continued, setting his drink once again on the bar and extending his right hand for a solid shake.

"Taylor Woodmere. Pleased to meet you."

"I see you're not in uniform, but from your age I wonder if you are stationed here at the naval base."

"No, sir. I am in adjunct services in my hometown of Chicago. Actually I am from a village outside of Chicago—Kenilworth, Illinois, north of the city, along the Lake Michigan shore."

Harold paused with a creased brow for an extended period of time before continuing. "You know, I believe that town is familiar to me. That name—Kenilworth. I am trying to recall. Someone from here lives there now. I just can't think that fast. It'll come to me."

"It couldn't be my neighbor, Jacques Van Shaw, could it?"

"That's it—the ultimate Sport—How is he?"

"Oh, Sport is doing well. He's actually the one who directed me here. Specifically to this inn."

"Well, I'll be. Now that is one coincidence—that I would be here right now, myself. Even I haven't lived here on any permanent basis for a while. Do you sail too? I remember that is the main activity I shared with Jacques from the time we were young. I know your lake has some good strong winds."

"Yes, sir, I do sail. I've never manned the lines on an ocean like you have here, but we cross the lake often—to Michigan or Indiana and back."

"I'm not sure of my schedule quite yet, but if I set out in the next few afternoons, perhaps you might crew for me and have a spin in our territories."

"That would be a great pleasure for me, I can assure you. I am here to visit a friend, but I will have some free time."

"Let me ask you one more thing, young man. Are you at all familiar with the game of bridge?"

"Actually, yes. My friends and I had been playing a little after college, but . . . well, let's just say, they found me a bit preoccupied when it came to leisure-time activities."

"I love to hear that—I mean that young people are involving themselves in the game. I am actually here to meet some friends—we're quite involved in contract bridge and working on the international bidding and club conventions. I'd love to invite you to join in a few hands, especially since you have a sense of the game."

"I would like to take you up on that, but I am anxious to acclimate myself to the area while it is still light out. Perhaps I could catch you another time."

"Yes, indeed, Mr. Taylor Woodmere. I will have a note delivered to your room if I find I am sailing again this week. But either way, you must send my highest regards to my dear friend Jacques."

"That I will do for sure, sir," Taylor answered and then was embarrassed because he knew it was too late in the conversation to ask for the man's full name. He signed his bill, excused himself and then exited the room, discreetly taking the manager aside as he approached the front stand.

"I am very sorry to bother you with this," he said, "but is there any chance you are familiar with the name of the fellow at the bar with whom I was just conversing? He was extremely friendly and wanted to reconnect with me and a former friend of his, but he introduced himself only as Harold." As he spoke, Taylor was noticing that the manager seemed to have an emerging smirk. "Has he been in previously? Might you know him?"

The manager turned back over his shoulder just to confirm his intuition and almost laughed. "Yes, I am quite familiar with the gentleman. I believe that I saw you take some materials on the history of the hotel. Well, you will find that in the 1920s he was part of a group of prominent men who actually financed the building of the Hotel Explorer to house their guests and to develop a tourist trade here. And it is rather funny—you would think that Harold, in particular, could have offered a spare guest room or two at his own home. Young man, you have just met Harold Stirling Vanderbilt."

Taylor looked down at his feet and now with his own grin, shrugged his shoulders incredulously. "Oh no, I have to think if I made a fool of myself from anything I said."

"Never worry about that with him. What a fine man. A class act. A graduate of the Harvard Law School, but he took his place in the family business—railroads. His great grandfather was—the Commodore—Cornelius Vanderbilt. But he's well known in his own right."

"I know—you don't have to say," Taylor interjected. "He's a revered yachtsman."

"And he literally wrote the book on contract bridge," the manager added.

Later that evening, when Taylor joined Emily and her entourage, he was anxious to pull her aside and share this story with her. She listened to him intently, never letting on that she also could count many of the Vanderbilt relations as friends.

He loved her new casual, unpretentious manner. She laughed and danced around with the other Newport Inn employees on the sandy shore with no regard for class distinction. And, of course, she was dressed as a waitress. Taylor found the white uniform outlining her slim body to be extremely intoxicating. For the first time in possibly a few years, Taylor was starting to be relaxed and maybe even happy. He would make no quick decisions . . . he would simply see where this road would lead.

His first kiss with Emily that was more than the casual greeting expected with close friends happened the third night. It was quick and impulsive on both parts, and neither of them knew what to make of it. The rest of that night they spent in a cautious avoidance, each by turn looking away when one caught the other's glance. But the following evening, when Taylor was late to meet the group on the beach, Emily was so visibly anxious for his arrival that she nervously paced around and eventually returned to an adjacent area where they had once lit a bonfire, thinking he may have gotten disoriented as to their meeting place.

And Taylor had been detained, but only because he had some errands to complete, because he wanted to do something special for the group. Until then, he had acted like the out-of-town guest that he was, simply enjoying the hospitality of the others, drinking their beer, eating the food they had rounded up, even borrowing their towels after they waded into the water. But now he was feeling a part of this resort fraternity, so this time when he met them after their workday was completed, approaching from the opposite direction, he did not come empty-handed.

And soon he was having a good time watching his new friends devour his groceries and become increasingly loud and playful from the addition of more liquor. Then he drew from his bag of goodies yet one more treat, a large rubber ball he had purchased to coordinate a game of coed dodge ball that he envisioned would end up as a rowdy merging of bodies on the beach. He sorted through the collection of towels he had actually bought at the five-and-dime, and then reached the ball at the bottom of the sack. And when he rose, he naturally began looking for Emily. His plan had been to ambush her first with his possession and get the game started, but he couldn't find her. The others were there, sitting in the sand, arms swaying to the guitar chords of a talented waiter, just beginning to slur their words a bit as they tried to sing along, but Emily was not among them. If she was there, she would no doubt have been in the center, waving her hands as the most accomplished musical director. But there was no Emily, and now that he thought about it, maybe no Mac either.

He was scanning the circle, the ball tucked in the crook of his arm. The sun-bleached hair of many of the boys in the pack made them almost indistinguishable from one another as the extended light of the summer evening had long since faded. Mac and Chase, especially, looked and dressed so similarly that he had often confused them and so now he walked around the circle for another angle to see who was missing.

"What you got there?" It was Chase, rising from the group and punching his fist to release the ball from Taylor's arm. And then they all rose in a throng and chased it before it was consumed by the waves. Just as Taylor had hoped, the ball was a hit as a diversion and they were forming a game as if they were in the school playground at recess.

"Wait, that's too hard," Rita whined as Chase made his first direct hit at her waist. When it bounced back to him, he repeated the maneuver until she caught the ball and went after him and they ended up tripping in the sand, laughing hysterically, and playfully pounding each other in an increasingly more intimate manner, with the ball now moving on to Doug.

But Taylor was standing back at this point, still looking around, envious of Rita and Chase on the sand, knowing now for sure his intentions with Emily. And he felt a nervous turning in his stomach, as he thought of Emily off somewhere and alone with Mac. One of the girls in the group, having been watching him closely, finally caught his attention and was pointing down the beach. "I think I saw Emily go down that path," she said. And then Taylor, nodding appreciatively back to her with his signature smile, took off in that direction.

He heard them first and then he saw them. Emily was standing against an old, grayish lifeguard post and Mac was leaning into her, with one arm braced on the wood at her back. But neither of them had heard or seen him approach.

"You're still hooked on that guy. Why don't you just admit it? I've been watching you and you've just been looking for him."

"No. I'm over him—we're friends again. I need that, but that is it."

"OK, then—if you want me to believe that—then you need this from me." He moved to kiss her, but she turned her head away. "Emily, this makes no sense. I can't take this. Either you are the worst sort of tease or you still love him. Admit it. You are not over him. I don't know if it is love or what. But I think you need his approval for your own self-esteem—like he knew you when you were riding high, and you want someone besides a hometown boy who will validate that image from your past."

"No—no. He hurt me too badly. He let me down. He's not great like everybody thinks he is."

"Don't you think I know that—I remember too that I was sad for you when he pretty much vanished from the picture when your father died. But maybe I was a little happy for me . . . maybe I've hung with you through these years, thinking we might eventually be together." Mac saw that she was crying now and wanted to hold her, to apologize, but he finally was getting it. She didn't want him. She never would. And when he turned away, feigning disgust so she would not see that he was simply distraught, he saw that Taylor was there and had heard it all. "You know what," he said, looking directly at his rival. "Take her—she sends me such mixed messages. I don't know what to make of her." And then walking away, he reiterated, "I'm done," pretending not to care, hoping to save his own dignity.

When she saw Taylor, she began straightening her clothes, wiping her makeup from under her eyes, pushing her hair back from her face. "He's right, you know." At first her voice was low and mumbling and she did not look at him. But then she lifted her head and firmed up her posture and her voice became louder and more direct. "I still want you even though you hurt me. You hurt me when I was most vulnerable. You should have really been there for me. And you are not the great person everyone thinks you are. Oh, you've got the brains and the charm and all that, but you're not just the nice image you portray."

He was blindsided and stung by her words. No one had ever called him out like that before. If he messed up, if people were disappointed in his actions, they rarely told him. He knew that he often got away with more than he deserved, that people he interacted with often found him intimidating in such a quiet, respectful manner, that they just reevaluated their own actions when his did not meet their expectations. If he was late for an event, perhaps they had called the event for too early an hour. If he didn't complete his full share of a school group project, then they hadn't correctly explained the assignment, or certainly he was so busy with his other demands that this was too much for anyone to handle.

But now she had said it. She had described him better than even she knew. And surprisingly, he found it a relief. For the first time he felt a burden lifted from him. Now she had verbalized it—that she knew he made mistakes in the past and would in the future—she knew he would be imperfect. He was before and he would be again. She knew it and yet, he was thinking, she still wanted him. He wouldn't have to feel he had to always be perfect for her in the future. And if she could forgive him, overlook his past actions, if she could want him back, maybe he belonged with her.

"Let me ask you this. Can you want me again knowing how I've let you down—knowing that to say I won't let you down again could be a lie?"

"You mean—can I want you again—knowing you are human—you are like the rest of us—a little bit battered—a little bit flawed—not . . ."

"Perfect," he interjected, as naturally, she was thinking, as couples do who finish each other's sentences. And so she repeated, "Yes, knowing that you are not perfect." But then he clarified—"No—when I said 'perfect' I was looking at your face, your eyes, your heart, if you can believe that. I meant you are perfect."

She was shaking her head now, rejecting that word, that medal of a label with all of its implied weight. "Just perfect for you."

And now that he was free to be just human, not the exceptional Taylor Woodmere, he allowed his human impulses to take their course. He bent down to kiss her, first to the rose tint of her ready lips, and then directly to the rising mounds of her breasts, scooping inside her swimsuit top, and then reaching under the half skirt of her stylish suit. And next he was maneuvering their bodies to the sand, gratefully eyeing the seclusion of the overgrowth of shrubbery in the landscape and quickly returning to the luscious landscape of her body.

He didn't know what he would do if she stopped him at any point, but he sensed by the movements of her body to accept his advances, that they would both take ownership of all that was happening, that they would each accept that they were acting on their natural human desires. Not too far in the distance, he could hear the others calling his name. "Taylor, come on. Thanks for the treasures. Taylor, you got some more?" But then, surprisingly, he heard Mac answer back to them to give Taylor some time alone with Emily. If Mac was a jerk, he was also a gentleman, Taylor was thinking. And so, although there was a momentary slowing of their passionate moves, they both relaxed again, her body continuing to respond easily to his, her hips rising rhythmically toward him.

He was trying to be objective. Was he truly attracted to her again, falling for her—or did he need someone to rescue? If he could not save Sarah, could he save her?

And a year later, in a simple, but elegant ceremony, Emily Kendall became Mrs. Taylor Woodmere.

Taylor

Kenilworth, 1945

The newlyweds began their first years of marriage not quite as separated as most couples during the war, although Taylor and his father did travel extensively to oversee and coordinate certain supply operations for the War Department. After the armistice, Taylor's father transferred many of the Woodmere Industries responsibilities to his son, as he and his wife began spending an increasing amount of time at the Palm Beach estate where the senior Woodmeres resided during the winter months. This left the main living quarters in Kenilworth for the younger couple for much of the year.

Taylor especially loved assuming his father's place at the massive leather desk chair. On the weekends, he would work in the front study, enjoying the landscaped front view of the rolling lawn. He would anticipate the smack of the newspaper on the drive and allow himself the work break of the long walk down the driveway to retrieve it. And then one day . . . there in the headlines—Potsdam—where he walked with Sarah—where she fell in love with a puppy that belonged to a family of picnickers. The paper was plastered now with pictures of the Cacilienhof Castle, which they had seen in 1937, after touring Frederick the Great's Sanssouci. Harry S. Truman, Winston Churchill, and Joseph Stalin, the three most powerful leaders of the world, the leaders of the Allied countries, the United States, Great Britain, and Russia, were meeting right where they had visited. Their mission was to deal with the future of Germany and the defeated Axis powers.

But his memories were much simpler.

"Promise me I can have a puppy and I'll consider running away with you," she had teased. "Papa is allergic and Mama is not a dog lover either. When she thinks dog—it is a German shepherd—a military dog. I think of a cuddly dog. What are your breeds in America?" He couldn't even remember what he had answered, but it didn't matter.

He couldn't help it. He walked back to his desk and knew that he was done with any work for that day. His depression had returned. Outwardly, he had made a normal, contented life, but inwardly he could never release his memories, his pictures of the past. Had he given up on her too soon? What truly had become of her? What would become of him? He was a husband now and hopefully one day he would become a father. But already from the first years he could tell, it would never be as he had dreamed, as he had verbalized to Sarah—just like her parents and like his—"that is what I want in a marriage."

Sarah

Europe, 1939–1946

Many times during her years with the Resistance, Sarah thought back to the day she was recruited and knew that her decision had been a rewarding, but difficult one. It was emotionally difficult, for she was saddened by her separation from her loved ones, her parents and, of course, Taylor, and she was no longer confident that she would be reunited with any of them. And it was physically difficult, not only with their work to bring the children to safety while eluding and even killing their pursuers, but also because the winter months seemed to offer no respite from the elements. And so she often found solace in remembering her own childhood.

For the first year, she missed books the most. No matter how inspired or exhausted she might be with her responsibilities during the war years, she would have loved to have ended a day either rereading the classics of her youth or raiding her father's library for a book on history or technology. He was still there with her, protecting her wherever she went, and sometimes she knew she spoke aloud. "Papa, what do you think of this growing field of psychology? I think understanding the mind can cure the body. And maybe cure aggression." By the end of the third year, she had only two desires. To be dry and to be warm. The cold wet chill of the damp forest was a thick blanket that she wore.

This is what she had once valued. Very, very soft pillows made of the most delicate plucking of feathers, the individual whispers of eiderdown so thin and thread-like that they often peeked through the weavings of her family's finest linens and floated softly on her cheek to be blown away individually by an allergic sneeze or an instinctive hand movement chasing a tickle sensation. And now she had to redefine pleasure. Now it was the most basic thing that she cherished—the soft spot of a bed of moss in the hardening base of the winter earth.

In her childhood, she would have described the forest as magical, would have sought out the most enigmatic animal footprint paths to explore, anxious to see which obscure mammal would eventually reveal itself. And she would follow the meandering streams, hoping to come upon a creative beaver dam. These were activities that she would be strongly scolded for, as she would be missing for long periods at a time, causing great consternation among the adults charged to her care. When she reappeared, always minutes before the time that they would be contacting the authorities to help search for her, they would attempt to punish her, to limit her boundaries. But she returned to them with such complicated narrations of her journey during this fall from grace—"So have you ever seen the pattern of three pairs of steps and a hop and then a turn and a disappearance that could drive you insane, and then you look up into the trees and . . ." that they knew they could never limit her imagination, the spatial context of her environment, and so they hired only nannies with the strength and energy of youth to closely accompany her.

Often, this was her solitary entertainment, the sounds she could hear and the sounds she could produce. Uncle Laurent, of that massive compound near Potsdam, the town she had visited with Taylor, had introduced her to the secrets of the forest. How often she would accompany her uncle with his brood of six children, her first cousins, as he did his rounds. He was a wealthy landowner who her parents labeled "idle rich," to his face and endearingly, while he shot back at them that they were "bourgeois intellectuals." As an accomplished birdwatcher, a card-carrying member of the Audubon Society of Germany, and an amateur biologist and botanist, he had taught her so much. On their walks, he would quiz all of the children, challenging them to identify the calls of the indigenous wildlife and cautioning them to understand the rich vegetation around them. Eventually, they all knew which leaves embellished poisonous plants and which flowers and seeds and bark would provide nutrition and even medicinal qualities.

Certainly she had no idea that she would use that storehouse of knowledge for survival techniques in her near future, that her compatriots would be drawn first to the lyricism of her pastime, the trill of a warbler or the calling of a finch, and then that they would empower her to be a leader of signals. She established an elaborate coding system, with one call alerting them to the presence of an ally, another to a passenger for the underground railroad, another, ironically the voice of the most graceful of the avians, the nightingale, as the warning for an approaching Nazi.

The mounting acuity of her sense of sound was a revelation to her and it made her think of the admonishment of so many piano instructors in her youth not to have a lazy ear. Whatever did that mean, she wondered. "I am trying my very best," her ten- or twelve- or fourteen-year-old self would whine back in her defense. As she grew older, she insisted that her ease with language must attest to her having attained a "good ear." But she was told, "No, you have a way with words—your mind has the ability to process language." Either she had not yet developed or they did not yet recognize her facility to interpret nuances of tones—to mimic the pattern of notes that might emerge from a classical piano piece. Oh, in this her classmate, the sallow-complexioned, spectacled, and dour-faced Helena wore the crown. And sometimes Sarah feigned self-deprecating appreciation and envy of Helena's gift, understanding that the poor girl should have some small joys.

But now there were no pianos. Oh, the thought of music would be so welcomed. But her sharpened hearing had only to do with the percussive sound of the leaves and forest beneath her feet. And when she was alerted to the crunch of leaves, she craved her once innocent response of youth. She wanted only to be transported again to a time at her uncle's home when they raked and gathered the leaves on the grounds at Potsdam and they would laugh and jump and play in the piles of elms and oaks and maples that had been the last of a fall too soon beckoning the crisp winter air. The oldest of the fallen leaves, the washed out brown ones replete with pinprick holes, those no longer bearing any green, red, or yellow tones of life and elasticity, would make the young group squeal loudest with delight. But now the images bore new meanings. In the stillness she would concentrate on the monotonous crawl of a beetle up a tree or a caterpillar inching its way along the ground. And then the crunch of the leaves became the sound of fear.

But in the forest there is also spring. There is renewal and rebirth, she continuously reminded herself—petals and blossoms and colors emerge from the brownish blackish compost. She tried to relive the experiences of her youth when she would have searched eagerly and optimistically for any small sign of burgeoning vegetation that would indicate the coming of the season, anticipating that around the next bend would be a meadow with hints of wildflowers. But now this forest was anything but enchanting; it was haunted and intimidating. And she held back from the pack, cautious now that each curve and line of the landscape would reveal a foreboding vision, not a fascinating treat.

Sarah had never met anyone like Gabriel Dressner. He had joined their ranks just weeks after the war had officially ended, when their group was transitioning from a war resistance pack to a Zionist band. He had been liberated from one of the concentration camps, one of only a dozen survivors from his location. Sarah had tried to befriend him, to get him to talk about himself, but he fought her efforts. Originally, he was from a small town outside of Prague; this was one fact he shared early on. But he was never satisfied with her pronunciation of its name.

"You are making fun of me," she would say to him— but he returned no tender words.

"You are a fool. You are a fool to think I would waste my time making fun of you. I don't even think of you. I think of killing Germans and I think of Palestine. I do not waste time plotting to antagonize a shiksa Jew."

The others in the group jumped to her defense. "You are invaluable to us," one of the leaders said to her quickly, as he physically took his place between them. And then he turned to Gabriel with a scowling, "Leave her alone—don't take your demons out on an angel." But everyone knew in their hearts what was going on. It was a strange courting ritual that would eventually play itself out and be resolved in love. Only the two main characters of the drama were in the dark.

Gabriel was proud to exhibit no manners. He felt he had survived by being strong and resourceful and he planned to continue in that mold. Although the term had yet to surface, he had no "survivor's guilt." He had "survivor's pride"—a sort of entitlement for what he had endured. Sarah was thinking that he was the antithesis of Taylor, who had been so mannered, so modest, for the hypnotic memory of her first true love was what she clung to most during her times of solitary despair. She often tried to imagine how his life had played out after he received her final letter. Was it true that they had already enacted their final scene together? Certainly she thought of her parents as well. She was desperate to know where they were, if they survived. But in all of her fantasies, whether optimistic or pessimistic, she pictured them together, and that was the one image that gave her peace.

Their first month together in the group, Gabriel continued to antagonize Sarah. "I can't stand you. I can't stand your German speech—even your German accent. You don't even look Jewish. Maybe you are a spy with your blond hair and blue eyes. If you were a man I would demand to see your circumcised penis."

She was mortified. In her life, no one had spoken to her like this—so blatantly showed her such disrespect. But she was a bright girl and now an extremely mature young woman. She realized his outbursts, his accusations, were part of the constant resurfacing of his recent memories of the war and the camps. If he were a child she knew she could work her magic to calm and comfort him and so now she searched for a way to reach him.

And then it came to her. She looked for a kerchief around the neck of one of the men in their party. She untied it and then unrolled it and then smoothed it into its original square shape and refolded it into a triangle. Then she placed in on her head, and let it hang loosely as a religious woman would a prayer shawl. And she began:

"*Shema Yisrael, Adonai Eloheinu, Adonai Ehad*—Hear, Oh Israel, the Lord our God, the Lord is One. *Amen.*"

It was the simplest and holiest and most identifiable prayer of the Hebrew litany.

After reciting it she paused and looked up at him. And then she continued. This time circling her hands three times over imaginary lit candlesticks in front of her, she said the Sabbath blessing:

"*Baruch Atah Adonai Eloheinu Melech Ha'olam Asher Kid'shanu B'mitzvotav V'itzivanu L'hadlich ner Shel Shabbat.*"

Now she could not look at Gabriel. She did not have to—she knew that he would have tears in his eyes and remorse on his tongue.

And then one night that was particularly cold—he came softly to her with his coat. And he wrapped it around her. But he was shivering so much that she felt guilty and made him take it back.

"Then please just let me put my arms around you. It is called body heat—it is always best when flesh touches flesh." And so he asked if he might put his hand around her waist under her sweater. And she let him, for she knew now he was gradually starting to become a different person—the man he was destined to be.

It was a long time before he shared his story even with Sarah—and as he became more mature and mellower in the following few years, he would cry to her, not for what he had endured at the camps—but for how inappropriately he had acted toward her those first months together after liberation.

"I could have driven you away. Why did you stay? I was so mean and bitter and self-righteous."

But she just held him in these moments. "No—I saw who you were always—you did not see it—you thought you escaped unharmed, but you were wounded. Not wounded like a puppy or kitten or bunny that crawls into hiding and licks its paws—but wounded like a tiger or lion or bear—a predator that comes out snapping. But yes, you are right."

"Now right about what?" he asked, confused.

"Lucky—that I stayed—very lucky at that." And then she ran her hands through the fullness of his revitalized, brown, wavy hair and brought his head to her breasts to rest as you would a sleeping child.

"Sarah—I loved you always, from the moment I saw you. From the moment I was introduced to you as Liesel Schultz."

"Yes, I know."

"You knew? Despite the way I acted?"

"You think you are the first to act crazy around me? Well, you are wrong—this is my gift—to cast those 'love at first sight spells' on all my suitors." Actually, she had just said it as a joke. She was not, finally, even thinking specifically of Taylor.

When Gabriel shared his story with the group, he once again began by teasing Sarah, but finally with warmth. "I think you were a parent pleaser," he told the group, but directing his introduction to Sarah. "But I was not," he continued. "Not at all. I loved the outdoors. I was not a student. I loved the physical—the brawn, not the brains. Our town was known for lumbering, and annually there would be a festival that we would all attend. For one day each year, Jews and Gentiles mingled and laughed together. I insisted on preparing for and then entering the many contests of strength. There would be prizes for the man who could throw an enormous log the farthest. I would never be the winner, but I would have ribbons of second or third place.

"'That is for the goyim,' my mother would contend. 'You should be studying. You are wasting your time. You should be more like your father, like your brothers,' she would say. But you know the end of the story and they do not. This physical strength—this is what saved me. I was so good at hauling things, a favorite pastime of the Nazis, that they could not afford to lose their best worker. More than one of the foremen slipped me an extra portion of food to make sure I maintained my strength and their work details would be successful. So what did the Nazis need most to haul in a concentration camp? Yes, you do know. The bodies of the dead, from the showers to the crematorium—moving them, stacking them on wagons. Sometimes, I was so sickened by my own powers that I contemplated sneaking early into the showers and exterminating myself. But then finally I knew my purpose. In that time when even many of the most observant Jews felt they had been abandoned by God, I found religion, for I understood my calling. As I carried my fellow Jews, I would quietly recite *Kaddish,* our prayer for the dead, for them. I wanted to do it individually, not in groups. I was obsessed with it. So I would remember their faces and give them the dignity of names, not numbers. And I would be their son or their father or their sibling and I would fulfill God's command—I would do it for them, of course, but mostly for myself. It gave me a will to continue, a reason to keep strong and survive."

Taylor

Atlantic Crossing, 1956

As difficult as his separation from Sarah was, he fondly remembered his time on the *Queen Mary*. It was not only that he held at the time of the 1937 crossing an optimism for his future with Sarah—having no idea that their separation would be anything other than temporary—but, on that trip, he had bonded with a wonderful new friend, Katherine Pritchard.

Katherine had married her bicyclist boyfriend, Edgar Spinner, in 1940, and in 1956, the Woodmere and Spinner families traveled together on the transatlantic voyage of that same ship, but now with an entourage of a total of five children and one mother-in-law.

Many times during the journey, Katherine would catch Taylor's eye and they exchanged knowing glances. And one evening, after everyone had vacated the deck chairs when there was a sudden drop in temperature, she was slow in gathering her belongings. She moved to join him by the railing, both of them trying to deal with the strong winds blowing their hair into their faces.

She didn't have to say anything and he gave her an answer, nonetheless. "Don't be sad for me. I am happy for you and you should be happy for me." He could tell from her expression that she could see right through him—knew he was taking moments now and again on the ship to think, *What if all my dreams came true also?*

"I can see it in your eyes," Katherine said finally.

"And what do you see, Oh, Omniscient One?"

"I see 1937, and promises and hope and longing."

"All that?" he returned. "Well, look deeper—you will see conciliation and contentment. I have a good life. I am blessed. Emily and I have Courtland, finally, although that road was a long, tough one."

"My God, yes—two miscarriages, while everyone around Emily was carrying babies and wheeling buggies. I ached for her, especially the first time when we were pregnant together—for a few months only."

"It was hard—but we were always happy for you," Taylor returned. "And now look at your brood of four. And I can tell for sure you and Edgar are a great match—always on the same page—a working team at home and at the business—always cheerful." Taylor started to turn from her, so that Katherine might not read the obvious envy on his face, but then he swung back with a slight smile. "But there is one funny thing that I have been remembering now about that first voyage," he said. "Your mother—I mean, did you hear her tonight in the dining room? A great contrast to our initial shared crossing. Now she is all over Edgar's accomplishments.

I heard her tell the others at our table, 'My daughter married extremely well. You know Edgar Spinner—yes, Spinner's Cyclery—top name in the field. Stores in half the states of the country.'"

"Yes," Katherine answered, nodding, "and I am fully cognizant of the incredible irony of those comments. But, it wouldn't serve me well to throw it in her face. She and Edgar have such a wonderful relationship now; he is the one that insisted she accompany us on this trip. He felt that now that she is a widow, she could relive some of her happy memories."

That night, returning to his suite, Taylor first looked in on six-year-old Court in the adjoining cabin he was sharing with the two Spinner boys. Their rambunctious energy of the day depleted, all three slept soundly. Taylor was happy that his son could enjoy this camaraderie of brothers that he did not have at home. And he was grateful to see that Court did not win the upper bunk that he had so forcefully demanded at the dinner table. Sometimes, he was so like his mother, Emily, exhibiting that spoiled and entitled side that still occasionally surfaced in her. Taylor was thinking that he needed to spend more time balancing her indulgences with his discipline. But that would require spending more time at home, more time with Emily also. In truth, Katherine was more than perceptive. Too often, Taylor was lost in his dreams, his parallel universe of happy endings.

Rachel

Newport, 1977

Rachel hadn't planned on being a career woman. It was just in her nature to become totally immersed in any project she chose to do for hopefully the brief time she would be working full time. She always envisioned having a big family—she had missed that herself as an only child. Richard had siblings, but they were out of town and fairly out of touch, having each been lured by the lyrics of a "California Dreaming" world, eventually marrying and settling out West.

Certainly, Rachel had wanted a brother or sister for Jason. She resolved to try to become pregnant soon after she married Richard so that the age span wouldn't be so great between children. Despite the surprising rise of her career, she was prepared at any time to switch to local projects, to stay home nursing a baby and occasionally freelancing. Jason was in school all day and Richard's pay could easily afford their Manhattan residence and a nanny.

And she especially wanted to give the gift of a child, one with his own impressive genetic makeup, to Richard, her Prince Charming, *sans* horse. But no such pressure was ever imposed by Richard himself. If there was not to be another baby, then he accepted the hand they were dealt, although he ached for both of them, but mainly for Rachel, when twice early pregnancies were diagnosed, but did not last a trimester.

It was one of the few challenges in Rachel's life that she could not surmount. Often Richard would reassure her with words—"we're lucky—we do have a family—we do have a child." And eventually, it was the emergence of Jason's personality that would help ease her out of even her brief periods of depression. As it turned out, his auburn hair aside, he *was* a little Richard. And it was a testimony to Richard's immersion in his fatherly role that Jason was channeling his impressive talent for numbers, and emulating the identifiable lift in his gait, and his mischievous smile.

So with no babies at home and Jason in school most of the day, her professional dream had time to develop into a successful reality. Rachel was now filming the third installment of eight in a series of television specials, which would actually be a forerunner to Robin Leach's *Lifestyles of the Rich and Famous*. It was called *Living the Good Life*, and featured estate homes and hotels, always including not just the properties, but a glimpse of the life and the people.

She knew immediately how she would introduce her piece. She was prompting the cameraman—dozing in the rear of the van—to begin his filming. "Shep, are you up? Are you on this?" When she saw that he was ignoring her, she became more forceful. "No, really, take out the camera—quickly—don't miss this. This is going to be extraordinary."

He eased himself forward with his elbows and opened his eyes briefly. From the backseat, he squinted through the front windshield and thought he was still dreaming. The fog was so thick that he had to remember for a moment that he was not on an airplane in the clouds. He shut his eyes again. "OK, Rachel," he said through closed lids, as he returned immediately to his reclining position.

"No. You don't understand," she persisted, turning from her place in the front, slapping the backpack on his lap and pressing it against the protrusion of his middle-aged paunch.

"Hey, stop it," he mumbled, still half asleep. "Is this a joke or what? There's nothing out there—are we even nearby?"

"Now—take out the camera now—you'll see . . ." And then she turned to the driver. "Dave, stop for a second by the side of the road; let Shep get everything ready."

"Jeez, Rachel," he moaned. "I hate to stop in this fog—if I stop on the street someone could rear-end us," he returned initially, and then added, "OK, maybe now, there's a real shoulder I can make out." Perhaps because of his lower position on the studio hierarchy, perhaps because he would do anything to please the beautiful Rachel Gold—to keep her lilting voice from reaching its manic phase—Dave did as directed. And finally, Sheppard Watts grabbed his handheld equipment, removed the protective cap, and focused in the precise direction she was pointing.

The fog was still dense enough that the driver, proceeding at no more than ten miles per hour, could barely see one hundred feet ahead. And so the slowly paced motion required for the shot was easily engineered, without Rachel having to say more.

Shep remained obstinate. "I'm wasting a good five more minutes of nap time here. I love you, Rach—but I am wasting good film here, too—fog is fog—plenty of stock footage for that."

"Just wait—be patient—it's rising—the sun is breaking through above—and I want you to capture the scene in real time. You'll hate yourself for missing it—think cinematography Emmy." There was silence for almost a full minute while they continued the approach to the mansion. "It's edging up. See, the fog is lifting. You can see almost to the end of the road now. Keep shooting—this slight wind—it's all working together. I've staked this place out and you are going to be more than surprised. We're already on the street so it will be right ahead of us where the road will take a sharp right curve at the junction of the estate gates."

Shep leaned out of the car now on the left side behind the driver, so as to be more aligned with the center of the street. If the image she painted was true, and Rachel was always on target with every detail, he would be even with the entry. And—as if on cue—as they were approximately one hundred yards away, the length of a football field, as Rachel continuously wiped the inside

of the windshield where the humidity was further limit-
ing the driver's vision, the fog began lifting. A victim of
the softly swirling wind patterns, the dense fog was disappearing, unveiling the magnificence of the property.

"No way," Dave bellowed un-self-consciously, as he
blinked at a home that would rival any museum in New
York. As a studio driver and the product of a lower-
middle-class upbringing, Dave was newer to work in the
entertainment field and Rachel loved the freshness and
naïveté with which he greeted each location. Of course
Shep, who had photographed royalty around the world,
was less overtly awed, but he was gracious enough to
acknowledge with a slight nod that, once again, she was
on top of her game.

At this more than impressive Newport, Rhode
Island, venue, Rachel knew she should be concentrating on the marvelous colorful array of fabrics being displayed before her as puddling draperies in the parlor.
But she couldn't help focusing on the antics of a seven-
year-old ballerina prancing in front of a mirrored wall
nearby, with a possibly twin brother imitating her moves
in a most obnoxious manner. They were playing for the
cameras, although the cameras were focused on Rachel
interviewing their grandmother in this renovated, turn-
of-the-century mansion, where one would expect F.
Scott Fitzgerald's character of Jay Gatsby to come up
from the sea entrance in his perfect white suit.

The girl, not to be upstaged, grabbed her brother's hands, at first seeming to curtail his movements,
but then she maneuvered him to be her ballet dance

partner, to hold her waist while she did a lengthy pirou-
ette and then a leap. Together, as if on cue, they ended
in a bow.

"Nana, Nana," they called in unison, "Look at me;
look at me; look at us now."

The stuffy and irritated grandame turned to Rachel.

"My Lord—do you understand now why I have each
line on my face? First their mother, my daughter, graces
me with an adolescence from hell, and then she marries
some sort of pitiful tattooed movie star and leaves on
my doorstep for half of the year these two totally undis-
ciplined charges. Why call me Nana—why not just call
me Nanny—that is what they think I am.

"And the beautiful art treasures you see here," she
continued, "my china, my crystal—Faberge eggs—twice
as much I have moved to closed storage rooms after
their fifth crashing episode. I apologize to you a million
times over. If you wish to reschedule or even cancel, I
will explain it to my husband. Lord knows I only hope
the tyrants don't short out your plugs with their shenanigans," she said, referring to the imposing network
of wires and cables that snaked within each room where
they were filming.

"On the contrary," said Rachel, "I'd love to use the
energy of these children to really highlight the property. Remember today's audience is extremely family
oriented," she explained to the owner. "They value that
casual lifestyle."

Rachel was actually surprised that her staff doing the
front work on this assignment at the estate of Judge and
Mrs. Simon Barrett had failed to mention these young

residents. But perhaps it was a period when they were with their own parents, as certainly Mrs. Barrett would not have been forthcoming about them.

"I can envision the promo right now." Rachel was thinking aloud. "Imagine playing hide-and-seek in a thirty-five-room estate."

During a break for lunch, the formal and sophisticated hostess seemed much more relaxed and approachable and actually interacted with the young children as the most endearing grandmother. Rachel was invited to tour the mansion at her leisure and to identify any other rooms that might have been overlooked on the initial scouting visit and where she would now feel that she might want to continue filming. Claiming that the humidity of the foggy morning was weighing heavily on her joints, Mrs. Barrett urged Rachel to explore the upstairs on her own. "Oh, I am really so happy that those vast rooms are used again by my grandchildren. These are the rooms of my childhood—I grew up in this very house, and then my husband and I moved in as a young married couple when my parents passed. And so my children were raised here, as well. And before I knew it, my daughter was sitting at the little vanity table in what was my bedroom. Don't miss it—the pink room, of course, third or fourth door down on the right. And now my little grandchildren are jumping on those same beds—playing with the same train set that my own father assembled. One day my daughter and son will inherit the house, but I don't see them fighting over it. They and their spouses are 'citizens of the world.' This is not their idea of modern. They will sell it, believe me, before they will settle here."

"Oh, but this is such a beautiful home—mansion really, or should I say castle?" Rachel finally was able to add.

"Oh, home. Yes, that is the highest compliment. My parents were 'old world money' and so they did not raise us to chase or covet materialistic things. But nothing is enough for my children—especially my Hollywood son-in-law. All of the history, the memories, the fact that senators and presidential candidates began their campaigns here, they roll their eyes at that." She stopped herself suddenly, as if afraid that her personal digression had seemed immodest to her audience, and so she went back to the specifics of the architecture.

"I knew that you would love the light and openness that the parlor would offer, especially the pillared loggia view to the backyard. But go on up the stairs, and excuse me that I will not accompany you. Anyway, I should be helping the real nanny to corral the little ones and get them appropriately dressed for a birthday party they will be attending."

Rachel recognized that the owner's exasperation had turned to tenderness. She could sense that Mrs. Barrett actually felt a responsibility and a love toward those rambunctious twins that overshadowed her pride in any of her material possessions.

And so Rachel accepted the invitation to proceed through the home. But when she climbed the beautifully curving central staircase and looked down at the patterned foyer floor, she had a déjà vu moment. Suddenly, she was back in time to her visit to the Woodmere residence in Kenilworth, Illinois. There were similarities certainly in the size and the layout of the mansion, the view out the rear, the grand entrance and multilayered chandelier; it was as if she had a second chance to survey that home that had so impacted the direction of her life, both personally and professionally. But for the first time ever, she had a pang of guilt. Before this, she had never looked back on her decision to keep Jason's real father a secret; certainly, that was not a choice that she had ever questioned. But for some reason today she tried to recall the image of another person she had noticed at the visit. While in Kenilworth, she had spoken only to Court and briefly to the butler, but she had seen this other man out of the corner of her eye, an extremely distinguished-looking, middle-aged gentleman. He seemed to have been shadowing them from a distance down the long hallway. Although she had dismissed him at the time, she knew that she must have understood that he was Court's father. And only now she allowed herself to wonder if perhaps the son was not a reflection of the father. Perhaps there was a grandfather who would have embraced Jason. Perhaps she had denied Jason a solid and impressive legacy. She was not thinking in monetary terms. No, it was the solid character of this grandmother that had impressed her and set her thoughts in this new direction. She would not go back on her decision, of course, and Jason had the benefit already of two sets of devoted grandparents, but all of a sudden she felt for this one man. Maybe he too was disappointed in his own son. Suddenly, Rachel was almost dizzy from looking over the banister, concentrating on the complicated pattern of the stone floor and her own complicated reflections, and so she literally shook her head and continued on her tour. As she peered into the playroom of this house in Newport, however, one more memory could not escape her. There was a little girl that Jason had insisted he had been playing with that day in Kenilworth. He spoke about her incessantly for a week after that visit, until, serendipitously, a new little boy about Jason's age moved into their New York apartment building and Jason became distracted enough to abandon all talk of the girl. And so Rachel could finally dismiss the incident as an overactive imagination at work.

Jason

New York, 1979

Jason Stone had always exhibited a maturity and strength of character beyond his years, and that is what his parents, Rachel and Richard, were hoping would surface when they presented him with the news that they were relocating to Chicago. The year was 1979 and Jason was ten years old.

"We're what?" was his initial response. "I can't leave my friends. What are you thinking? What is this really about?" Instinctively, tears were welling up in his eyes. "You're not hiding something, are you? You're not getting divorced, are you?" he ambushed them accusingly.

Richard and Rachel looked at each other more than lovingly and couldn't hold back little laughs. "No, darling," his mother had said quickly. "You know that is not true."

"I'm not sure I know anything anymore," he returned. "It's just that every day it seems like the parents of someone at school are getting divorced. And half the time at games the kids have one mom dropping them off, a stepdad picking up, a stepmom cheering—another having a tantrum with a dad and then the next thing you know my friend has left school and moved farther uptown or to Long Island."

Rachel and Richard again were sharing knowing looks and shrugs. Their young son had so graphically articulated the scenarios at many of the pricey Manhattan prep schools, where parents had too much money and too little time for anything but themselves—where children were often one more commodity for display. Husbands were leaving families for colleagues, secretaries, and nannies, and wives were multitasking with jobs, workouts, lovers, or any list of priorities that did not include raising kids. Their son needed the strongest reassurance at this point that they were an extremely intact family.

"Jason. We are moving—all three of us—together—and happily—back to my hometown of Chicago. All the reasons are good. Your New York grandparents, Dad's parents, have relocated to Florida, and since Aunt Ida and Uncle Chal married, they are away for half of the year themselves. If we move to Chicago, my parents can enjoy watching you grow up and we can be there for them as they have needs. It all began because Dad's firm presented him with a wonderful opportunity to be a managing partner in their Chicago office. *Architecture Today* is anxious for me to work out of that area and has given me the title of Midwest editor."

Rachel knew she was speaking quickly and in an almost artificially upbeat manner, as if her tone and cadence could obscure the reality of what enrolling in a new school and separating from old friends might entail.

"I don't suppose it's like I have any choice in this decision, anyway; at least you can be honest with me in that," Jason said.

At this point, Richard took over. "Jason, one thing you can be assured of—to us you are number one—we would never do something that would in any way hurt you. We know that Chicago is going to be a wonderful hometown for Mom again and now for all of us. Our job opportunities will mean security for us and for our futures, including your education. And we like the pace of Chicago. It is a big city, but maybe a little less intense than New York.

"You asked if you have a choice and you do. If you truly feel that you cannot cope with the news, then Mom and I will reevaluate our decision. But we hope you will choose to be happy and excited and to welcome this adventure."

"By the way," Rachel added, not above sweetening the pot with a small bribe, "your grandpa is waiting for the word that we're really going to live by him so he can pick out a new racing bike for you. He's so happy that you will live where there are safe streets and bicycle paths."

Suddenly Jason's sullen look was lifted—he was still, after all, a ten-year-old boy confined to walking and taxi riding in his Manhattan environment. "Well, that would be nice," he said softly, trying to maintain his pitiable attitude for he was enjoying the sympathy it was evoking. But he couldn't restrain himself. "No," he finally interjected to his parents' initial dismay. And then he quickly added, "No, he can't pick it out himself. I'll go with Grandpa to Spinner's Cyclery—I remember I saw that they have one in Chicago too. I want to pick out the bike."

And three months later, as the school term ended, Jason and his grandfather left the bicycle shop rolling the sleekest royal blue and steel gray bike, the newest model—The Courtland.

Taylor

Kenilworth, 1987

While his wife, Emily, constantly protested his traveling for business, in reality, when Taylor was home, he was inattentive and distant, even dismissive of her. Earlier in the evening, she had approached him while modeling a new formal gown and reminding him to begin preparations for that evening's charity event. Once again, however, he accused her of caring more about her looks than about any cause and challenging her to choose an existing dress from her wardrobe and to donate the difference. Naturally, she stormed off in tears. But Taylor made no move to placate her or to apologize. He was content to spend time alone in his study, simply using the remote to scroll through the channels on the television set, when suddenly something caught his attention. It was some sort of special presentation featuring a hotel dining room, with the cameras scanning everything from the rich, textured wood furniture to the antique dishes. He was attempting to raise the volume when the venue changed to highlight the veneer of a massive and lengthy maple wood bar. He knew he had been to this location, but he could not immediately place it. He had a familiarity with the spot to the point where he could say to himself, "I sat on that chair," or he could picture the bartender drying a wine goblet and then holding it up to the light to check for water spots.

Taylor was becoming increasingly frustrated. He could put no name to the property. He had turned to the program after it had started—but the familiarity of the lobby, the details of the columns and arches of the foyer, pulled him in—and then finally, fading to the commercial, the name was revealed. It was the Waldorf=Astoria Hotel in New York City—the venerable institution where he stayed at the end of the summer of 1937. Those were the few days he had spent in deep contemplation of his future as he returned from Europe, from meeting Sarah Berger, when he delayed venturing on to Chicago where Emily Kendall would be waiting. Could it really have been fifty years ago that he ate in that dining room and planned for a perfect future that did not materialize?

He was glued to the television set like a child returning from school, ignoring all other stimulus while nibbling on a snack. He was, in fact, just reaching for the bowl of mixed nuts and pretzels at the corner of his expansive desk when once again he was magnetized to the screen.

"And now we return to our special presentation focusing today on New York City's Waldorf=Astoria Hotel, with host, Rachel Gold."

He heard her name and his reaction made him spill half of the assortment on the floor. He moved closer to the set.

"Thank you," Rachel was saying, "and welcome back to the glorious ballroom of this grand hotel. Imagine it is 1940 and you are a descendant of Mrs. Astor's famous 400 list. How many events during any one year might you have attended here? The hotel itself has meticulously documented many of the society weddings. Picture the elegant bride entering this room filled with hundreds of roses—her train so long that it extended down the first five rows of seats. In one bridal party alone, two of the attendants fainted from standing straight and still during the extended procession and ceremony . . ."

At this point, Rachel turned to the escorting hotel manager. "We have with us Mr. Jay Montgomery, manager of the Waldorf for the past twenty years. Mr. Montgomery, you run quite an establishment here. Can you take our viewers on a behind-the-scenes look at what it takes to keep this place ticking?"

"Thank you, Rachel." He beamed into the camera, but then turned back to the hostess in a less self-conscious manner. "It is my pleasure to introduce you to the world of the Waldorf=Astoria."

"May I ask one more question before you continue, as our audience may be intrigued by your unusual logo, as I was."

"You mean the double hyphen, the equal sign between the words Waldorf and Astoria. It is no mistake. It is just one more thing that distinguishes us. It was meant as a symbol not only combining two original hotels, but combining the original established standards with the newly constructed edifice."

Mr. Montgomery seemed to feel comfortable as a speaker and Rachel appeared impressed with his next segue. "Yes, if you are thinking the name is sounding familiar," he said, again almost to the camera. "Your Waldorf salad at lunch is a creation of our very own maitre d'hotel, our most illustrious Oscar Tschirky. And credit him also with your veal Oscar at dinner."

Continuing her walk through an ornate corridor of the hotel, she noted a gallery of photographs delineating the history of famous events and guests. "Here is a picture from 1933 of a gathering of chefs of the hotel, all in their tall white hats, led by the stripe-suited and robust Oscar. They are holding up champagne glasses of Dry Monopole, dated 1925, and toasting the end of Prohibition.

"Now we move to a picture of Crown Princess Ingrid of Denmark dining with Thomas J. Watson, president of IBM. It is May 1939." The picture is not flattering for the princess who towers over her dinner companion. She is caught in a wide-mouthed speaking pose, her royal jewelry, from her necklace to her crown, overpowering his display of medals—her earrings competing with the hotel chandeliers.

"And in 1956, Prince Rainier III of Monaco and his fiancée, actress Grace Kelly, announced their engagement in the Waldorf's Conrad Suite." The camera closes in on this photograph, as well. As Miss Kelly sits in a glamorous evening gown with long gloves and a pearl choker, her handsome prince stands by her side, leaning on her chair. The rows of medals on his tuxedo are even with the top of her head, his trademark thin moustache adding to his distinguished European look.

Taylor was mesmerized by Rachel Gold. She was not hard to recognize; she looked as young and fresh as the day she entered his home, but perhaps more polished. She must be about thirty-seven years old, he was thinking. The same age his son Court would have been. She was beautiful and self-assured. "I know he is eighteen—he'll be in college soon," he actually said aloud to himself. He was thinking now of Rachel Gold's son, his grandson, "Rusty," who had been Jason Gold Stone for many years, and he tormented himself once again, wondering if he shouldn't try to connect with him. *But no*, he thought, *that would only be good for me and I want what is best for him.*

Luckily at that point, as if on cue, his precious granddaughter, his ward, seventeen-year-old Sylvie, distracted him as she entered his study dressed elegantly in the prom dress she had just purchased, and she approached him as a young princess wanting the approval of the king. And then he was confident again he had made the right decision. As Sylvie maneuvered through adolescence and the woman she would become peeked out ever so slightly now and again, he would not risk reintroducing her father's chaotic past and disturbing the stable environment he had created for her.

Taylor

Kenilworth, 2004

Even as he approached his ninetieth year, Taylor Woodmere was not a man of idle pursuits. While he enjoyed the serenity and seclusion of his study, with the comfort of his weathered leather chair and the cavernous walls of his volumes of books, even there, he was always at work. Though his father and grandfather before him would be credited with amassing the family fortune, Taylor had been responsible for maintaining the tremendous growth of the company during his tenure as president and chief executive officer. He had loved making money—and spending it. He was not immune to the lure of luxuries—automobiles, vacations, art, and the like, but he also loved that he employed a great number of people—that more families than his own depended on his business acumen. He was a pioneer in health benefits for company employees. Through the years, he had sat on government advisory boards for labor practices. He was a big businessman with a strong social conscience.

Years ago, he had prided himself on his beautiful handwriting, though he now considered it a lost art. Then, he would stay up late into the night and pen letters to friends, business associates, and government figures. And now with the onset of arthritis, he was proud to have transitioned to the keyboard touch of the computer, even e-mailing his newer associates, as, naturally, so many of the old colleagues were gone.

He especially enjoyed communicating by computer almost daily with Sylvie, the beloved granddaughter that he had raised. Often, Taylor would recall when Sylvie transitioned from being a weekend visitor at her grandparents' home to a permanent resident in Kenilworth. As she matured into a bright, confident and capable woman, he had actually hoped that Sylvie might step into a position of authority in the company, since her father, Court, had never met that potential, and had died before the age of thirty-five. But Sylvie had chosen her own path in her efforts at self-discovery. She had become a respected psychologist, the author of several articles in professional magazines, which today were among his library collection.

They did, however, work together on one major project. Taylor was still often seen about his community and even downtown in Chicago, still active in the Woodmere Foundation. The foundation funded grants in many areas, from medical research to work internship programs for minority young adults, targeting both high school graduates in the trades and college graduates. The foundation had been his true baby. He had certainly received more pleasure from it than from his own child.

This failure with Court had been a deep pain that Taylor had carried through his life. Whether valid or not, he bore tremendous guilt for his son's behavior and shortcomings. Why had he not been more empathetic and nurturing as Court was growing up? Why had he not remembered his own struggles with adolescent insecurities, his own fears of disappointing his father? Initially, he had tried to place the blame on Emily's poor influence, remembering the positive role that his own mother had played in bolstering his self-esteem. But eventually he blamed himself for not being at home enough as Court was growing up, for not recognizing that Court did not possess a constitution strong enough to shoulder the weight of the Woodmere legacy. Although Taylor, himself, was not so dissimilar from his father, Addison Woodmere, Jr., and his grandfather, "the senior Addison," both men of great accomplishment, they did each expound that the son of the next generation, the continuation of the dynasty, was of primary importance. In this, Taylor had failed his family. His son, Courtland, had basically peaked in high school and had become an incredibly challenging young adult, even before he was asked to leave Northwestern University after his second year. How ironic, that this son had achieved the one milestone that none of the Woodmere patriarchs could. He was, unbeknownst to almost anyone including himself, the father of two children.

More and more lately, Taylor's thoughts reverted back to that day in 1975, when a beautiful young woman, looking for Court, had entered his home with her little boy, and how he had followed the life of that little boy,

Jason Gold, for over thirty years. No matter what, he knew that Court had come through in one respect— given him two wonderful grandchildren, one to be openly proud of—and one to clandestinely enjoy.

Taylor

Kenilworth, 2005

Taylor Woodmere, with his granddaughter, Sylvie, by his side, read the article that appeared in the newspaper that morning.

The Woodmere Foundation from Status to Scandal
Chicago Tribune, **February 17, 2005**

The article surrounded their photograph at the previous day's news conference, with the picture of *Jeune Fille à la Plage* interposed.

A scandal has emerged involving the well-known industrialist, philanthropist, and lifelong Francophile Taylor Woodmere, ninety, of suburban Kenilworth. Pieces of a puzzle have been coming together in an onerous way for Woodmere, who supposedly developed his lifelong attraction to France during a visit to Paris before continuing on to Berlin in 1937. It is alleged that Woodmere was in possession of and then eventu-

ally donated a painting to the Art Institute of Chicago, which has now been challenged as a Nazi theft from a Jewish family. The painting is *Jeune Fille à la Plage*, by French Impressionist Henri Lebasque.

According to eighty-two-year-old Gerta Rosen, the painting had been the property of her neighbors, the Emanuel Berger family in Berlin, just prior to World War II. Taylor Woodmere, accompanied by his grand-daughter, Dr. Sylvie Woodmere Hunt, held a news conference yesterday explaining that the painting that has stirred this controversy as a Holocaust theft and that had hung in that Berlin home in the late 1930s was actually Taylor Woodmere's property. It had been sent to him from the Berger residence prior to the war.

In truth, Taylor was not ready to reveal the full story of how he left the painting with his love, even if the story would have exonerated him.

When Woodmere was asked why he did not donate the painting sooner and in the Bergers' name, he responded that he had spent years and resources trying to see if the family survived, but that he had always been the owner nevertheless.

The controversy brought Taylor back, once again, to his memories of the summer of 1937, when he had left the painting as a surprise for Sarah. In his first note to her when he arrived back in the States, he had writ-ten, "Someday it will hang in the home we will have together." But he could not say this to the press while his wife, Emily, was still alive. Although Emily knew of his desperate search for Sarah Berger, and in her heart she must have known the truth that he had fallen in love with Sarah, he had always kept the charade that he was following a humanitarian effort of friendship in trying (desperately) to locate her. He had explained to her that he and his father had been business acquaintances of the Bergers. But Emily was no fool. She must have understood that Taylor did not reconnect with her, did not present her with a ring, until he had exhausted all efforts in locating Sarah, until he understood that she had fallen into Nazi hands when the *St. Louis* was rebuffed from an American landing.

Even after his eventual reunion with Emily and their subsequent marriage, a certain cloud of sadness and longing continued to envelope him. He never fully gave himself emotionally to his wife. And so, in a news conference so many decades later, Taylor Woodmere held to his brief account, although the full truth would have better cleared his name and truly turned a scandal into an intriguing human interest story. He owed that, at least, to Emily.

After generations of accolades attached to Woodmere Industries and the Woodmere family name, it is shocking that it should now be clouded with rumors and actually accusations of anti-Semitism. In the past, the only negative publicity associated with the name involved Taylor Woodmere's son, Courtland (Court) Woodmere, who was charged with driving under the influence of drugs in the accidental death of his young

wife, Lilly, in 1973. It is reported that Court spent many of the following years in drug rehabilitation facilities, never fully emotionally recovering from the tragedy, and that he died in 1985. Dr. Sylvie Woodmere Hunt, the daughter of Lilly and Court and the only surviving heir to the Woodmere fortune, was present with her grandfather at the news conference.

Solomon Garber, a spokesman for the Jewish community, expressed great surprise and skepticism at the charges. "Taylor Woodmere, although not Jewish, has been a strong supporter of the Jewish Federation and Israel Bonds for decades. My inclination is that there is more to this story and I would withhold further comment and continue my support for Mr. Woodmere until a time when these reports would be proven reliable."

A spokesman for the family of Gerta Rosen, the Holocaust survivor who had originally recognized the painting in the Art Institute of Chicago and questioned how Woodmere was associated with its provenance, suggested that "perhaps his lifelong support of the Jewish community might be further acknowledgement of guilt feelings."

Jason

Chicago, 2005

So many evenings throughout the early winter, the waves can have a thunderous effect along Chicago's lakefront, as strong, cold winds set them pounding against concrete barriers. This sight and sound of the relentless presence of nature in its most glorious form always seemed to give Jason Stone a renewed energy. But by February, a thick coating of white ice will often blanket the waters, offering a quieter, though equally ominous view, and Jason would be drawn to the peace and tranquility of that scene. It helped him to put in perspective the demands of his own schedule. Depositions and documents, the essence of his day as a lawyer, seemed as ephemeral as the imprint of the cars also in his sight, dashing and disappearing along Lake Shore Drive in the rush hour. Within minutes it gave Jason the feeling of contentment that he sought, proud to live in this fascinating location on the city's Gold Coast.

Inside the residence, Lara Stone had finally found a moment to glance at the paper, as she slowly stirred the fresh pasta marinade she was preparing on the stove. She actually set the *Tribune* so close to the burner that she had to wipe the spattering red sauce from the front page section. It was then that she saw it. It was the article on the Woodmere Foundation and the picture of Sylvie Hunt that caught her eye. Lara took a minute to process what she was reading. Then she called to her husband— "Jason," she said once, and then louder a second time, so he could hear her across the rooms. When he was nearer, she began. "Remember the woman on the first day of school?—You've got to see this article."

Jason looked over her shoulder, as she continued. "Remember, I told you about Sylvie Hunt—mother of Jessica Hunt—the mother who was a little too interested in Marcus, who offered some incomprehensible apology the next week." She looked back at him and saw she had more than captured his attention. "Well, this is her—here. Dr. Sylvie Woodmere Hunt—there's a whole story about her family."

Jason, responding immediately to the repetition of that familiar name, moved closer to his wife to better view the article, while she read it to him.

Again—the names—and now the painting itself in the paper—with controversy. He was done with niceties. He would digest all of this overnight, but tomorrow he would be determined—he needed to meet with his mother, and, if need be, he would confront her about this. Whatever memories they may stir for her—he needed to know what all this meant to him.

Jason's assistant was surprised at his unusual late arrival, and later, when all things were revealed, would remember his uncharacteristic frenetic manner, request to get his mother on the line and then to arrange a lunch reservation for three people at a nearby restaurant. She overheard him almost demand that his mother meet him there and then witnessed a similar, but less hostile, call to his wife.

And in a booth, in a corner of La Fontaine Restaurant in Chicago's Loop, Rachel finally told him her story (his story)—the whole story, with its love and disappointment and then its happy ending—her son, Jason. "Oh, sweetheart, your memories are valid," she began. "I had no idea the strong specific images you held of that brief visit to the Woodmere Estate. You have to understand, that I had never been there myself until that day, and then I found it so unnerving and disappointing that I refused to think further about Court as your father and proceeded with marrying Richard and having him adopt you. You may remember that after that day, I never called you Rusty again; you were only Jason. Even I had no idea of the roots of your birth father until that day. And until you just showed me this article, I never knew the story of his decline."

When Jason responded, he turned to his wife Lara to speak, his back symbolically to his mother. "My mother would never talk about my father. She always told me that I was special, 'the child of a beautiful love.' And I accepted that—remember that at six or seven, I was adopted by Richard Stone, and I had a wonderful life, feeling safe, secure, and loved. By the time I was old enough to perhaps want to search for my father, I was old enough to understand the social history during the 1960s and I thought maybe she was involved in 'free love' or a commune and maybe she just didn't know who he was."

Now he turned back to his mother and tried to put tenderness in his words, although there was a palpable edge to his tone. "I was old enough to know that my strong mom did not deserve to be denigrated by my researching my birth father. And my true father, Richard, who raised me with such devotion, deserved my faithfulness. In truth, he was such a distinguished man that I was afraid he might not know about my mother's past, that he might love her less if I disturbed whatever story she had told him."

He was almost crying and both women ached to see him in such pain. His mother could barely offer her words through her own choked emotions. "Jason, darling, I am so sorry that you held your questions in, and especially that you did it to protect my privacy. Your maturity has always amazed me."

And although he hated to see her anguished, he knew he had to continue. "But, my God, how naïve I was. Don't you understand what this means—forget the provenance of the painting—it is not a living thing— what about me? What about my provenance? My real father was what—anti-Semitic. He came from Nazi sympathizers. This is my heritage—this is my provenance? No thank you—give me ignorance—knowledge isn't power; it is devastation."

And now, he did finally look directly at his mother as he spoke. "You raised me with a proud Jewish identity. But here is the truth now—here is my true provenance. I am the son and grandson of anti-Semites and I should have known sooner.

"My memories were kept alive for a purpose—that one day, in my complacency for my good and privileged life, one day when I would return home from my good job to my beautiful wife and healthy, handsome son— just as I reveled in my contentment—that I would be knocked down to the lowest level of existence. I don't come from a proud heritage—I come from filth.

"That woman, Sylvie, from what you told me, now everything is clear—names and places and events. She was living at the Woodmere Estate with her father and my father, Court. Sylvie, my afternoon playmate, who would recognize my son, my young double, years later, actually is my half sister."

Sarah

Haifa, 2005

S arah Dressner was enjoying her morning cup of coffee before her busy day would begin. Thankful for her good health, she wanted to treasure every moment and breath and help others when she could. And so she was finishing her daily routine before taking the bus to the nursing home where she was a volunteer. There, she would read portions of the newspaper to her eager following, knowing that maybe soon she would be a listener herself.

And so it was her custom to sip her coffee and peruse the paper for the most interesting articles to share with the residents of the home. And then she saw it. It was common that stories involving the provenance of Holocaust-era paintings not only appeared in local papers, but also circulated in the Jewish press around the world, and especially in Israel. In her hand was a photograph of the painting he had left with her almost seventy years ago. *Jeune Fille à la Plage*, by Henri Lebasque, was back in her life once more.

She became excited, almost frantic. Her eyes were tearing and she could barely read—but there was no one to turn to for help. Her husband, Gabriel, was gone for many years now, and her children and grandchildren lived in Tel Aviv. She wiped her eyes; she had not been overcome like this for a long time.

This was the painting that her first true love, Taylor Woodmere, had given her to hold on to until they could be reunited. And once again, as so often in the intervening decades, she relived the timeline. She had met Taylor in Paris in 1937, when she was only seventeen and proud to accompany her father on a business trip. She and Taylor had made an instant connection and he followed her to Berlin. He was honest when they first met that he had actually bought the painting for Emily Kendall, his girlfriend back home. But soon after they met, he knew it was meant for her, just as he was meant for her. He had left the painting for her, until both she and the painting made their way home, back to him in Chicago. In the time they spent together, she returned those same wondrous emotions. And she would carry the memory of the passion of a first true love throughout her life.

After their brief, whirlwind romance, he returned to America, and they both planned that she would be joining him in the near future. But circumstances of history and war intervened. And so it was that the painting hung in the Berger house for a year until it accompanied her aboard the ill-fated ship to America, the *St. Louis*. How ironic, she thought now, that this painting made it back to him and she did not.

For when they docked in Cuba, only certain passengers and some cargo with American tags were allowed to reach their destinations. The great majority of passengers were returned to Europe. Later, even she would learn from statistics the Holocaust Museum would reveal that 908 passengers were returned to Europe on the *St. Louis* and over 250 died in the Holocaust.

In truth, while Sarah never knew if the painting had made it back to America, she did know that Taylor had eventually married Emily. It was years before Sarah could finally resurface following her experiences in the war. After being sent back on the *St. Louis*, she spent the remainder of the war years maintaining the identity of Liesel Schultz. Just as the leader on the ship had foreseen, with Gentile looks and her affinity for children, she was a strong asset to the Resistance Movement. Eventually, she made her way to Palestine, helping to establish the new State of Israel. Although she was happy and settled in the routines of her new reality, she made inquiries about Taylor. She was so changed then, no longer the innocent, young girl with whom he had fallen in love. She could understand that after so much time had passed Taylor had probably thought he had lost her and so he had returned to his life. She did not blame him at all. She thanked him silently for her wonderful memories, for adding to her will to survive. She became devoted to building the new land, accepting and returning the love of a fellow Resistance leader, but never forgetting the flames of passion and desire that Taylor had first ignited in her.

Sarah smiled to herself as these wonderful, strong memories were allowed to return to her. It had been years since she had focused on that period in her life, but now she knew she could not read this and sit idly in her reverie—she had a responsibility to set the record straight. Taylor Woodmere did not deserve this treatment. He was a good, compassionate man, and she needed to clear up any misunderstanding and to clear his name.

Within hours after a phone call, her daughter and son-in-law rushed to Haifa, to her side. Parts of this story were not unfamiliar to them; Sarah had been generally open about her personal history and the Holocaust. Even the name Taylor Woodmere was not new to them, as she had told them of his efforts to bring her to America before the war. But she was always vague regarding their romantic involvement.

The following day, her son-in-law was able to connect with the appropriate authorities so that Sarah could detail over the phone and eventually by certified letter that this painting was indeed the property of Taylor Woodmere. She explained that she knew Gerta as a neighbor and appreciated her concern in the matter, but that Gerta did not know the whole story.

But most importantly, she felt she needed to contact Taylor Woodmere directly.

Emily

Kenilworth, 2005

Despite the fact that her pneumonia had kept her bedridden and she rarely spoke on the telephone anymore, Emily Woodmere was agitated by its relentless ringing during this stressful time. And so on this day, she was the one who answered the call from Sarah. Sarah explained that her name was Dressner now, but she was Sarah Berger—that she needed to speak to Taylor Woodmere regarding the painting. No, she told the woman that answered, she was not a reporter. She was calling from Israel. She was the woman in whose home the painting in question was temporarily displayed, but Taylor Woodmere was always the rightful owner.

Unlike her husband who still had a strong constitution, Emily's mind and body were showing all the signs of her age. But she still remembered the story of Taylor's trip to Europe and how he returned to her less loving, more distant, and how it was many years before they became a couple again. She remembered the pain that Sarah had caused her. And she was disturbed, even confused, when this woman insisted on talking to her husband. She did not even want to tell her husband that Sarah was on the phone. Even after all these years the past still haunted her.

"I don't think this could be Sarah Berger. I know that Taylor searched for Sarah Berger after the war—that woman was lost decades ago," Emily said.

"No, you don't understand. And—you must be Emily. I **am** Sarah Berger, now Sarah Dressner, and I eventually settled in what became Israel. Your husband was a special, wonderful person, and I know there is controversy now and I want to help clear his name."

Even with this said, Emily was hesitant to reconnect her husband with Sarah. And somehow, across the wires, Sarah understood that to Emily she was not an older woman who had survived the Holocaust, but a contemporary rival, who tried to steal Taylor, her precious love. And then Sarah, knowing that she could help this woman and still hold onto her own cherished memories, told Emily that she had verified to the authorities that this painting was always owned by Taylor Woodmere, that she was only holding it for a brief time, that it was bought as a gift for **her**, for Emily.

And with those words, for one more moment in time, Emily was young again. Her handsome suitor, Taylor, had not abandoned her when he went to Europe.

Audible across the lines, Emily was sobbing, yet it was as if her faculties were revitalized. Finally she spoke to Sarah. "Thank you—you are a good person—You have now given me the greatest gift at the most crucial hour."

The Woodmere Estate

Kenilworth, 2005

I n the following week, as Rachel Gold Stone deliberated how to handle the situation, to restore Jason's confidence in himself and in her, the papers carried the resolution of the scandal and the clearing of, even the acclamation of the Woodmere name. But still she knew that she had to clarify and rectify the past. With support and encouragement from her husband, Richard, she made a call to the home of Taylor Woodmere, and was surprised that Taylor not only took her call immediately, but did not even question or resist when she requested a meeting with him. She even wondered if he had misunderstood her identity, perhaps thinking that she might have been a reporter following the story. And she was further confused when he insisted that she bring her family, as his family would all be present. Of course, that was her intent—but how could he have known—that on this visit she would not let Jason be overlooked.

It was on a beautiful Saturday morning, with the sun glistening off Lake Michigan a specter through the eastern windows, that Jason Gold Stone, accompanied by his wife, Lara, and his parents, Rachel and Richard, revisited the Woodmere Estate, for the first time in thirty years.

And greeting him in the foyer, as if resurrected from a dream, was his grandfather Taylor and his half-sister, Sylvie. Introductions were made as they were ushered into the dining room and presented with refreshments. As if leading a board meeting, Taylor said he would like everyone present to listen to a story from the past.

Taylor went on to explain how in 1975 he had overheard the conversation between Rachel and Court and correctly surmised that the wonderful little boy, called Rusty, was actually Court's son. He then made it his business to follow the life of his grandson. Immediately, he put him in his will to provide for his inheritance. But since Taylor felt he had failed with Court, he kept his money reserved for Jason's future and let him become a man who could fulfill his own promise without his interference. But through the years he interfered a little, providing anonymously his grant for Northwestern Law School. Many years prior to that, Taylor had even clandestinely helped Rachel secure initial interior decorating writing assignments on Chicago's North Shore, until she established herself as a writer in the field. Since his investigation revealed that Rachel was marrying a good man—and he felt his son had done enough damage—he chose to remain only in the background.

But he was glad that he finally had the opportunity to clear up the stigma of the anti-Semitic remarks by his son, Court; it was Court's misunderstanding of a situation. In truth, the Woodmere family had been strong Jewish supporters for generations. Taylor recounted the story of Court's grandfather Addison, who encouraged Taylor to establish relations with a Jewish businessman when he sent him overseas before World War II. At this point, Taylor apologized for Emily's absence, explaining that she was ill, but that her anti-Semitic leanings, which Court had picked up on, stemmed only from a valid jealousy of a Jewish woman Taylor had met who presumably perished in the Holocaust. He was careful not to identify her as his "true love," although the words almost slipped from his lips. (As it turned out, Emily would not emerge from this last convalescence and her funeral would be the following week.)

By the end of the afternoon, tears and hugs and forgiveness united a family with such diverse roots. Sylvie and Jason could not stop exchanging instances of how the haunting, but pleasant memories stayed with them all the years. And Jason promised his grandfather Taylor that he could soon meet his great-grandson, Marcus, another little "Rusty."

Later that afternoon, content now with the satisfaction of a heartening family reunion, Taylor was finally focusing on a recent memory, when less than two weeks ago he was called to the phone and it was Sarah Berger Dressner from Haifa, Israel. For him, it was like speaking to a ghost from the past . . . an angel really . . . as he did not know that she had survived. There was the sound of age and experience in her voice, he was thinking, just as he knew there was in his. But it was recognizably her voice. It was Sarah. It was her beautiful German-accented English, just a little broken by the mechanics of time on the body. And now he was back in time, back to the exact moment that was the movie playing in his head through all the intervening years.

He was not holding a telephone receiver, not in his study focusing on the memories of a lifetime—pictures lining his walls—a wedding and an assortment of events that accompany the raising of a son and then a granddaughter and then great-grandchildren. He was not seeing photos of handshakes with Supreme Court judges and even presidents. He was focusing on one uncaptured picture of the past. It was the moment when he turned his head in the Paris restaurant and he was introduced to the most beautiful young woman he could imagine.

"Sarah, you have to know. I searched for you—I searched for your parents," he had said to her when he could finally manage words. "Eventually, I found only your father's name among the victims of the concentration camps . . . Emanuel, that wonderful and accomplished man. He was an inspiration to me. You must believe that . . . And when I finally knew his fate, I cried." The words were not coming quickly or easily. "I cried for the tremendous loss. But your mother, like you, I could not trace."

She was equally slow to answer him, her abbreviated, tearful breaths audible across the lines. "My sweet Taylor, you have the same soul that I last knew. You could not have known that I used Aryan identification papers during those war years. Yes, we lost my father to the terror, but my mother survived. It is a very long story, and, of course, she was never the same. But eventually I located her after the war in a displaced persons' camp in Germany, and I was able to bring her to Israel. But as you can imagine, she is gone for a long while now." And then Sarah was too overcome to continue. There would be time ahead to fill in the story.

"Sarah, you have to know. I never stopped loving you," he finally said, choking back the emotional tears that in all of his life seemed to only surface for her.

"And I was never complete without you," she responded softly. "I never stopped thinking of you, dreaming of our time together, honoring the pledge that I would love you forever," she continued. "But I did not realize that you still felt the same. I thought that you had found happiness and peace."

"I made a life—that was all," he responded quickly, "but now I am whole again."

They both wondered if despite the constraints of age and distance, it would be possible for them to meet in person once more. Or would they have to remain content with this acknowledgement of their constant connection, this mutual validation of their love and their memories?

Through a series of phone conversations, they would bring one another's histories up to the present. But it was on that very first call that she thanked him profusely for trying to save her then, and he thanked her for saving him now.

Epilogue

On Taylor's instructions, the spokesman for the Woodmere Foundation had been successful in misleading the press as to the day the El Al flight would land at Chicago's O'Hare International Terminal. Taylor would not deny the reporters their story; he felt even grateful for the role they had played in crafting its conclusion. But just as his introduction to Sarah and their long separation had been private for decades, so he wanted this reunion to remain out of the spotlight.

He was visibly nervous as he waited for her, his assistant straightening his jacket for the second time at his request. He alternated between studying the batches of pictures that she had sent him and pacing within the reception area. Emily had been gone for five months now, and he held Sarah's condolence card, as her words carried a warmly supportive, empathetic message.

In the most recent photograph Sarah had sent, taken at a child's birthday party, he could probably best recognize her smile and her eyes. "I don't want you running to some young, blond Alice who is walking off that flight," she had told him on the phone. "And then you find out I'm really that old great-grandma in the rear." In the photo, she was still a striking woman; her physique was lean, without the stoop of age, but her exposed hands betrayed an appropriate frailty. Her blondish-gray hair, at chin length, was pulled back by two tortoise shell combs. Of course, the soft, cream perfection of her seventeen-year-old face now had the lines and color that a harder life reflects, the biography of years in the Israeli sun. But it gave her a strength of character that a fully lived life deserves.

Finally, as the Customs doors opened for this next wave of arriving passengers, Taylor rose and his hands could not help a slight shake. The exquisite bouquet he was holding dropped to the floor. As he bent down frantically to retrieve it, his aide began gathering the flowers and tightening the bow.

And then when Taylor lifted his head, she was there—laughing at him, then laughing with him, then feeling his arms drawing her to him, cocooning in his embrace as he kissed her forehead. They separated and looked at each other, simultaneously smiling and nodding approval, but both finding it hard to speak. Taylor took her hand and kissed it in the style of an old-fashioned suitor, and then brought his lips to hers.

People surrounding them, each involved in the drama of their own lives, enacting similar meetings spiced with a potpourri of international dialogue, were drawn for a moment to the magnetic attraction of this handsome, elderly couple. Perhaps they were each envisioning this as a symbol that time would not diminish their own feelings for the loved ones they now greeted so eagerly, taking it as a hopeful sign that true love endures forever.

Although the initial scandal of a stolen painting had a short-lived play in the papers, it was only the resolution that caught and kept the national and international media's attention. Even *Time* magazine saved some pages to retell briefly what they termed "a heartwarming story, spanning generations, finally giving peace to those seeking provenance, giving closure to those clinging to pictures of the past."

Acknowledgements and Historical Notes

Writing this novel has been a fascinating journey, where a relaxing project became a consuming passion. Attending the Santa Barbara Writers' Conference and New York's Book Expo early in the book's development, I was truly surprised and validated by the encouragement of writing colleagues and publishing professionals. During the process, I met and corresponded with two extremely talented writers, Tatiana deRosnay, author of *Sarah's Key*, and Betsy Carter, author of *The Puzzle King*, who so graciously provided me with their contacts. The enthusiasm for the story from Mitchell Levin of Dream-Works was one more step in keeping my dream alive. Much thanks to respected editor Ann Patty, who has worked with such esteemed novels as Jenna Blum's *Those Who Save Us*, and who helped to identify areas to expand in the narrative of *Pictures of the Past*.

I am especially thankful for the love and support of my family as I worked on the book—my husband Michael, our children and their spouses, Carlee and

Keith Londo, Rob Eisenberg, Abby and Chad Eisenberg, and my littlest inspirations, Skylar and Jace Londo. I was guided in my endeavor always by the memory of my beautiful, supportive parents, Berdie and Bernie Rothblatt, and I actually began the novel as a diversion to cope with the untimely loss of my brother Steve, a highly regarded director at the Federal Environmental Protection Agency, and a loving husband and father.

I am forever grateful to more than one hundred readers, friends and relatives (and their friends and relatives) from the Chicago area, Florida, New York, France, Germany, and Israel, who anxiously asked for their turn with the manuscript and so enthusiastically embraced the story that it compelled me to follow it through to publication. Although so many people deserve to be listed by name, a special thanks for their encouragement goes to my very earliest audiences, my husband, of course, and Judy Farby, Essie Landsman and Stan Stein who indulged me to read it aloud to them over iced tea breaks, and Gail and Bruce Greenspahn, our traveling companions, who followed Taylor's adventures as we had our own.

In some ways I wrote this novel for the Sisterhood Book Club of Congregation Beth Shalom in Northbrook, Illinois, where I have been the leader for over sixteen years. Like the family of book club readers everywhere, they are such a bright, interesting, warm and supportive group of women. They want to learn about people in contemporary times and in the context of history, but they also want to fall in love with a good story. When we are particularly challenged by the literature, I remind them that this is why we are in a book club. We want to expand our vision of the world and enhance our experience with language. And I thank them, as a teacher without a classroom, for joining me in this rewarding venture.

Long before I was drawn to books that influenced me to become a writer, I discovered the books that made me become a reader. Among my favorite classics are Leo Tolstoy's *Anna Karenina* and Emily Bronte's *Wuthering Heights*. Chaim Potok's *The Chosen* and *My Name is Asher Lev* drew me at an early age toward the wealth of Jewish literature, and then I discovered the strength of Holocaust literature with Leon Uris and *Exodus* and *Mila 18*. Taylor Caldwell's *Captain and the Kings* introduced me to intriguing family saga, and soon I was captured by Jeffrey Archer's *Kane and Abel*, Herman Wouk's *The Winds of War* and *War and Remembrance*, and James Michener's *Hawaii*. Of course today, with such a proliferation of good literature in every format, people are drawn to the hottest, the edgiest, and the most current best sellers. But I do encourage young people to visit many of the best books from the past.

In researching the people and periods covered in *Pictures of the Past*, I must give credit to the following: The Illinois Holocaust Museum and Education Center; The Art Institute of Chicago; *Refuge Denied*, by Scott Miller and Sarah Ogilvie; *Rise and Fall of the Nazis*, by Claire Welch; *Jews in Berlin*, edited by Andreas Nachama, Julius H. Schoeps and Hermann Simon, English translation 2002 by Henschel Verlag; *Inside Hitler's Germany, Life Under the Third Reich*, by Matthew Hughes and Chris Mann;

Can It Happen Again? Chronicles of the Holocaust, edited by Roselle K. Chartock and Jack Spencer; *The Holocaust Chronicle,* Louis Weber, publisher; *Memories of My Early Life in Germany 1926-1946,* by Ralph Neuman, and *We Survived, Berlin Jews Underground,* by Inge Deutschkron.

While the general framework of the story for *Pictures of the Past* played for me as a movie in my mind, oftentimes my characters, mainly Taylor and Sarah, told me what would happen as the story unfolded. And this was especially true for the incorporation of the *St. Louis* episode. Some years ago, our friend Steven Safran, in relating to us his treasured family history regarding his grandmother, Dorothea Heymann, who had been a passenger on the ship, must have placed the kernel of an idea in my mind. When I reached the point of the story where Sarah and her mother Inga sought to escape Germany, I was drawn to the *St. Louis* along with them. It happened that I had become aware of a lecture regarding the historic voyage scheduled at Chicago's Spertus College of Judaica, where the speaker was Scott Miller, director of the Benjamin and Vladka Meed Registry of Holocaust Survivors at the United States Holocaust Memorial Museum. I was not surprised to see the Safran family in the audience, as well. Scott Miller and Sarah Ogilvie, director of the National Institute for Holocaust Education at the museum, had researched the fates of all nine hundred thirty-seven passengers on the doomed voyage of May, 1939, in their book *Refuge Denied.* I owe a special debt of gratitude to them, as I found their work both informative and inspirational. Sadly, Dorothea Heymann was among the two hundred and fifty-four passengers who did not survive the Holocaust when the *St. Louis* was turned back to Europe from Cuba and America. Dorothea, Steve's maternal grandmother, went first to Holland and eventually to Auschwitz, where she was said to have lived no more than a week. I hope that in some small way I have honored her memory.

Although the basic facts of the voyage of the *St. Louis* are true to the documented history, the passenger group meetings, the character of Joseph Levin, and the formation of a Resistance force from the ship, if actual, would be a coincidence of the merging of fact and fiction.

As for Henri Lebasque, while he was an actual French Impressionist painter, both of his paintings described in the book, *Jeune Fille à la Plage* and *Fille de l'été*, are not, and their true provenance can be traced only to my imagination.

In structuring the novel, I chose 1937 as a realistic year prior to World War II when Americans might still seek to travel to Europe for business or pleasure. I admit to having had no prior knowledge of the famous, and for me fortuitous, Paris Exposition of 1937, which revealed itself to me in beautiful detail through internet research. Serendipitously, I had already chosen Henri Lebasque as the perfect artist for my story, accomplished, but not well known, when his showing at the very real Exhibition des Maitres d'Art Independants at the Petit-Palais was confirmed.

Deby Eisenberg
www.debyeisenberg.com

Book Review Discussion Guide

1. *Pictures of the Past* illustrates our constant striving to maintain endearing human relationships despite the challenges of life, from the simple trials of young love to the complex terrors and heartbreak of war. Discuss the many examples of this within the book, including the quote, "How ironic that one wonderful man had changed her small world's perception of love at the same time that one evil man had heightened the larger world's perception of hate."

2. What effect do family heritage and expectations play in a person's development? Do "only children" bear an added weight of responsibility in a family? And just as with the lineage of a work of art, what impact does our provenance have on our future?

3. Readers should discuss the randomness of survival in the Holocaust. Draw on familiar stories in literature or in family histories. Does this lead only to survivor's guilt or also survivor's pride?

4. Man versus society, good versus evil, the loss of innocence . . . so many of the traditional literary themes course through the novel. How does Taylor fit as

the archetypal "tragic hero?" Was Taylor actually a complex individual? Discuss perfection and flaws in characters.

5. Which characters change and grow in the story? Is Taylor's return to Emily understandable?

6. Follow the examples of parent-child relationships and discuss which are the most healthy. What is the result of strong or weak mothers and fathers?

7. How does Rachel's profession work well with the novel? What epiphany does Rachel have when she visits the Newport, Rhode Island mansion where she conducts her interview?

8. The author, herself, states that once she molded her characters, they began to tell her where they would take the story. This was especially true when she realized that Sarah's mother, Inga, did not intend to join her daughter on the St Louis. Do you understand her action?

9. Explain the many references that could have created the title, *Pictures of the Past*.

About the Author

As the leader of an established Chicago area Book Club, Deby Eisenberg challenged herself to write a novel that her avid readers could not put down and would love to discuss. With a Masters Degree from the University of Chicago, she is a former English teacher and journalist. Inspired by so many wonderful books and formidable authors, and drawing on her love of literary research, art, architecture, Jewish history, and travel in the United States and Europe, she tried to envision a multi-generational love story that would inform as well as entertain, that would broaden the mind and open the heart. Deby and her husband Michael, an obstetrician-gynecologist, live in Riverwoods, Illinois. They have three grown children and two grandchildren.

Visit her at www.debyeisenberg.com.

CPSIA information can be obtained at www.ICGtesting.com
Printed in the USA
BVOW04s2248250913

332192BV00001B/17/P